Orphan Warrior

Reluctant Princess

By
Paul Johnson

ISBN 978-1-8382981-1-1

Cover design by: Rebecacovers

Dedication.

To my father Peter Henry Johnson
6th April 1936 – 5th May 2012

Chapter 1

Anouk was a happy child now in her seventeenth summer; she was tall for the women of the township with flowing golden hair, which was most often tied back in a ponytail. She was slim with slightly pale skin and an almond-shaped face, bright green eyes, a small nose, and full, but not to full, lips. Anouk had what some would call a muscly build, due to the hard work and lifestyle of living on a farm holding, but over the last few years, she had developed curves in all the right places, much to the notice of the local boys, who came by the farm paying her a lot more attention of late.

She considered herself as a simple sort of soul, quite content with her lot in life. She had lovely foster parents, a beautiful house to live in, and a bed to lay her head. But outside is where she loved best, the rolling fields where she could run through the corn brushing the ears with her hands. Feeling the tickle of them on her palms, or running over the soft grass barefoot letting the wind blow through her hair, as the rabbits darted for their burrows on her approach.

Sometimes she would go to the woods where she loved smelling the damp musty smell of the soil, listening to the cheery songs of the birds, and watching how the sunlight plays through the branches and leaves of the tall trees. She would always sit by her favourite tree, it was a big old oak with a recess in the trunk on one side. Sitting there with the tree around her made her feel safe and protected as though the tree was her protector. Whilst sitting there quietly, she often saw squirrels playing in the branches, one of which had got quite brave and would approach her. On future visits she would always make sure she had a few nuts in her pocket to give him, should he visit her.

Very often at the end of her day, after having done all her chores, she would take a walk down to the lake, where she would swim and bathe, washing any worries away with the clear, fresh, water. She had become quite a good swimmer, Pata had taught her, but her regular trips to the lake gave her ample chance to practice. She loved to go under the water and just swim for as long as she could hold her breath, everything was so quiet and serene, with the feeling of her body moving through the water.

On one occasion she heard whispers whilst getting out of the water, after having dressed, she spotted two of the town lads hiding behind a bush spying on her, "Get out of here", she shouted at them. They both took off running, "I will be telling Pata about you two" she called after them. She never saw them again, so the threat of Pata did the trick, but of course she never told Pata about it, she wouldn't have liked for them to get into trouble.

Anouk lived with her foster parents Pata and Katcha. Pata was a big man, the tallest in the township with muscles on muscles. He cut an imposing figure wherever he went, and Anouk was always in awe of him, but he was a kind soul, at least to her. She had many childhood memories of him playing with her out in the fields, or sitting on his shoulders as they walked through the woods, and bouncing on his knee in front of the open fire on cold winter nights. Katcha was a portly woman with untidy short brown hair, who always wore a floral apron. As a mum she was loving and attentive towards Anouk, teaching her cooking and how to look after the house and one day how to become a good wife.

Pata and Katcha loved each other very much and very rarely was a crossword uttered in the house, both of them doted on Anouk. Katcha would tell her "you came along at just the right time for us, a blessing from God himself ". Pata and Katcha were unable to have children of their own, they tried for many years, the healer eventually telling them "It just isn't meant to be for you ".

The holding Anouk lived on was a large one, in comparison to many of the others, it stood a mile or so from the closest town called Belcher. The house had a long pathway which led down to the Belcher road, and fields stretched out in all directions. To the south was a large lake where they got their water, swam and bathed and to the north stood the woods.

The town of Belcher was large, busy, and sometimes smelly, not like the sweet country air she was accustomed to. It was laid out in a circle with roads leading in from several directions, forming a wagon wheel layout. There was a large market where you could buy all manner of things, and some of the house residents set up stalls outside their houses. In the centre of the town was a large building called the Ossary, this was where Pata would go on regular occasions for town business.

Anouk always got to go to town on the big market days with her parents, where they would purchase supplies and seed for the farm. Sometimes she would meet up with her friend Minit, the two of them would go and look at the many dresses on display, imagining what it would be like to own such gowns. They would look at the many combs, hairbrushes, mirrors, and face powders the rich ladies would use, that always made them giggle, why would you ever want to put powder on your face. They always ended up at their favourite eatery where they would sit and have fresh bread and cheese and talk about anything new in their life.

The only real friend in her life was Minit; she was the only one she could confide in about her sadness at not knowing her true mother and father, the only one who would not chastise her for talking about it. She was the same age as me, so she had no answers. She would listen out for anyone who may say something, but no one ever did. It was as if they never existed, but they did because I am here. What could be so bad that two people would be erased from their very existence, in the memories of all who knew them? I thought back to our last walk together.

Minit and I would spend many hours walking and talking. Sometimes we would go somewhere quiet where we could dance and laugh and just enjoy being young. She would say on occasions, "I wish I looked like you; you will make someone very proud to be their wife". Minit was relatively short in height even for the township. She had dark brown hair and a round almost chubby face, and a build to match, but her breasts hadn't entirely developed fully, and her backside was a bit on the round side. Anouk laughed out loud, "No you don't, you are built for comfort Minit. You will bear many strong children who will help work your husbands' land. Have you thought who you might choose to become your husband?" Minit's cheeks reddened a little, her eyes got a faraway look in them as she slowly said, "Well Chanda has been paying me a lot of attention, and visits just lately. I think he is building up to asking my father for my hand". I stared at Minit with thoughts racing through my mind, but all that came out was "But you're not eighteen yet!", Minit giggled looking at my face "Well I will be in a couple of months, and if he does ask you will be one of my bridesmaids, won't you?". I could not help but smile, "I am so happy that you have found the one and of course I will be your bridesmaid, although Pata might not be happy having to buy me a new dress".

Anouk had her own set of chores on the farm, she loved the animals. Feeding the pigs, who were always pleased to see her. There were three pigs, Spot, Pinky and Nudge, Pata told her not to name them as one day they would be used for meat, and he didn't want her getting too attached to them. But Anouk had given them names because all living things should have a name, at least she thought so. So, Spot had lots of black spots, Pinky had no spots, and Nudge would always come over to her and nudge her legs. They were probably only pleased to see her because she brought their food and filled the water trough, but that didn't matter she was happy to do that for them.

Next came looking after the horses, there were two of them, a large brown mare called Bonny and a large black Stallion called Oakley. If Pata was using the big plough then they would be in the fields with him, and she could clean the stables much quicker, but more often one or both were there, and she would get to stroke them.

Bonny was the more mischievous always pushing her around whilst she tried to do her work, many times she had to scold her to get her to behave. And finally, the cattle where she had to get the hay from the haystack and take it to the field, there were too many cattle to name, well she tried once, but they kept moving around, and she got so confused she gave up. After filling the water troughs, she would make her way back to the house to see if Katcha had any housework needing doing. She didn't mind the work as she would rather be busy, after a good day's work, she always slept soundly that night.

Ever since being a little girl, for as long as she could remember, she loved the end of the day. After everyone had eaten dinner and the tidying was all done. She would always sit with Pata, Katcha would sit opposite doing her sewing, and he would tell her incredible tales about where he had been and what he had seen. He had travelled many miles from home and seen mountains as tall as the sky, forests so big you could get lost in them, white stuff he called snow, which he described as frozen water, falling from the sky. He would tell her of the animals with long noses, others with horn noses, and some with necks longer than a man. But her favourite was hearing about the sea, Pata described it as a vast lake as far as the eye could see, and the water was always moving. Boats that would float on it, the men in them catching fish. But what fascinated her the most was the stories of the enormous boats called ships, Pata said they would sail on the sea, going to other lands where the strange animals lived. Many a night, she fell fast asleep listening to his voice, dreaming of one day being on a ship bobbing on the sea, travelling to the other lands.

Anouk had never known her true father or mother; she was forbidden even to mention them within the household. In fact, she was forbidden to ask anyone within the township about them. In the early years, this was easy as she looked upon Pata and Katcha as her parents, but as she grew older, her mind started to wonder, who were my parents? Why can I not know about them or what became of them? It all seemed to be a dark secret the town was hiding from her, forbidding her to learn, to talk about them, to know them.

All orphans start to have questions about where they come from, but Anouk was denied these answers, by all she knew. Her mind ran riot with all the questions; she knew her mother must have been pretty, as everyone was always complimenting her on how lovely she was. She liked to think her father would have been a strong, handsome man, maybe one day she would find the answers.

Once she tried to talk to a neighbour Berm, he was an older man who had worked the land all his life. He had what looked like thick leathery skin, baked by too many summers, he was a big man and held a prominent position within the township as head of the Ossary. The Ossary ran the town, upheld the laws, dealt with anyone who broke the law and decided what their punishment would be.

When she had run an errand for her mother over to Berm, she tried to ask him about who her real mother was and why she must not speak of her. Berm seemed to become enraged, his craggy brown face turned red with anger, and he lashed out his bear paw of a hand hitting her square on the cheekbone, sending her flying across the yard. As the pain radiated across her face, he stood over her and bellowed "Don't ever utter those words to me or anyone else in the township again, next time it will be more than the back of my hand". With that he turned and walked into his house slamming the door behind him.

By the time I got home, my face felt like it was on fire, the side Berm had struck started to feel puffy, and the bones in my face ached. My father saw me first and with great concern came over to inspect my face. He held my chin between thumb and forefinger turning my face away so he could look at the swelling, "Who did this to you"? I could see anger flash across his flint grey eyes, his face cold as stone. That look scared me, but also comforted me seeing the concern for my wellbeing. As I looked up into his face, I said "It was Berm, he got so angry with me", a quizzical looked passed over father's face, it was like he could not believe what I had said, for a long moment we stood that way. When he spoke it was with an exact measured tone "And why would Berm have reason to strike you"? Now it was time for me to feel a little scared, my stomach dropped as if there were a lead weight added to it, making me feel queasy. I could feel the sweat starting to bead on my forehead as I looked into those flint grey eyes "I asked him about my mother, and why I could not speak of her, I was curious father and him being..... ". I stopped short as I watched the same sort of anger pass over my father's face as had Berm's. Fathers thumb and forefinger pinched together like a vice on my chin, causing my eyes to water with the pain; his flint grey eyes turned to stone as he looked deep into my eyes. "We have told you many times that you must never ask such questions to anyone. You have only yourself to blame ", I could feel the tears rolling down my cheeks, and my knees begin to shake as I looked into his granite-like face

"Go to your room and do not come out until your mother has been to speak with you".

He pulled his fingers away, causing my head to jerk sideways. I staggered back away from him, turned and ran for the house as fast as my legs would carry me. Rushing through the house to the small room I had at the back, I burst through the door slamming it closed behind me. Throwing myself on my bed face down in the pillow and bursting into tears. My cheek ached, and now my chin hurt. But that wasn't why I cried, it was because I didn't know who I was, where I had come from, who I was supposed to be and why all the secrecy. I was beginning to hate my life, question my very existence.

Chapter 2

The Ossary building, which was at the centre of the town, was the largest in the area. A single-story circular building with a large solid wooden door, outside the door, stood two massive pillars painted gold with carvings of animals and Celtic symbols, which held the entrance roof aloft. The building itself was painted white with a thatched roof and many windows around the wall. Stepping in through the door brought you into the public chamber, several doors lead off to the left and right, giving access to the many offices occupied by the town clerks. Directly in front of the entrance was a similar door to the front of the building, which granted access to the main Ossary meeting chamber. The public hall was more of a waiting room with many chairs for people to sit and wait their turn, the walls adorned with the weapons and shields of now dead knights. To one side stood a small altar adorned with two lit candles and a Celtic cross, in the centre was a wooden plaque carved with the names of the fallen knights.

Berm was seated in the head chair of the Ossary; the chair was of dark carved wood imposing in size, indicating the importance of the person seated there. The carvings on the chair depicted wild animals, a boar's head, the fox, a badger, and an eagle. There were also religious symbols such as a Celtic Cross and knots; it was a precious item within the room very much like a throne.

The table before him stretched out in a horseshoe configuration almost filling the room which was round in shape with a stone floor. There were two doors, one directly behind the head chair, which led to the Ossary heads chamber and one directly in front, which led to the public hall. Looking up, one could see a roof constructed of straw with large wooden beams which stretched across the room. Seated around the horseshoe were the members of the Ossary, six to Berms left and six to his right, all older men. The Ossary, made up of twelve members who would vote on issues, laws, judgments, and punishments. In the event of a tied situation, the head of the Ossary would get the final vote. Berm's role was to present the case to the Ossary and question any person brought before them so the others could make a decision.

Berm Banged on the table three times and a quiet descended over the room, he spoke loudly and slowly "We are here today for a grave matter, it is one we have known will come for many years now, and one we will have to deal with, with total impartiality. It will, of course, be a challenging time for Pata".

Berm looked to his right and directly at Pata who was seated two seats away from him, Pata did not look up but continued to stare at the tabletop in front of him fully aware all eyes were on him now. Berm continued "A difficult time for the township occurred seventeen years ago involving two people whom we do not utter their names, they were the devils spawn within our towns' breast. They were cast out and judged in this very room, for their wicked deeds, disgracing us all, creating a rift between us and all surrounding townships".

He paused to look around the room at each individual seated at the table, as his gaze travelled over them each looked away until he got to Pata, he was now looking directly at Berm, but there was a moisture in his eyes. Berm could see there was a significant internal struggle going on within him, but that was because he knew him so well. Berms mind cast back to the battles they had fought, side by side, the countless times they had saved each other in the field. The good times they had shared as well as the bad, like when he had lost his first wife, Pata had been his rock, his stalwart companion.

Berm continued "The surrounding townships have not forgotten nor forgiven, but they have come to terms with the deeds of the two. When they were stoned to death by our town the other townships began a healing process, coming closer to us than they had. Seventeen years later we are almost back to where we should be within the towns standing". Berm paused again to take a sip of his ale, looking at Pata, he saw he was once more looking at the table. "A meeting of the township heads was held here in this room just two days past; the heads were making me aware of our obligation to them, that when the spawn of the two turns eighteen, she too must be put to death by stoning, that day is tomorrow". The room was deathly quiet; no one moved, no one breathed for what seemed ages. A small catch in the throat caught Berm's attention, he looked right and saw Pata desperately trying to control his emotions. A loud bang sounded in the room making everyone jump, Berm looked to his left and saw it was Shan who had banged his goblet, "Shan has requested to speak; the head allows it"

Berm said.

Shan although one of the elders was a bit younger than the rest in the room, he still had blonde hair although greying at the sides, he was of solid build and small faced, some might say a pinched face. But he had proven his bravery on the battlefield more than once and earned his place on the Ossary. "I thank the Head for a chance to speak. I have heard what Berm has said so far, and know of the deeds of the two. However, it was seventeen years ago, we have done so much for the other towns since, why does it have to come to this? Because we saved what we considered to be an innocent baby, does that child get to choose who her parents are? No. Will that child act in the same manner? No. Then why must we punish her for her parent's sins?" He paused for his words to take effect on the others, "I know this child, she has not displayed any of the qualities of a witch, she is just a child enjoying life and sees the good in all around her".

Several hands started to bang the table in agreement with the speaker. Berm waited for the noise to abate to silence, a tankard hit on the table to his right, looking he saw Dard was the owner of it. "Dard has requested to speak; the head allows it," Berm said with his hand outstretched to Dard.

Dard was the oldest in the room, his grey hair untidy and uncut for weeks, his face creased by age and weather, he had seen many summers as had his clothes, which were a bit threadbare in places. "I thank the Head" his voice was cracked and weary, "Seventeen years ago we decided to save a baby because no one was up to kill it with its parents. I don't criticize anyone; we talk of devil's spawn and surely to kill a babe in arms is the devil's work. BUT, we did undertake an oath to all the townships that when the child becomes an adult, she shall suffer the same fate as the parents, and if that fate is not delivered, we may well receive the wroth of the towns once more". He waited for his words to sink in, slowly looking around the table seeing quite a few nodding heads. He continued "We have all come to know, and like the girl, we all know she does not deserve the same fate as her parents, we all knew this day would come. It is up to us, here today, to decide her fate and that of the town. What is more important, one life or all the lives of the township".

Many more hands banged the table than before. Berm looked to Pata; he was still looking to the tabletop his shoulders imperceptibly shaking with emotion. Pata's thoughts were racing he could see which way it was going, and it may be him who would have to plea passionately to the Ossary to save his little girl's life. What could he say? What will sway the Ossary to save her and possibly go in open conflict with the townships, and what will he say to his wife if he loses.

Berm waited for the quiet to return and then turned to Pata "Pata my dear friend, the time has come for you to speak, let us all know your mind". Pata looked up around the table, making eye contact with each, and every member, a little shakily to start with, Pata started to speak "You all know me, we have all lived good lives here within the town. I would lay down my life for each, and every one of you, we have fought together, drank together, laughed together, and sometimes cried together. Seventeen years ago, a baby came to my house; at first, I did not want her, the devil's spawn. But as she grew and became a person my feelings changed, she became the child my wife and I could never have. A child I have played games with, read to, comforted, and protected, a child I have grown to love and cherish. That child has now blossomed into a beautiful young lady any man would be lucky to have as a wife. Don't let the townships dictate whether she lives or dies; let your conscience make that decision. Does she have to pay the price for her parent's deeds? Does she have to die to appease the royal town?" Pata then fell silent looking down to his hands in his lap, dreading the upcoming vote.

Berm allowed a few minutes for Pata's plea to fully sink in, the gravity of the situation weighing heavy on his shoulders. "We have discussed the matter at hand today, every one of us has to reach into his heart, and decide for themselves". He looked solemnly around the room; the tension was palpable, never in the history of the Ossary had such a decision had to be made, against a potentially innocent person. "All those in favour of upholding the town's promise raise your hand". As Berm looked around the room, members raised their hands which he counted. Berm continued, "I count six hands raised; all those not in favour of upholding the towns promise raise your hands". Berm looked around again, "I count six hands not in favour therefore, I declare a draw. I will cast the final vote".

Berm closed his eyes and searched his soul and heart for the answer; Berm was a townsman through and through. His thoughts travelled back to the day she had stood in front of him asking about her parents, in his heart, he knew that would never stop. He opened his eyes and found all eyes in the room were on him. Berm looked at Pata with eyes that said it all "I have decided; I will uphold the towns promise to make it seven for and six against. Tomorrow at noon she will be taken to the stoning circle where the townships promise will be upheld, that is the final ruling of the Ossary".

Pata leapt from his chair sending it skidding back into the wall, not saying a word, he looked directly into the eyes of Berm, and for the first time in his life, Berm felt fear. Pata looked around the room at each and every member, his face cold as stone and a fire in his eyes. But he didn't utter a word; the look was enough. He stormed out of the room, slamming the door behind him.

Chapter 3

Anouk awoke in the morning, as she lay in her bed listening to the morning sounds, she felt comfortable, warm, and safe. She could hear Katcha moving around the kitchen area in the next room, the pigs outside snuffling and a horse whinnying, probably the one Pata had chosen for the day's work. Anouk stretched working out the kinks in her muscles, rubbed her eyes, and sat up in the bed. Her room was very plain and basic with a washstand in the corner, I bet Katcha has been in to put fresh water there for me, she thought. A simple wooden wardrobe Pata had built for her few dresses and clothes stood against the wall. He had carved AB on the doors, one letter on each door for her name, Anouk Bower, she had taken their surname. And there was her bed with a straw mattress, not precisely a palace but it was hers, a place to call home, a safe place.

Anouk heard the front door bang and Pata's voice, although muffled through the wall. That's odd, she thought, Pata must be talking very loudly for me to hear it. As she listened, she could hear Katcha's voice; she seemed to be shouting at Pata, and Pata was now shouting back at her. Whatever could have happened? they never shout, she thought, as she tried to listen for more, all she could make out was Pata saying her name. Oh god, whatever have I done? It must be awful for them to be shouting and arguing about me. How have I upset them? Anouk sat stock still in her bed barely breathing, the argument continuing next door. Her mind began to race, replaying all she had done over the last few days, trying to see if she had done something to upset the most important people in her life. She racked her brain, desperately trying to make some sense of the situation, but she couldn't think of anything she had done or said that would have caused this. Think, think, there must be something, what have I said? Think, suddenly the front door slammed closed again with a bang which made her jump out of her thoughts and back to listening, all seemed quiet again.

Anouk thought, Well, whatever it was about it must be bad and I really should go out there and face the trouble head-on. She looked up at the window; the sun was relatively high; she must have slept in this morning. Realizing this, she leapt from her bed, stripping off her nightclothes, hurriedly washing her face and hands at the washstand. As she was doing this thought, it can't be because I have overslept, could it? No, they would have just come and woken me surely, she hurried to get into her work clothes. She needed to speak with Katcha and her jobs still needed to be done, she had arranged to meet up with Minit that afternoon at the lake for a swim. As she ran a comb through her hair trying to get the knots out, she wished for a brush but they were expensive, and she hadn't wanted to ask for one. After putting her hair in a ponytail, she rushed out into the kitchen area, Katcha was standing at the table with her back to her, her shoulders rounded looking like she was carrying a great weight. Anouk could hear the soft sobs escaping from her lips. She stepped up behind her and slipped her arms around her waist, hugging her, not saying a word. Katcha's hands dropped to hers and squeezed them tight; a big sob broke from her lips.

Anouk and Katcha stood that way for some minutes, not saying a word, just hugging. Katcha released her hands and turned around to face Anouk, her face was red, and her eyes were puffy from crying and had dark rings under them as if she had not slept last night. Raising her hands to Anouk's face she held her, one on each cheek looking into her eyes. When she spoke, it was with a feeling of profound loss, sadness, and love in her voice, "You need to run along and get your chores done, when you're finished go to the lake, bathe and put your best dress on. We have to go to the town today, and I want you looking your best". Anouk just looked at her, taking in her face, seeing the sadness held within it. "But what was all that about with Pata? Have I done something…."? Katcha cut her short, "No my sweet angel, you have done nothing wrong, do not let anyone say any different to you. We just have to work something out, now run along to your chores".

As she hurried on with her work, she could see Pata far out over the fields working with the horses, stopping and shading her eyes from the sun. She tried to make out what he was doing, he appeared to be just standing still in the field with the horses close by, well he is doing something out there she told herself. I wonder should I go speak with him, he is very angry with me, enough to upset Katcha. No, get your chores done girl, then we should talk, she told herself. Anouk continued with her chores, and when she was nearly finished, she looked over to where Pata was again, she couldn't see him, but the horse was still standing in the roughly the same spot. Now that is odd, she thought, what could he be doing?

As she was nearly finished, she decided to run over and see what was happening. It was a lovely day with a clear blue sky and the odd fluffy white cloud, a slight breeze blew over the fields which carried a whinny from the horse to her. She looked at the horse, which was watching her approach over the fields. Oakley was attached to the plough, and some of the fields had been ploughed, but that was an odd place to stop she thought mid furrow. As she got closer, she noticed what looked like a mound in the field behind the plough, she started to run faster, the closer she got, the more she began to realize it wasn't a mound, it was Pata.

When she got to him, she dropped to her knees at his side, she could see he wasn't moving. Standing erect from his chest were three arrows, the arrows were of dark wood and had black fletching feathers. Anouk tried to shake Pata, to get him to move, the blood was starting to soak into his shirt, joining together from the three arrows into one big stain. Anouk could see he was dead, and tears started to well in her eyes, she let out a loud wail "Nooooo". As huge heart-rending sobs tore up from her chest, she sat and sobbed inconsolably in front of Pata's lifeless body unable to comprehend why or who would do this. For many minutes Anouk remained on her knees, head down with the feeling of her world crashing down.

"Katcha" she thought aloud, using her sleeve to wipe the moisture from her eyes, looking up and over to the house. Black smoke was billowing from the roof of the house; she wiped her eyes again to be sure, yes black smoke. Jumping to her feet desperate to get to Katcha she turned and hurriedly released Oakley from his plough harness, leapt onto him bareback, and rode as fast as she could back to the house.

As she approached the house bright orange flames started to burst through the roof consuming the thatch like a fire breathing angry monster, she brought the horse to a skidding halt. Anouk leapt from her mount and ran towards the front door shouting, "Katcha, Katcha where are you?". Entering through the door, her eyes started to burn with the smoke; she breathed the air which burned deep down into her chest, causing her cough. Burning straw was falling around her and sparks wisped through the air in front of her blurry eyes. She spotted Katcha slumped over the kitchen table and started to make her way to her through the burning smoke, making it to Katcha's side. Katcha wasn't moving, she grabbed her shoulder and shook hard, trying to rouse her, but still, she did not move. The fire was getting hotter, she could feel her skin begin to burn and the smell of her hair starting to singe, she pulled one last time at Katcha who slid from the table to the floor landing on her back.

Her clothes were covered in blood and Anouk could now see her throat had been cut, she just stared at the body on the floor as the house burned around her. Suddenly a huge crack sounded over her head. Instinctively she looked up and saw the roof was giving way; it was all about to come crashing down. Anouk could see Katcha was dead and started to back up to the doorway, unable to take her eyes off of Katcha's lifeless body lying on the kitchen floor, as she got to the door the roof collapsed inwards into the house sending flames and thick black smoke towards her. Anouk turned and flung herself sideways out of the door to the ground to avoid the flames. She lay gasping on the ground, dragging in huge lungsful of air. Lifting herself from the ground on very shaky arms, she felt a sharp pain at the back of her head, and everything went Black.

Chapter 4

Dug was an amiable sort of guy, a little down on his luck of late but things always came good sooner or later. A bit of a drifter, not putting down roots to speak of and jack of all trades but certainly a master of none. Drifting from village to village, town to town, the only thing he could claim to be good at is a bit of thieving, but then you can't brag about that can you.

Dug was in his thirty-somethings, he didn't care to remember nowadays. He was of heavier build now than when he was in his youth, the middle getting bigger and hanging over his belt. But he was happy in his day to day life. Only yesterday in Stockling he managed to pinch a loaf and a spit of meat from a lonely farmhouse, he had finished off the food this morning and still had a full belly, a road to walk and the birds to talk to. So, all in all, life was good at the moment. As he wandered along the road towards the next town, Belcher was its name, he whistled a happy tune and looked up at the blue sky and white fluffy clouds. As he walked, he became aware of a horse trotting down behind him, turning to look back and stepping to the grass verge, he saw a farmer type coming down on a large brown mare. As he got closer the horse slowed to a walk and the rider called out "You going to Belcher", Dug replied "Who wants to know", the rider shrugged his shoulders as he passed. Calling back over his shoulder, "The names Sam and there's gonna be a stoning today, we haven't had one of those in seventeen years, bound to draw the crowds". Dug watched as the rider continued down the road, thinking, odd he has got such a valuable horse and can't afford a saddle, ah, probably spent all his money on that fancy long leather coat. As he continued to watch him, his attention was drawn to the large war bow on his back and the black fletched arrows hanging out of the quiver. If I could get my hands on that it would be worth a pretty penny, he thought to himself.

Dug had a good memory, he had to in his game, marking out faces who had money or other valuables he could steal. Where he spotted food and items he could sell. Yep, he was pretty good at his craft. His thoughts changed to what the rider had said, Crowds! Could be a good chance to pick a few pockets, maybe a few stalls to get supplies from, when they weren't looking of course.

His mind made up he hastened on down the road towards Belcher, looking up he could tell by the sun that it must be about mid-morning and he knew any execution was always set at mid-day, so that should give him plenty of time to walk to the town. It was then he noticed a huge black cloud of smoke rising in the sky on the horizon, well someone is having a big bonfire over there he thought.

As he walked, he reminisced over what might have been his life, he was born to a rich merchant in the Royal town town of Regis. He and his parents lived in a large house with many servants, and life was good for them. Always food on the table, his parents had plenty of money to lavish on their only son, he used to want for nothing. As he got older, the ladies paid him a lot of attention, mainly because of the money, he knew that, but the attention was always welcome. Lavish parties, royal parties, he used to mix with all the upper crust at that time. But then some big scandal happened with the royal family, only the elite inner circle knew what had happened, but it caused a real upheaval within the royal town and his father was blamed for some of it. As a result of that his father was stripped of all titles, land, and money by the royal family, Dug was cast out, and his father and mother were stoned to death at the Regis stoning circle. A short while later, the Royal family had their own sorrow to deal with when their only son and heir was killed in a tavern fight of all things, something to do with a lady's honour.

Dug looked up and saw he was already approaching the town of Belcher, judging by the sun he would still have some time to kill before the stoning, reaching into his pocket he pulled out what few coins he had and saw there should be enough for a flagon of ale. He had not been to Belcher before but looking around it all seemed pretty much the same as all the other towns, the main road he was on led through the houses towards the centre of the town. The road would continue down to the end where a bigger more imposing building stood, which would be the local Ossary. Dug knew the stoning circle would be directly behind the Ossary, so at the appropriate time most people would move away to that area, leaving him to ply his craft.

He walked down the long road in the direction of the Ossary looking left and right at the many market tables set up outside the houses, some containing food, he made a mental note of those. Others had clothes, mostly farmer drab-coloured overalls, shirts, and hats, and some had trinkets and baubles laid out in brightly coloured patterns to attract the buyer. Soon he found what he was looking for, a house with several benches next to rough wood tables set outside, most were occupied by people drinking flagons of ale and talking in hushed tones between them. He saw one table with two men sitting on one side having a heated conversation, and the bench the other side was empty, as he approached the two looked up at him with little real interest. Dug asked "Anyone using this bench, ok if I sit and rest my weary legs?" The two glanced at each other then back at Dug, the skinny one replied, "Help yourself, stranger".

Dug sat down taking a better look at the two men, the skinny one to his left had red hair under a large brimmed hat, really pale skin and a scar running down the left side of his face, starting just under his eye and curving down and around almost to the corner of his mouth. He was dressed in tidy town clothes and didn't look as if he did much hard work. The second was a larger man with untidy black hair, browned skin, and bad teeth. He wore a black eye patch over his left eye, now he looked as if he could handle himself. The two had gone back to talking quietly, and red was using his hand to shield his mouth in an attempt not to be overheard, which was working as all he could hear was hushed whispered words.

"What can I get you stranger", the voice made Dug jump as he had not seen the owner approach him, looking up he saw a tall solid man with a full beard and happy eyes looking down at him, he had a large belly over which hung a dirty white apron. Ah, the owner he thought.

"Can I have a flagon of your best ale, good sir"? Dug asked.

"Have you got coin? I can't be doing with people who don't, and I don't know you stranger".

Dug fished the coins from his pocket and put them on the table for the owner to see.

"Ah, all good there then, I see you have enough for two", the owner said with a beaming smile, "Be right back" he called over his shoulder as he hustled off to get a flagon. Dug looked down at the coins and thought, *ale is cheaper here than Stockling, this would have only bought one there.*

As he waited for his ale the two men stopped talking and started sipping their ale. Red was looking at him now, putting his flagon down, he spoke.

"So stranger, you here for the stoning"?

Dug pondered the question, replying, "No not really, I was travelling through the area and just happened here today", the owner returned and thumped a flagon down in front of Dug spilling a little of the ale, taking his coins from where Dug had put them on the table he turned and walked away to another table. "So, what's this stoning all about, was the poor bugger caught with someone's wife"? He asked jokingly.

Red looked at Dug with sad eyes shaking his head slowly, "Nope, and that poor bugger as you put it is a woman, nobody has been stoned here in the last seventeen years, its barbaric and shouldn't be allowed. But no, the powers that be say....".

Red stopped as the other man poked him in the ribs whilst shaking his head. Red went back to sipping his ale, and the dark-haired one said "Right, well I am off, some of us have a job to do. Don't get too drunk Tam, you will miss the stoning", he laughed out loud as he rose from the bench and walked off. Dug sat and looked at Tam for a short while; he was holding his flagon in both hands on the table, staring at the contents deep in thought.

"Tam is it?" Dug asked, Tam looked up but didn't say anything, so Dug continued, "Well I am Dug, and you were going to say something before your friend stopped you, want to tell me now?" Dug continued to watch Tam and could see he was having an internal battle with himself, so Dug let the question hang whilst he took a few more sips of ale. Tam looked around making sure no one was close enough to earwig.

"As I said the person is a woman, well only just becoming a woman at eighteen years today, all I know is she is an orphan who lives out on a farm in these parts. But no one can say what she has done wrong or why she has to be stoned. I ask you, just how barbaric is that, stoning was stopped years ago, anyone deserving of a death penalty nowadays gets beheaded".

Tam looked down staring into his ale again, and Dug tried to process what he had just said, "So no one knows what this girl has done? Surely if it was such a heinous crime to warrant a death penalty then everyone would know, how can it be justice if you don't know what you are being accused of"?

Tam looked up into Dug's eyes and replied "Exactly my point, that poor girl will be going to her death never knowing what she was supposed to have done, and if she has done nothing then why is this happening?". Tam looked around again, took the last swig of his ale and stood up "I have to go my friend, out of town before it starts, I cannot be a part of this". Walking around to Dug's side he laid a hand on his shoulder saying, "I would advise you to do the same, for your own soul".

It was now Dug's turn to sit and ponder over his ale, a young girl being stoned for no apparent reason, he could understand criminals being punished, as long as it wasn't him of course. But this is so wrong, has this town gone mad. This was going to take him a bit longer to process. He spun around on the bench leaning back against the table, holding his ale in his lap. Looking up at the blue sky and wispy clouds deep in thought, suddenly a movement caught his eye, a man stepped out of the house opposite. He was wearing a long brown leather coat, and as he turned to shout something back through the doorway, Dug saw the bow and arrows on his back. Ah, it was the rider he had seen earlier, Sam he said his name was, well Sam I now know where you live, he thought, making a mental note of the house.

Shan was sitting in his comfy chair with his head leaning forward onto his hands, which were clasped together into one big fist on which his chin rested. He was deep in thought, and very troubled thoughts they were, "How can this be allowed to happen? The poor girl is not responsible for the actions of her parents; she was but a babe when it all happened. She could not choose who her parents would be much less who should be her sire". He looked up around the room, it was a good house, commensurate with his standing in the town and his position on the Ossary. The floor was of stone but upon it was a beautiful red, black and gold rug almost the size of the room, two large comfy chairs facing the finely carved small table in front of the fireplace. The fireplace was made of dark oak carved with wood animals, horses, and birds, in the centre was a coat of arms of two rampant stags supporting a shield. On the shield was a large blue cross, an arrowhead pointing upwards displayed in each quarter and atop the shield was a knight's helmet, with three feathers flowing backwards from the helm. His eyes fell to the motto emblazoned below the shield, Semper Honos Semper Veritatem, "Always Honor Always Truth" he thought to himself.

Shan rose from the chair and started pacing around the room. He could hear the gathering crowds in the street outside; the time was getting close. He felt physically sick with the thought of what was to come. Shan continued pacing thinking out loud "What would possess Berm to pass such a decision? Was he being pressured by outside forces? The other town leaders had been to see him, did they threaten him with something? Or was it the Royal family who had a part in this, god knows they have the biggest reason for seeing her gone". Shan stopped pacing by the window, looking out at the crowds he watched them as they meandered around. He spotted two men, they were dressed in farmers clothes, but the clothes looked brand new and of very high quality, not what farmers are usually dressed in, he thought. As he watched the two getting closer, he could see their faces more clearly, I know that man, he thought, staring at his face. Shan cast his mind back to where he had seen him before, he had been on an official visit to the Royal town of Regis, and when he was introduced to the King in the royal chambers, that man had been stood behind him, a knight, a Royal protector. So, the Royal family must have a hand in this if they are sending their people to see if the execution takes place.

Shan turned from the window his eyes moving to the opposite wall where his broad sword and shield were mounted, on the shield was the same coat of arms, his eyes fixing on the motto once again. Always Honor Always Truth, Always Honor Always truth, kept ringing through his brain.

Chapter 5

Anouk awoke, she was face down on a cold stone floor. She lay there listening to see if she could hear anything, am I still alive, she thought. The answer came as a searing pain came from the back of her head, grimacing she raised a hand to where it hurt, her fingers came upon a large bump which had been oozing with blood. As she explored the wound, the pressure of her fingers caused more pain, grimacing she moved her hand away. She lay there just breathing and trying to deal with the pain in her head for a few minutes. Eventually, she thought, well I need to sit up and see where I am, it was at this point the memories of the last few hours came flooding back. Pata in the field with arrows in his chest, Katcha in the kitchen with her throat cut, the house burning, it was like an avalanche of sorrow and pain cascading through her brain. Her whole world had gone, been destroyed, taken from her forever. The tears welled in her eyes; she started to sob uncontrollably.

After many minutes she started to get control of herself and thinking more clearly again, placing her hands on the stone floor she gingerly raised her body, but very quickly the room started to spin and she felt sick, laying back down she decided she was going to have to do this slowly. Over time she slowly raised herself further and further up until eventually, and after what seemed ages she was sitting on the floor. Her head still hurt horribly, but she could now look around the room, it was round in shape with one door which looked very solid with metal bands horizontally across and no handle. The room was empty except for her, and the walls were bare, a small window was set high on the wall opposite the door. Looking up, which hurt her head to do, she could see heavy wood beams that had bars affixed covering the whole roof. Is this some kind of prison, or dungeon? She asked herself, but why would I be in prison; I didn't kill Pata and Katcha, it has to be some terrible mistake.

Slowly she climbed to her feet, wobbly at first but managed it to the door, Anouk started to bang her fist on the door shouting "Hey is anyone there, can anyone hear me, this is all a big mistake, let me out". A loud bang came from the other side, making Anouk jump and step back, a gruff voice said, "Shut the hole in your face, or I will come in there and give you another lump on your head". Anouk slowly backed away from the door until she reached the wall behind, sliding down she sat putting her arms around her legs and hugging herself into a ball. As she sat there, she tried to think, why is this happening? Pata was a respected member of the Ossary and the town. She was sure he had done nothing wrong, the town should be up in arms about his death, and Katcha. Oh, poor Katcha, a lovely lady who never had an unkind word for anyone. The town should be out seeking the killers of her parents not locking young girls in prison.

The door to the room suddenly swung open, a large muscly black-haired man stood in the doorway, his hair was untidy, and his skin was brown from being out in the sun a lot, over his left eye was a black eye patch. As he smiled at Anouk, she could see he had really bad teeth, some missing, some broken, the rest standing out like black tombstones. "On your feet girl, it's almost time for your grand appearance", he started chuckling with a leering look in his eye. Anouk shivered with disgust and tightened herself into more of a ball. The man strode across the room, "So it's going to be like that is it girly", reaching down he grabbed her wrist in his large meaty hand and tugged hard causing Anouk to lose grip on her legs.

He yanked her arm upwards so hard her body had no choice but to follow, pain blossomed in her shoulder, it felt as if he would pull her arm off. As she rose from the floor squealing in pain, he spun her around, so her back was against him, his other arm closed around her waist like a vice, pinning her tightly back against him. Letting go of her wrist his hand dropped moving to her chest where he gripped her right breast in his big meaty hand, squeezing so hard she again squealed in pain. Moving his lips close to her ear he said, "It's a shame I didn't get to keep you overnight, oh what fun we would have had", he ran his tongue slowly up her cheek leaving a trail of saliva on her.

Anouk squeezed her eyes shut, the stink of the ale and bad breath in her nose, the wet of the slime he left on her cheek, and the violation of her body began to overwhelm her. A rage she had never felt before started as a ball in her stomach, expanding bigger and bigger until her whole body was needed to contain it. The pressure, the rage, the anger, the loss, the final humiliation of violation coalesced into a ball, so powerful her body could not contain it anymore. The two of them started to rise from the floor, floating in the air until the rage exploded out of her like a thousand gales.

The pressure wave sent the jailer flying against the wall killing him instantly; the heavy door was ripped from its hinges flying through the air outside, the roof to the prison blown clean off up into the sky flying away like a giant play toy, a loud bang preceded the rushing air as it tore upwards through where the roof had been like a giant tornado, carrying the body of the jailer high into the air. Part of the explosion shot through where the door had been in a horizontal column across the road, flattening all who was in its way and striking the house opposite. The merchant tables lifted with their contents, one going through the window of the house the other flipping up and over the roof and far off into the fields scattering merchandise along its path. The front door, open at the time the tornado hit allowed it inside, swirling within the house like a giant cauldron being stirred, churning the contents and occupants alike into a broken mess.

Anouk fell to her knee's still facing the wall, naked. The pressure wave had blown every last stitch of clothing from her body, for a moment she felt serene and calm, but then the questions starting running through her mind, what happened? Was that me? How can this be possible?" She thought. I have never felt like that before, what am I? What have they done to me? So tired, I need to sleep, god I am so tired, just close my eyes for a bit.

A figure appeared at the door; it was Dug. He had been up the road at the house tavern when the roof flew off the building to his left down the road; he saw the gale shoot across the road, hitting a merchant's house. Concerned, people might be injured, and there might be something to lift within the debris, he ran across the road to the open doorway. When he arrived, all he could see was an empty room except for a naked girl kneeling on the floor facing the opposite wall. Her back was to him; he could see she was quite young, maybe early twenty's, she had long blonde hair tied back in a ponytail and looked as if she were praying. Taking his long coat off, he approached the girl and draped it over her shoulders; she didn't move. Holding her gently by the arms, he lifted her to her feet, but her knees gave way almost falling back down. He caught her and wrapped the coat around her and lifted her into his arms. He left the devastated building and started walking up the road away from the Ossary. The town was in chaos with people laying all over the road and others rushing to help them, he could hear some shouting "What the hell happened?" and "Did anyone see what happened?" As he walked no one paid any particular attention to him, I need to find a healer somewhere here, he thought whilst looking down at the face of the girl he was carrying. Her eyes were closed, but he could see she was blessed with a particular beauty.

As he was walking past the houses looking for a healer symbol, a door flew open, in the doorway stood an imposing figure of a man, tall and strong with blonde hair starting to grey at the sides, showing his advancing years. "Quick, come here". Dug veered to the doorway, "Are you a healer? The girl needs to be seen by one", he said as he walked. The man stepped aside clearing the doorway, "No, but you need to get inside now before anyone sees you". Dug entered the house, and the blonde man quickly closed the door, he reached down lifting the corner of the red, black, and gold rug laying on the floor, with a flick it rolled back and revealed a trap door. With a hefty tug the blonde man lifted the trap door to reveal steps going down to a cellar, the cellar was dark, and Dug eyed it suspiciously. Glancing around the room he could see this person was well off and the sword and shield on the wall indicated to him this man might be a knight, he read the motto on the shield, Always Honor Always Truth.

His dad had made him learn Latin as a boy, the motto and the coat of arms rang a bell from his childhood. He made up his mind to trust this blonde knight; he hoped he would not regret it. The blonde man spoke again in hushed tones, "My name is Shan, quickly go down to the cellar, you will find a cot and candles down there, but go now, you must hide. I will join you later when it is safe and explain what I can". Dug descended the steps into a cellar which was of a decent size, a cot stood against one wall, and a small table against another, candles and flint were on the table. Dug gently laid Anouk on the cot, and went to light the candles, as they burst into flame the hatch closed and he could hear the rug being slid back in place. Dug went back to check on Anouk and concluded she was sleeping, picking up a blanket from the end of the cot he laid it over her, sitting down on the floor with his back to the cot he pondered over the events of the day and his conversation with Tam, could this be the young woman who was supposed to be stoned today? Looking over his shoulder at Anouk's sleeping face, she looks as though she is of that age, and Shan rushing to hide us in his cellar would fit with that, but then why would he, a knight, be doing this? Surely, he should be upholding the law of the town, not hiding a fugitive in his cellar. The questions whirling around his head made his brain hurt, and his eyelids were getting heavy, oh well a little nap and I will be better disposed to figuring some of this out. Dug closed his eyes and started to doze.

Dug awoke to the noise of the trap door opening, looking back over his shoulder he saw Anouk was awake. Sitting huddled back against the wall with the blanket pulled tightly around her, she was looking fixedly at him with great suspicion in her eyes. "Who are you?" Her glare boring into him, Dug cleared his throat and wiped the sleep from his eyes; he explained he was a traveller who just happened to be in the town today, and then went on to describe the events leading up to their being in the cellar. Dug looked over to the steps and saw Shan sitting there watching and listening.

Anouk sat and thought through what he had said, throwing a sideways glance at Shan she asked "So where are my clothes? Who took them from me?" Dug shrugged "I don't know; you were naked when I found you", Anouk looked over to Shan, "And who are you?". Shan smiled and ran his hand over his hair, "I am Shan, a knight of Belcher, an Ossary member and friend of your father Pata, I also own this house we are sitting in". He looked at Anouk thinking, thank god she is safe for now, but we are going to need a plan to get her out. "I came down to see if you two were hungry, would you like some food?". Both Dug and Anouk nodded their heads, "Ok, back in a minute", Shan disappeared up through the hatch returning a short time later with a tray containing a loaf of bread, some meats, cheese, and a jug of ale. Placing it on the table he turned and headed for the stairs saying "Just getting some tankards", he went up the steps returning quickly with three cups in his hands. Looking at Anouk, he asked "Would you like some bread and meat?", Anouk looked to the tray "I would prefer some bread and cheese if possible", Shan selected a platter and tore off a chunk of bread, using his knife he cut a wedge of cheese placing it next to the bread on the platter before taking it over to her.

She accepted it gracefully and started to eat hungrily; she hadn't realized how hungry she was until now, her stomach growled in acceptance of the food. The three sat and ate in silence, Dug having more than his fill and was on his second cup of ale when Anouk broke the silence asking Shan for a cup of water which he quickly went and got for her. "I need to go and do a few things, but when I get back, we all need to discuss what has happened today and what we are going to do from here". Shan disappeared back up through the hatch which closed behind him, the sound of the rug could be heard covering the trap door, then the front door opening and closing came next with silence above after.

Anouk lay back against the wall feeling contented with a full stomach, as she sipped her water, she looked at Dug who was looking at her. She could now make out kindness in his face and concern for her in his eyes; she started to feel safe with him, the beginnings of trust and friendship. "Tell me about your life Dug and how you became a traveller". Dug looked away at the other wall, cleared his throat, and started to tell his tale, about the big house in Regis, the splendid lifestyle, the ladies and the balls he used to attend, embellishing it a little bit to make it all sound grander. Then told her of the downfall of his family, how the Royal family stripped them of their lands, money, and titles, ending with how his parents were put to death and he was cast out. Dug finished talking and was looking down at the last of his ale in the cup he was holding. When he looked up at Anouk, he could see her eyes were watery, she was looking at him with sorrow written clearly over her face, “But that was a long time ago now, so don’t you go fretting over me lass”. Anouk attempted a smile and quickly wiped the moisture from her eyes.

Chapter 6

Shan returned to the house carrying several bags, he slipped quietly in through the front door and deposited the bags on the floor. He then moved about the house making sure the windows were covered and locked as were the doors. Satisfied all was well he headed for the bags and selected one, moving the rug and opening the trap door he descended into the cellar. Dug was sitting one end of the cot whilst Anouk, still wrapped in the blanket, was sitting the other end, the two were talking quietly but stopped as he entered, both looked at him as he strode across the room pulling extra candles from the bag which he placed on the table. Noticing the food tray was empty, "Do either of you need more food"? Looking over to them, he saw them shaking their heads. "Ok," he said, walking over to the cot and standing in front of Anouk. Shan dipped into the bag again and pulled out a light green shirt followed by brown trousers; they were of the rough farmer type material and pretty non-descript. "I am sorry about the quality, but we are going to need you to blend in as far as possible. Also, these are boys' clothes, so you are going to have to pass as a boy". Anouk's eyebrows shot up at this and said, looking down at her chest, "And how am I going to possibly do that"? Dug chuckled in the corner causing Anouk to shoot a look of distaste his way. Pulling the next item from the bag Shan let it unravel down onto the cot, it was a length of soft white material, Anouk eyed it with suspicion. "Well you will need to wrap your um, chest with this to flatten your um, well I am sure you get the idea".

Anouk looked up to Shan's face as he was speaking and was sure she could see a bit more colour in his cheeks, she wanted to giggle but thought better of it. Lastly, he pulled a black brimmed hat and brown boots from the bag, "You will need to wear your hair up under the hat, and I do hope the boots fit ok, I had to guess a size". Shan then threw the empty bag into the corner by the table and turned to Dug, "Ok, I think you and I should go upstairs and leave the lady to get herself dressed", Dug nodded, and Shan turned back to Anouk, "When you are done just knock on the hatch, and we will open it for you, ok?", Anouk smiled at Shan and nodded.

When both the men had left the cellar and closed the hatch, Anouk stood up and let the blanket slide from her to the floor, removing the long coat, she stood naked. Looking over her body to check there were no injuries, she noticed her right breast, four-finger bruises ran down the side of it near her breastbone. The sight of these brought back the memory of the disgusting, horrible man who had caused them and the pain he had inflicted on her. She started to feel angry again at the way he had violated her, a tight ball of fury started to manifest itself in her stomach, her memories of the day were coming back slowly, and she realized this feeling wasn't good. Closing her eyes, she pictured being in the fields of corn on a hot summer's day, the wind in her hair, and the summer smells of the holding. Calming herself, she felt the ball of fury lessen and dissipate from her stomach. "I will have to watch that in the future," she told herself.

Having dressed and bound her chest as requested Anouk knocked on the hatch and waited for it to open, Shan stood to one side as she climbed up out of the cellar. Dug was seated in one of the two comfy chairs in front of the fireplace, Shan moved to the other and indicated his chair with a graceful sweep of his arm, "Please use my chair, young lady, or may I call you Anouk?" She lowered herself into the chair whilst smiling up at Shan; she could see his face more clearly now as this room was lighter than the cellar. He had a smallish face but handsome, clear blue eyes and a small scar above his right eye. His teeth were nice and white, which stood out from his tanned face. Shan had now sat on the table between the two of them, and realizing she was staring she looked down to her lap with a small blush creeping into her cheeks. "Well, may I call you Anouk?" Shan repeated, "Oh, sorry, yes, of course, you may", Anouk replied blushing even deeper for not having answered. "Ok, Anouk you and I have met before, some time ago I know, but it was when I was over visiting Pata, you were a lot smaller then, running all over the place like an angry wasp. How the years have changed you, and very much for the better, I must say", Anouk blushed again, "Why thank you". Shan continued "Anouk, I need you to tell me the events of today up to why you were imprisoned in the town jail".

Anouk took a deep breath clasping her hands in her lap and started telling her story; she started with waking up to the massive row between Pata and Katcha in the kitchen, how upset Katcha was, and how she had told her to hurry her chores as they were going into town that day. She went on with having done her chores she went over the field to where Pata was ploughing, as she started to describe the scene of what she found tears welled in her eyes, she described Pata laying on the ground, and the dark arrows with black feathers sticking from his chest. Dug made a noise at this causing Anouk to stop, she and Shan looked at Dug who held up his hand "Sorry, please carry on Anouk, I may have something to add later". Anouk continued describing being with Pata when she saw the house was on fire, of using the horse from the plough to get to Katcha and the house. Anouk paused, her shoulders shaking a little as she held back the sobs, in a shaky voice, she described the scene inside the farmhouse with Katcha and how her throat was cut. Finally, she told of how she escaped the fire, but something hit her head, knocking her out, and later she woke inside the jail.

After a short while, Shan spoke "I can't believe Pata and Katcha are dead", his words hung in the air for a short time, then Dug spoke, "Whilst I was walking to town, I was passed by a man on a large brown mare, he was riding bareback which I thought was odd, as he passed me I saw he had a large war bow across his back and a quiver with black fletched arrows". Anouk looked at Dug, "Black arrows! And I bet that large brown mare was Bonny, I didn't think of it at the time, but Pata was using the large plough, which takes two horses, but only Oakley was there". Shan spoke "Dug can you remember anything more of this rider, we need to know who it was". Dug looked to Shan with a mischievous smile, "Shan, I remember everything, he had a long brown leather coat, his name was Sam, and he lives, but five doors down from where we sit". "Sam Longshot" Shan exclaimed, "He is called that because he is so good with his bow, but why would he want to kill Pata? There has to be more to this; he wouldn't kill an Ossary member for no reason", the three sat in silence digesting what had been said so far.

Shan looked around and said" Ok, it is time for me to impart my story and what I know of this situation. When I was younger and just a page I worked with several knights of the time, so you got to hear what was happening in the world and more importantly how the knights were tasked. There were people throughout the land who had what you might call, a special power; the men were called sorcerers and the women witches. Their powers ranged from controlling fire, water, wind and some could control the very ground you stand on". Shan was looking at Anouk whilst saying this, and Anouk's eyebrows were rising higher and higher on her head, whilst staring intently at Shan. Shan went on "Your parents were regular visitors to Regis, where a Royal scandal emerged involving the young Prince and only male heir to the throne. The prince was a handsome man turning many heads in court, he was also an accomplished swordsman and fighter, the best in the land some would say. But he had an eye for the ladies, and he had many conquests, married and unmarried, most were willing although it was said, some were not. Anyway, he met his match in a town tavern one night where he was found dead in a back bedroom; his body had been crushed as if by an invisible giant hand, his hair and clothes were scorched, and yet there was no fire in the fireplace. It was decided it must have been the work of the sorcerers and witches, your parents returned to Belcher shortly after the death of the Prince. They never talked of or went to Regis again, but within a few months, your mother started showing signs of being with child. They disappeared a few months later, and when they returned, their child had been born". Shan paused to sip some ale, whilst Anouk tried to process what had been said so far, so I am not the only one this has happened to. He is talking about my parents, so he must have known them, I have so many questions for him, but she didn't want to break his train of thought so decided to remain quiet for now.

Shan continued, "A few months after the death of the Prince these people were decreed by the Royal family as ungodly and sacrilegious and ordered that all knights of the towns were to find them and round them up. They were to be stoned to death in the villages they came from. Anouk, after your birth your mother was seen to control fire in the woods, by a villager, and your father bringing down trees with just his hands. He reported this to the Ossary, your parents were arrested and put to death because of what they were". He paused before continuing, "Then came the question of what to do with their baby", looking straight at Anouk, "That was you, Anouk, no one was prepared to kill a babe in arms, so it was decided to place you with foster parents out on one of the farms, and hope that you did not develop any special powers. Pata and Katcha was chosen, and that's where you lived. However, the Royal family learned of your existence and fearing you were the daughter of their son and could also become a witch they ordered that you must be stoned to death on your eighteenth birthday".

The room had started to darken and Dug got up to light some candles; Shan continued to sit on the table deep within his thoughts and Anouk had drawn her legs up into the chair where she hugged herself, rocking and thinking. Suddenly a commotion down the street caught all of their attention; Shan leapt to the window looking out "Oh god they are searching houses, quick you two need to get back in the cellar, go, go" he shouted softly. The two of them ran for the trap door and disappeared through it as fast as they could, Shan gathered up the bags he had left at the door and threw them down to the cellar, dropping the trap door quietly and quickly pulling the rug over it. He quickly moved the chairs and table to sit directly over the trap door and sat down in one of the chairs. No sooner had he sat down the front door burst open and there stood Dard with several townsmen behind him. Shan gave Dard his hardest stare and demanded, "What is the meaning of this, how dare you burst into my home without knocking, I demand you treat me with respect, and knock next time".

Dard just glared back declaring "I am here on official Ossary business, all homes are to be searched to find the witch", speaking over his shoulder, "Go on boys, leave nothing unturned". Shan leapt from the chair and stood directly in front of the door and Dard, he drew himself to his full height and stared down into Dard's face. In a low growl Shan spoke loud enough for all to hear, "If you damage anything you will have me to answer to". Dard just continued to stare at Shan whilst the men outside exchanged fearful looks, they all knew full well what he was capable of. Shan returned to his chair, sat, and crossed his legs, watching as the men filed into his house, the last one to step through the door was a face he knew well Sam Longshot. Two of the men looked around the front room, neither thinking to lift the rug, whilst the rest went off to search his other rooms, Dard just stood by the door staring at Shan. As the men started to return reporting no sign of anything untoward, Dard finally spoke "You are expected to be at the Ossary shortly after sun up tomorrow, there are matters that need to be discussed", with that he turned on his heel and walked out of the door followed by the last stragglers of his men. The last of them disappeared through the door when Sam appeared from the back of the house, seeing he was the last to leave he hastened towards the door.

Shan stood and looked at him, "Sam might I have a word", he stopped with a nervous jerk as Shan slowly closed the front door, Shan spun and covered the few paces to Sam in a blink of an eye, his right fist shot out, and landed like a battering ram on the side of Sam's head, his knee's buckled as he fell to the floor unconscious. Shan knew he needed to act quickly, moving the rug and chairs he opened the trap door and rolled Sam down the steps calling out to Dug and Anouk, "Sit on him and keep him quiet". Replacing the rug and chairs, he sat down again as if nothing had happened. Shan sat there for quite a time, but no one came back to his door, rising from the chair, and looking out the window he could see nothing more of consequence going on up or down the road. He breathed a sigh of relief and thought "Now to find out what that murderous rat has to say".

As he got to the bottom of the steps, he saw Anouk and Dug were sitting on the cot staring across the room, on the opposite side of the cellar was Sam, seated on the floor with his back against the wall. His hands had been tied behind his back with some rope Dug had found in one of the bags, and his mouth was stuffed with a corner of the blanket. Sam was awake now and staring fixedly at Anouk, a mixture of anger and fear in his eyes, even as Shan entered, he didn't look away. "Is this man the rider you saw earlier Dug"? Dug looked up, "Oh aye, he's the man I saw". Shan stepped between Sam and Anouk blocking his view, squatting down, so he was level with Sam and looking him in the eye's, "I am going to remove the gag, if you shout or try to make any loud sounds, I will beat you as you have never been beaten before, do you understand?" Sam nodded slowly; a look of puzzlement was on his face whilst he thought quietly to himself, what is Shan doing? An Ossary member harbouring a witch doesn't he realize they will stone him for this too. Shan reached over and removed the piece of blanket, Sam smacked his lips and tried to replace some of the moisture the blanket had sucked from his mouth.

"Ok, I am going to tell you what we know, and you are going to tell us what you know, understand?" Sam nodded so Shan continued, "We know you were out of town today as Dug saw you riding back from the direction of Pata's farm, you were riding a large brown mare which you took from Pata's farm", Sam just stared at Shan not showing any emotion or surprise, after all, he remembered seeing Dug on the road as well. "Dug also saw you were carrying your war bow and black arrows, now, Anouk saw Pata's body in the field, and your arrows were in his chest, so this brings me to my question, why did you kill Pata and who ordered it?". Sam sat looking down as if he were thinking, but actually what he was doing was working the knot on the rope that bound his hands, years of archery had given him strong agile fingers, he was starting to loosen the rope, just need to buy a little more time, he thought.

Looking up at Shan he replied, "Well it was all my idea, the man had it coming for sheltering a witch all these years", his gaze moved across to Anouk, "That thing should have been put down at birth". Anouk flew off the cot towards him, but Shan's strong arms stopped her in her tracks, "Not now" he whispered in her ear, he could see the fury in her face and worried she might lose control again. Dug stepped forward taking Anouk by the shoulders and ushered her back to the cot, Shan spun around reaching down he grabbed the front of Sam's clothes lifting him from the floor before smashing him back into the wall, where Sam's head bounced off it, setting off a ringing in his ears, and black dots swirled around his vision, but he stayed conscious, this time. So was able to go back to working on the rope. Shan's hand moved from his clothes up to his throat where the big man's hand closed tightly around it cutting off most of his air. Leaning in close to his face Shan growled "One more comment like that, and you will have a horrible death", Sam gulped as best he could. Shan continued "Now one more time who ordered the death of Pata? I know it wasn't your idea because you are too weak and pathetic to dare kill an Ossary member without some protection, tell me the truth or so help me I will snap you like a twig". Sam at this point was going red in the face and gasping for air, so Shan released his grip a little and waited for him to reply, "It was Dard, he told Jem and me to sort the parents and get the witch to the jail, so you see I was only following orders". Shan's eye's narrowed and bore into Sam's, "And why would Dard order such a thing, he knew the decision of the Ossary?", "Because he thought the parents might take off and not bring the witch to the circle", Sam replied.

Shan felt anger well up inside him at Dard "He is going to pay for this most dearly" he thought, but as he only had his lackey to hand his anger fell upon him, pulling Sam forward he shoved his head back against the wall, there was a dull thwack, and Sam fell dazed to the floor. Unseen by anyone in the cellar Sam's hands finally released from their bonds. Shan turned and joined the other two, "This is bad", he stated, "If the oldest and most revered member of the Ossary ordered this, then someone with more power and influence must have pressured him into this course of action". Dug stood nodding, and Anouk spoke, "Why are they so dead set on killing me? I haven't done anything bad to anyone, well maybe that man who molested me, but he deserved it, and who is this Jem?". Shan answered her "Jem is a lout who they use as a jailer sometimes, bad teeth, black eye patch, you can't miss him", "Oh, I don't", Anouk said quietly, "He was the man who molested me in the jail, and now I know he was the one who killed Katcha, I don't care that he is dead".

Dug and Shan looked at her knowing what that feeling felt like, suddenly a movement behind Shan caught her eye, it took a moment to process, but Sam was on his feet and coming at Shan's back, with no time to shout a warning, Sam was on him. Shan's face crumbled with pain as the knife punctured his back, he started to fall forwards and down, causing Sam to be pulled forward slightly, putting him off balance. Dug instinctively reached to catch Shan as he fell, Anouk quickly realizing what was happening started to feel a rage build within her, the man who had killed her father was now plunging a knife in her saviour's back.

Reaching out, with no concern for her safety, she grabbed Sam by his shirt front, Sam looked to her and started to smile until he saw her eye's. There was a glow to them, not a bright glow but a very definite source of power acted within them, her face was almost serene as she fixed upon him, now he felt true fear coursing through his body making his knees weak and his mind recoil in terror. Anouk felt her power build, not as much as when she had been violated in the jail but enough to know she could deal with Sam. Thrusting her hand forward to get Sam away from Shan, her power travelled through her body and down the arm holding him, bursting through her palm into his chest. It broke free like a mini-tornado throwing him the few feet into the back wall, the force was so powerful that when he hit the wall, nearly every bone in his body broke, and the back of his head shattered and flattened, Sam slid down the wall, dead.

Shan was on his knees, blood staining the back of his shirt, and was obviously in great pain, Dug continued to support him but was looking at Anouk with wide eyes, "I hope to never to get on the wrong side of you", he said starting to grin. Anouk took no notice of his comment, reaching under her shirt, she quickly removed the binding material from her chest, then bundled it into a pad and pressing it to Shan's back to stem the flow of blood, "We need to get him a healer and quickly, come on and help me get him up onto his bed, then you can go get the healer". "But what about you, we can't let anyone see you here" Dug replied. Through gritted teeth, Shan said, "No, it is too dangerous, you both need to leave immediately and go somewhere safe". Anouk ignored Shan's comment, "We need to get him to his bed, then you go for a healer, and when he comes, I will hide in another room until he has gone, now come on there is no time to lose". The two helped him to his bedroom where he laid on his bed, "Go", said Anouk, but Dug dithered by the door, Anouk looked at him annoyed at his dithering "What now?" she asked tersely, He replied "I don't know where the healer lives". Shan spoke up although muffled as his face was in his pillow, "Two doors up and across the street", "Ok, I will be as fast as I can" Dug said over his shoulder as he disappeared from the door. On his way through the front room he closed the trap door and pulled the rug straight over it, before disappearing through the front door.

Anouk sat quietly with Shan keeping the pressure of the pad on his wound; he was groaning, gripping the bedclothes up in his fist, quietly she said, "Thank you, Shan, I don't know why you have helped me, and now you have been injured doing so, but please know I am and will always be grateful for everything you have done", he mumbled something into the pillow which she couldn't make out. The sound of the front door opening filtered through the house and Dug's voice came clear and loud, "Thank you for coming, he is outback, I will show you through to him". Quickly and quietly Anouk slipped through to the room next door closing the door as softly as she could, standing with her back to the door she listened to the footsteps coming down the hall into Shan's room. She could hear a soft woman's voice, but the words were indistinct through the wall, then Dug spoke explaining he had found him outside the front door, how he helped him in and then went for her. "Somebody must have attacked him in the road outside, stabbing a man in the back, just how cowardly can people be? I ask you". Good story Anouk thought, she slid down the door and sat on the floor, the voices continued next door, but she had stopped listening. She was running all that had happened through her head, trying to make sense of this crazy day.

Pata and Katcha were dead, moisture welled in eyes, she dabbed at them with her sleeve, killed by Sam and Jem which was ordered by an Ossary member, I was taken to jail, and they were going to stone me to death. Anouk shuddered at the thought of that. My true parents were a sorcerer and a witch, *in their terms*, and were stoned to death, so what does that make me? Am I also a witch? And what the hell has this dead Prince and the Royal family got to do with anything.

The questions kept coming, but she had no real answers, a knock at the door brought her out of her thoughts, "She has gone now, you can come out" she heard Dug say from the other side of the door. Stepping back into Shan's room she could see his torso was bandaged, and he was now sitting up in his bed, "How are you feeling? What did the healer say?" she asked as she perched on the side of his bed and taking his hand in hers, he could see the genuine concern in her face and smiled weakly. "I will be ok, missed all the Squire bits just lost quite a bit of blood, rest she said, Ha". "You and Dug", he said looking from her face to Dug, who was standing behind her, then back to her, "Must leave immediately", Anouk started to protest, but Shan continued, "The Ossary will get to hear of my wounding, and members are going to start to visit, the two of you must go, now listen carefully". Shan paused as he winced from the pain, "I have purchased supplies for you which are in the packs in the cellar, collect them and leave, head west and travel for at least three days on foot where you will come upon a forest, travel at night and sleep during the day, less chance of being seen and speak to no one! Once at the forest travel into it for one day still heading west, then turn north, after another day you should hear a waterfall, go to it". Shan tried to move but winced and gave up, "At the waterfall make camp and someone will find you, tell them I sent you and what you can do with your power", Dug gasped "Is that wise, you know what they do to people like Anouk?", "I assure you it is safe. I know these people and trust them with my life, I will join you as soon as I am fit to travel, now go before it is too late". Dug spun and rushed off to get the packs whilst Anouk continued to sit and look into Shan's eyes, "We will get to see you again, won't we?", He smiled at her concerned face, "Try and stop me, once up and about I will travel to you my lady", Anouk rose from the bed and leaning over kissed him on his forehead, she tuned and as she left the room she called back "I shall be waiting, and I am not a lady". "Oh, but you are my sweet lady, you most definitely are", Shan thought as he lay back.

Chapter 7

The two crept out of the front door each carrying a pack on their back, the night was dark but not dark enough as there was a nearly full moon, pausing in the shadows Dug looked up and down the road, no one seemed to be out at this hour. They continued to creep along the wall of the house, keeping to the shadows, just as they turned the corner of the house a door banged open across the road, people laughing loudly emerged walking into the road. Dug and Anouk quickly scurried to the back of the house where they squatted in the darkest shadow, "That was close" Dug whispered. Looking up Dug could see a large cloud heading for the moon, "We'll wait for that cloud before we run for it, run straight ahead and as fast as you can, ok?", he looked at her and could see her nod.

They waited until the cloud covered the moon and the night was at its darkest before making a move, springing from the wall they both ran as fast as they could over the fields, continuing to run for as long as possible when eventually they had to slow to a walk, both panting loudly, looking back the town was far in the distance and fast disappearing from sight. No one had seen them; they had got away, thank god, thought Anouk. They carried on walking putting distance between them and the town, "Are we going the right way? Shan said to go west", "Yes we certainly are, I am not many things in this life, but a traveller I am, my sense of direction is impeccable, young Lady" Dug replied. "Why does everyone insist on calling me a Lady, I am not a Lady, I am a farm girl, a maiden", she grumbled quietly, kicking her feet through the long grass as she walked. "I also have excellent hearing and I heard that, so in answer to your grumblings I will say this. Today you turned eighteen, you have grown up to be a beautiful woman, so now you have the right to be considered a Lady in anybody's eyes. If anyone should contradict that, you send them to me and I will sort their thoughts out for them", Dug was looking back at her with an impish look on his face which made her smile, all of a sudden Dug pitched forward falling to the ground face first. Landing hard enough to make an oomph sound, scared he had been hit with an arrow or something she rushed to his side, only to find he had tripped over a log buried in the long grass. Anouk giggled "Shouldn't traveler's watch where their putting their feet" Anouk giggled even more which set Dug off chuckling, they both sat on the ground together and decided to take a five-minute rest.

"How old are you Dug? If you don't mind me asking", "Not at all, I am thirty-something, nearing forty summers, why do you ask?", "Well," Anouk continued, "You must have been around my age when all this sorcerer and witch thing was going on, I was thinking what do you remember of it"? "Hmm, I was living with my parents when it all started, I remember the round-ups, but I never went to any of the stoning's, far too barbaric for my taste".

"But you lived in Regis, did you ever come across my parents? Do you know anything about them?" Anouk persevered. "I can't say I do; I may have met them at one of the many parties or in one of the taverns. I used to frequent the one which the Prince's body was found, but they could have been any one of the many people I met back then". Anouk felt disappointed, but if he didn't know anything then that was the way it was, she shivered as the cool night air started to get to her. Dug noticed and handed her his long coat, as she slipped it on Dug announced, "We need to get moving again, only so much darkness left, and we have a lot of ground to cover".

The pair trudged on covering as much distance as possible, watching their step and walking in silence through the darkness as the moon watched on overhead, witnessing their passage over the vast grasslands. They had crossed no roads or saw any farm buildings as they walked, they could have been the only two people to exist in their cocoon of darkness. As light gathered on the horizon threatening the approaching sunrise Dug started to keep his eye out for somewhere to hunker down for the coming day. The sun had risen by the time he spotted a place suitable; it was a large round hollow in the ground, at the bottom stood some jagged boulders in a rough circle, in the centre of the boulders was a circular hole in the ground. The boulders looked as if they had been rolled in by some giant hand, but it was the best they were going to find out here on the flat grasslands, making their way to the bottom, Anouk sheltered next to one of the boulders whilst Dug went to inspect the hole. Looking down, he could see it was very deep, maybe a well he commented to himself. Going through the packs Shan had supplied for them, Anouk found there was several rounds of bread, a round of cheese, some meat, and a few apples, there were also several water skins in one of the bags as well as some spare clothing, rope, a knife, and some candles.

Anouk ripped a round of bread in half and handed the bigger half to Dug, each took some meat and ate hungrily, having finished her food Anouk took one of the skins and pulled the stopper before sniffing the nozzle. "Urgh" she muttered, "What's wrong, is the water bad?" Dug inquired, "Nope, not water, ale" she replied in disgust flinging the skin over to Dug, he grinned widely, as he caught the skin. "Good old Shan, he knows me better than I thought" and started to take a big swig from the Skin. Anouk continued through all the other skins, pulling the stoppers and wrinkling her nose each time, eventually declaring, "There's no water, it's all ale, what am I to drink" she said downhearted. "Well you will need to get a taste for ale my Lady" Dug replied with a mischievous look on his face, "But I don't even like the smell of it and stop calling me that will you". Anouk pulled a stopper and sniffed again at the nozzle wrinkling her nose once more, with a deep sigh she poured some of the liquid into her mouth and swallowed, the taste was worse than she thought it would be, her face screwed up as if she had bitten into a lemon and started to cough, "Urgh, tastes like ditch water". Dug watching all this take place, burst into laughter, it was the funniest thing he had seen in a long while. She shot him a look which showed she was not amused, turned and laid down on the ground with her back to him, curling into a ball to sleep. Dug watched as she snuggled down and thought, "Sleep well my lady", as he settled back against the boulder, ale skin in his lap.

Shan lay in his bed listening to the pair of them leave through the front door, that was the last sound he heard of them, but he still lay quiet for some time trying to hear if any hue and cry went up outside. After what seemed ages and no sound reached him, he decided that they must have made good their escape. The pain in his back was inescapable; it felt as if the knife was still being pushed into him, the elixir the healer had given him was starting to wear off, which made it worse. Closing his eyes, he started to mull over what he knew; the Prince had been a womanizer. Known to have taken many ladies against their will, could that have happened to Anouk's mother, leaving her with a child. If so, had they lured the Prince to that tavern and killed him in revenge. If that were the case, then Anouk would indeed be a Princess of the Royal family, who now only had a daughter of their own. "How old was Geraldine now"? he thought aloud.

He cast his mind back, she was younger than her brother by quite a few summers, she must be about thirty now, some twelve summers at least, older than Anouk. Shan and Geraldine had courted for a short time, long enough for the both of them to fall in love. But the King had prohibited him from seeing her anymore, sending him away to Belcher, never to return to Regis. He did not agree on their union as Shan was not of noble blood, he was a knight through his own determination and hard work. What could have been? He mused. But getting back to his thoughts he continued assessing the situation, so there would be no threat to the line of ascension to the throne. So why were they so set on getting rid of Anouk, just in case she becomes a witch? You don't kill someone for what they might do or might become, or were they just out for revenge. Shan started to doze, adjusting to the pain in his back.

Shan jolted awake, opening his eyes he saw the kindly healer was at his bedside, as his thoughts came back to him, he realized the sun was just coming up, and the room was becoming brighter with the daylight. He greeted the healer "Good morning Ada", she was an old lady of at least sixty summers, her face lined with wrinkles, kind blue eyes, and chubby cheeks. She was large of build but short of height, which made her sort of waddle when she walked. "And how is my patient feeling this fine morning"? She had a soft almost melodic voice which put people at ease almost straight away, "I am still in quite a bit of pain, and your elixir has worn off" he replied, "Well, we shall sort that before I take a look at what is happening under your bindings", she said whilst fishing around in the pocket of her apron, finally coming up with a small vial. "Head back and tongue out please" she directed and dropped a small splash into his mouth, "Now swallow and let it get to work whilst I get a bowl and some water to clean your wound". When she returned, the elixir had started to take effect, she removed his bindings and rolled him on his side to get a better look. Washing the wound whilst making approving sounds behind him, she finally spoke "The wound has closed nicely due to my neat stitching if I do say so myself. I will bind you up again, and you are to take it easy for the next few days to let the cut heal further, do you understand?"

A male voice cut in across the room making them both look to where it came from, stood imposingly in the doorway was Berm, "Is he fit enough for visitors"? "Yes, but I don't want him walking anywhere as that will put pressure on his stitches", she replied continuing to treat the wound with a green coloured compound, which she smeared thinly over the stitches. Berm made his way into the room, walking around the bed to the side Shan was now facing. Looking down into his face, Berm continued, "How are you, my friend? Did you get a look at whoever did this to you?", "I have had better days", he replied, "And no I didn't see who it was, they snuck up and stuck me in the back like a pig, leaving me for dead on my doorstep". Shan left it at that as the best lies were the simplest ones. "Ok, we will discuss that later, but now I have sad news, my friend, Pata and his wife are dead, and their daughter is missing, people are saying that she did it before running". He watched Shan's face as he gave the news assessing his reaction, Shan made a wide-eyed look of surprise and replied "What, how did it happen? Were there any witnesses?" he said feigning complete surprise at the news, "Have you got search parties out looking for her"?

During the conversation, Ada had finished replacing his bindings and stood back to admire her handy work, "Yup, that will do a treat", she said, more to herself than to them, she continued "Now young man, no walking around or getting physical else you might pop those stitches, I will come by tonight to check on you again", "Thank you, Ada can I ask if you would leave the elixir so I can top up when it wears off?". Ada looked at him squinting her eyes in thought, "Ok, but just a drop as I have done, and not too often if you wish to keep your wits about you", she said placing the vial on his bedside table. "Thank you, you are an angel, if you look in the top drawer of the dresser over there, you will see some coins, please take your fee", Ada waddled over to the dresser and opened the drawer muttering "I don't know about being an angel, but I will take my fee".

As she left the room, Berm moved back to the door closing it, Shan made himself more comfortable in his bed propping himself up against the headboard. Berm approached "Yes we have search parties out at the Pata's holding and also fanning out from the town; tracker dogs are being brought over from the next town, so we should find her, soon I hope". "I see," said Shan filing this information away, "Other strange things have been happening around here too, the jail has been destroyed and poor old Tom Chandler, the merchant opposite, has been killed in his house, looked like a tornado had gone through his house everything was smashed to kindling".

Shan continued to feign his surprise, "Shan, you know I wouldn't ever want to see anyone stoned, don't you? I had no choice but to uphold the townships promise, it wasn't the town chiefs who were pushing for it, it was a Royal decree, and we can't fight against that can we!" Shan nodded slowly "How have the Royal family taken her escape"? "Badly by all accounts, they are sending their knights over to take control of the search", Berm stood chin in hand thinking for a short while "Anyway, I have taken up enough of your time, and I need to get to the Ossary meeting", leaning forward Berm placed his hand on Shan's shoulder and smiled. "Rest my friend, you do not need to attend the meeting today, I will make your excuses for you", as he made his way to the door Shan spoke "Berm, be careful of Dard, I think he may well be a snake in the grass", Berm's hand was on the door handle as he looked back, nodding with a knowing look on his face, "I will, my friend, the snake has not gone unnoticed".

After Berm had left, Shan pondered over his words, the most worrying of which was the dogs being brought over, but they shouldn't arrive until later today and probably won't start until tomorrow morning, by which time any scent track would have disappeared, wouldn't it? He asked himself. Another thought popped into his head, why did Berm change the subject so quickly mid-conversation, did he feel he had to justify his reasons for ordering Anouk be executed? Or was he trying to let me know, in some round-about way it was the Royal family behind it?

Looking to the bedside cabinet he knew he had quite a few days' worth of pain relief in the vial, that should get me through, he thought, his mind made up he got off the bed and started to pack some clothes and supplies into a large pack which he hid in the spare bedroom, next he looked out his old armour, which was already packaged, took his sword and shield from the wall in the front room and hid it all in the spare room with the pack. As he checked it all he said to himself, "right that's everything ready for the off", his back was paining him once more so he returned to his bed and took a drop of the elixir before laying down to rest, he closed his eyes and ran through what he was going to do that night, first I will go down to Sam's lean-to, I'm sure the brown mare will be there, saddle her up and bring her back here for the bags. He didn't get any further as he fell asleep.

Chapter 8

Regis was the capital town of the realm, it was similar to the layout of the towns surrounded it but many times bigger, and had at least three times the population. At the centre stood the Royal palace instead of an Ossary. The Ossary was located within it, and was made up of nobles and presided over by the King or Queen, whoever was available, on the day. The building was huge with miles of corridors and hundreds of rooms; all the corridor walls were adorned with tapestries and torch sconces at regular intervals. Some of the corridors had statues of past Kings and honoured knights; others bore weapons, armour, and shields. There were windows, on the ground floor, every so often, but they were narrow and didn't let in much light. The floors were made of polished granite, making the whole atmosphere dark and foreboding for the newest of visitors.

The Palace was in an uproar, servants scurrying around fearfully in their white tabards with gold crowns emblazoned on the chest, and a scared look on their faces. The King had received bad news and was now in a terrible rage, screaming at anyone who dared to approach him, throwing pots, vases, and anything else that came to hand at anyone who came into sight. "Incompetent, useless fools, can no one do a simple task around here? One thing, one thing I asked for, and still, nobody is capable of getting the job done". The King's servants were cowering in the corners of the room, some had taken cover behind the heavy ornate furniture, "Get out, get out all of you, and where is my advisor", the King roared.

As the last of the servants scurried through the door a weaselly man with untidy black hair, thin pointed face, and shifty black eyes, poked his head around the corner of the door. "Glitch, get in here" the King roared making Glitch wince with fear as he stepped through the door and closed it behind him. Glitch was a tall but thin man, dressed in flowing black robes, around his neck hung a heavy gold chain of office, he was the King's advisor and had been for several years now. He made his way across the room to the King who had quietened for now and stood looking out of the window. King Uther was a very large man; some would say fat, *not so he could hear, of course*. He stood head and shoulders above most men so carried his weight well; he had a pudgy face, bright green eyes, and white hair which was now thinning. Dressed in fine robes of red, gold, and blue with intricate stitching, inlaid with gemstones of many colours, the value of which would keep a lowly farmer and his family for a lifetime.

The King turned to face Glitch, his face still red with rage, "They have lost the girl, and now she is in the wind, what are you going to do about it?", Glitch gulped and thought quickly, "Well, we shall dispatch a cohort of men to the village immediately, and I will instruct the knight's to go and search the realm, she cannot get far unless somebody is helping her, sire". "Somebody helping her!", the King bellowed, "Let it be proclaimed that anyone found to be aiding that girl will be put to death, now go and get it done", Glitch bowed. "It will be done sire", turning on his heel and heading for the door, "Glitch, where is my daughter"? Stopping at the door Glitch turned, "I believe she is in her quarter's sire", bowing again he quickly left the room.

Glitch knew she was in her quarters as he had designs on her. When the King dies, she would be the only heir to the throne, once the other girl was dead of course. She was still unmarried, so he intended to be there as her husband when she took it. The only fly in the ointment was, she didn't like him, but he had time to work on that, one way or another.

Princess Geraldine was sitting in her quarters with her three handmaids, playing cards and laughing, the mood was light and airy in the room. The Princess was now 34 summers old and strikingly beautiful, she had long black hair brushed back into a plait wrapped in a web of gold mesh, dressed in the finest dress of green and light green, embroidered with gold and silver thread. The dress fitted her perfectly accentuating her curves and hourglass figure.

The handmaids had been with her a long time, and she considered them friends rather than servants, she didn't like the term servant, people should do things because they like to, she was often heard to say, much to the annoyance of her parents. The Princess's outlook on life was so much different from most others in the palace; she liked people to be happy in their work and respected for who they are. She knew there were bad people out there in the realm, and if they needed to be punished then so be it, but people shouldn't be punished just for who they are. That was her philosophy, and nobody was going to change it.

The door flew open, and the King stomped in, he was red-faced and slightly out of breath, "Begone servants", the handmaids flew out of their chairs, hustling across the room to the door of the inner bed-chamber. Once the door was closed, the King turned to his daughter, "Have you heard? That little witch has escaped, she should be dead dammit, but she got away and now poses a threat to the very throne, our throne. I should have sent the knight's in the first place; they wouldn't have let this happen". The King was pacing the room, getting more agitated as he spoke, but Geraldine stayed sitting, remaining very calm as she watched and listened. "That fool boy of a son has brought this upon us, his reckless acts and insatiable taste for women, if he weren't dead already, I would kill him myself". Shocked by his final outburst she thought for a second before speaking, "Father, how could you say that, he was your son, my brother, you are talking about, that is a terrible thing to say".

The King stopped pacing and faced his daughter, "Stop being so nice about everyone, it's his fault we are in this mess now, and it's me who is going to have to sort it out. I've sent soldiers and knights out to scour the realm, the little witch will be caught and killed only then we will be able to rest easy". This did not sit well with Geraldine; it offended everything she was, thought, and felt, "But Father, we don't know she is a witch, why does she deserve to die for what she *might* be. Wouldn't it be more humane to capture her and see what we are dealing with?" The King strode the few paces to his daughter, gripping her upper arms and pulling her to her feet, his grip tightened vice-like on her arms causing her to gasp with pain, standing face to face, he looked at her with a dangerous stare. “That girl will be a witch if she isn’t one already, she is a threat to us, you, your ascension to the throne and she will be put to death, you hear me”.

Geraldine just looked fearfully at her father, she had never seen him this angry, he was bad-tempered at the best of times, but this was pure fury and hatred in his eyes. The King released her and turned away. Geraldine thought for a second then said in her best placating voice, “But shouldn’t we at least find out what she is considering....”. The King spun around his hand, slapping her full in the face causing her to fall back onto the seat shocked, the pain started to radiate over her face, and tears formed in her eyes. The king loomed over her “Why do you make me do that? You know it’s your fault? You need to get a backbone if you are to rule this realm. She will be dealt with how I see fit, not you”.

“Uther! Whatever is going on”, it was the Queen's voice, coming from the doorway. She cut an imposing figure of a woman, flame-red hair topped with a tiara, wearing a sky-blue figure-hugging dress and dripping with gems. She was a woman who took great pride in her appearance and enjoyed the attention of the men around her. Second wife to the King and stepmother to his daughter, Amelia commanded great presence wherever she went. The king looked over and seeing it was his queen smiled, “We were just discussing what needs to be done about a certain problem, but we are finished now”, he shot a look at his daughter deep with a warning not to cause trouble. “I have to go my dear, things to do, always things to do, as you know”, he said as he left the room.

The queen walked to the couch and sat next to Geraldine,

looking at the tears in her eyes and growing red mark on her cheek, feigning compassion she asked, "What was that about". Whilst thinking, I expect the bitch deserved it, little miss do good. "He was telling me that my alleged niece had escaped her execution, he was beside himself with anger", Geraldine raised her hand and gently touched her fingers to the painful area on her cheek, she could taste the blood in her mouth and just knew she would have a bruise on her cheek, again. "Oh yes, I had heard she was on the run, but it shouldn't take them long to track her down", and kill her. Removing one of my main obstacles to the throne, then the fun part will begin getting rid of you and your father, she thought quietly. "But he is going to kill her without a trial or investigation, that is just murder, she has a right to be heard. If the rumours are true, she is my niece, his granddaughter. This would never be happening if Harold was still alive".

Amelia sat, holding her hand and nodded sympathetically. If Harold had still been alive, I would have married him, and things would have been so much easier she mused. "You have to look at it from your father's perspective, she is an illegitimate child, her mother was executed for being a witch, and she grew up on a farm, a commoner. And if we don't deal with it, she could lay claim to her royal heritage; it would be a massive scandal for us". "Yes, I know all of that, but we don't know what she wants, she may be happy on her farm, she might not want anything to do with us, and we will never know how she feels if she is killed without ever being asked". Amelia let her ramble on for a while, not taking too much notice, more concerned with her own thoughts of, it will be very different when I am in charge. A page knocked and came into the room, "Message for you your highness" he said holding out a silver tray. Amelia took the note and read it, "I need to go to a meeting, keep your chin up my dear I am sure all will be well". She rose from the couch and headed to the door, "Don't think too badly of your father, you know he means well".

Alone in the room, Geraldine sat and brooded over the events of the morning. Her thoughts turning to her brother, Harold, it had been a great shock to her when he died, there were many rumours, and story's about how he had died, but she never really found out the truth of it. They had been quite close, he had always tried to include her, but she wasn't very good with swords, bows, and the manly things he used to get up to. But he always found time to sit and talk, telling of the antics he and his friends would get up to, he always knew how to make her laugh. She was six summers younger than Harold when it happened. She was inconsolable for weeks after, and she still felt the loss deeply even though eighteen summers had passed.

I wonder what she looks like, would I be able to see my brother in her? She pondered what it would be like to have a niece to share her life with, she wasn't lonely, she had her handmaids and plenty attention from others in the court. But to be able to sit and laugh with another member of the family, without having to worry what they are thinking or plotting, now that would be a thing to savour.

Geraldine's handmaids returned to the room, having waited an appropriate amount of time to make sure she was alone, and immediately started fussing over her. Nesta, she had been with her the longest of the three, checked her face and tutted, "Not again", was all she said and disappeared off to get more face powder. Nesta was the eldest of the handmaidens, some thirty-five summers, but she wasn't sure of that, she was plump and short with brown hair and a kindly face. She was married and had two children of her own, and lived outside the palace with her family, the only one of the three that did. The other two, Mary and Fina, were younger and lived in adjoining rooms to her quarters, so they were on hand during the night hours. When there were special occasions in the Palace, Nesta would bunk with Mary, which made them naturally a little bit closer with each other than with Fina, but they were all good friends.

Nesta returned with the powder, standing behind the couch with her back to the main door, she tilted Geraldine's head back and started to apply powder to her hurt cheek, covering the redness and emerging bruise. Mary and Fina sat either side of her holding a hand each, concern in both their faces. None of them noticed the King return to the doorway behind them. Whilst Nesta applied powder to her cheek; she spoke softly to her "No man should hit a woman, doesn't matter if they are King, father, husband or stranger, should never happen in my book, and may the Lord strike them down for their sins, that's what I say".

Nesta suddenly let out a yelp as the King grabbed the back of her hair, pulling her backwards and forcing her to her knees, "Guards, Guards", he bellowed. Geraldine and the maids turned to see the King holding Nesta by her hair on her knees, "Father, No, please" shouted Geraldine, "Don't do this", the maids just looked on in total fear. Two Royal guards hurried into the room, the King threw Nesta forward towards them, "Remove all our finery from this woman, and take her to the public square for flogging, on the charge of disrespecting the crown", looking down at the prostrate woman, "You are released from our employ forthwith". Geraldine leapt from the couch making her way to her father, dropping to her knees and gripping his robes, "Please father, she meant nothing by it, I will deal with her, please I implore you, don't do this". The guards picked up Nesta escorting her from the room, the King looked down at Geraldine. "Humph, you couldn't deal anything, you are too soft. I came back to tell you to prepare yourself to receive a suitable suitor I have selected for you, it's high time you were married". Pulling his robes from her hands the king stomped out, as the doors closed Mary and Fina went to her. She was crying, as were they, all three sat in a huddle behind the couch consoling each other. Geraldine vowed, *I hate you father, and I will never marry or bear children to carry on your hateful line.*

Chapter 9

Anouk woke up with a start, someone was shaking her, and there was a hand over her mouth, panic started to build, the power started to manifest in her stomach. She heard Dug whisper, feeling the hotness of his breath on her ear, "Quiet, somebody's coming". Opening her eyes looking up at him, she noticed the sun was well past mid-day. Dug's face was full of concern; she settled slightly, the power ebbing away. "Hide behind the boulder and I will go look to see who It is".

As Dug scrambled up the slope, she slipped around the boulder pulling their bags with her. Nestled behind the rock, she strained her ears to hear what was happening. A strange gruff voice said, "Whoa", she heard two sets of feet hit the ground above and the same gruff voice said, "You there, what are you doing skulking around out here in the middle of nowhere?". Dug replied, "Me sir, I'm just a traveller making my way from town to town, not doing anyone any harm sir", "Ok have you seen a young woman with blonde hair walking around here"? "No, can't say I've seen anyone at all for the past day or so, what's she done?" Dug enquired. "Never you mind that, just know there are a great many people out looking for her, if you see her and bring her in, I am sure there will be a good reward in it for you". As the knight started to turn, he looked back at Dug, a quizzical look on his face. "Have we met before traveller? you look familiar". "Nope, don't believe so sir, I would remember meeting a knight", as Dug said this he saw a look of recognition pass over the knight's face, the knight started to draw his sword. "YOU, pickpocket and thief, you stole my purse in the Stockling tavern".

Dug stepped back losing his footing and falling back down into the hollow coming to a stop halfway down, the knight followed him with the second knight stepping forward to the rim of the hollow. As the knight got to Dug, he raised his sword high in the air above him, "You are a thief and a liar, it is my duty to dispatch you forthwith". Anouk now peeping around the boulder saw her friend in real trouble, the knight was going to kill him, I have to do something. Fear, terror, and sorrow at possibly losing a friend all helped to fuel her power, feeling it build once again, she stepped from the boulder, "STOP", she shouted.

The knight's looked to her, quickly realizing this was the witch, her hair beginning to flutter and her eyes starting to glow, she began to float up from the ground. Raising her hand towards the knights who found themselves frozen with the sight of this witch in full flow. "BEGONE", she shouted and pushed her hand out, palm first, as she had done to Sam. The power ripped from her palm in a mini-tornado, spiralling over Dug and striking the knight full in the chest plate of his armour. The chest plate quickly crumpled inward crushing the knight's chest beneath, his sword fell from his hand dropping into the tornado of wind. Like an arrow shot from a hunter's bow, the sword flew through the air striking the second knight, point first full in the chest, his armour unable to stop the blade, it passed through his chest puncturing his heart.

Both men, within that split second, fell to the ground, dead. Anouk dropped to her knees letting the power wash away from her, she was still slightly out of breath as Dug knelt at her side “Are you ok”? He asked, “Yes, just give me a minute, I will be fine”, she replied. “Thank you for saving my life my Lady, I will be forever in your debt”. Anouk looked up thinking he was joking again, but what she saw was sincere gratitude and respect in his eyes”, taken aback she placed her hand on his, “Don’t be silly, anyway I need you to show me the way to this waterfall”, she said with a wry smile. Dug huffed, “We need to do something with them and the horses, you go get the horses I will deal with the knights, bring the horses down into the hollow”.

Anouk set off to do her part as Dug went to the body on the rim, pulling the sword out, with quite some effort, he then dragged the knight down to the hole. Before pushing him in he removed any weapons and found his purse which contained quite a few gold coins. Having dealt with the first he went back for the second going through the same process. Once he had finished, he returned to Anouk and the horses, removing anything from them which could identify them. Each horse had saddlebags and a quick search revealed they had tripled their food and there were several skins of water. He took one to Anouk who drank thirstily from it.

Dug announced he needed to get some sleep and it was her turn to keep watch, for what was left of the afternoon. As Dug settled down Anouk made her way to the rim of the hollow and settled there to keep a lookout, nothing was moving in any direction as far as she could see, so she started to think about the night before in Shan's house. So, I am not the first to be able to do what I can now do, but the others like me have been hunted down and killed like my parents, she thought. What did Shan say about this Prince? He liked the ladies and was killed in a manner that showed powers were used; Shan said he was handsome, what if he attacked my mother making her pregnant? That would make me a Princess! She chuckled out loud, me, a Princess, never heard anything so absurd.

She knew little of the Royal family apart from they lived in a Palace in Regis and they had a daughter, what did Pata say one night long ago? Ah, yes, she would be in her thirties now, and was called Geraldine so she would be my what? My Aunt, she tried to imagine how she would react if she rolled up on her doorstep, calling her Aunty. She continued running these thoughts around for the rest of the afternoon when she saw the sun was down to the horizon; she made her way back to Dug.

He was lying flat on his back and snoring like a pig, sorting some food and ale for him, water for her, she woke him from his slumber, Dug snorted and opened his glassy eyes, looking up at her, "An angel in my bed-chamber" he declared. Anouk laughed, "Get up you lummox, we need to eat before heading off, the sun's nearly down. They sat and ate in silence, then cleared the camp of anything that would show they had been there, "Now we have horses we will make much better time, might even make the forest by morning if we are lucky". She replied, "I hope so, it will be much better under cover of the trees". They led the horses to the top of the hollow, as they settled into the saddles and started west once more, the night slowly darkened around them.

The two rode for several hours without talking, each with their thoughts keeping them company, the moon had come up and again was quite bright enabling them to see where they were going, and keep the horses at a good pace. Anouk was riding alongside Dug when her curiosity got the better of her, "Dug, that knight back there called you a thief and a pickpocket, did you steal his purse?" He thought for a second and decided honesty here was the best, "Yes, I did, he was drunk, and I thought he wouldn't remember, boy was I wrong there". He then told her the story of his life after being thrown out of Regis, how he survived, and lived on his wits. He told of the towns he had visited and the people he had met; he rambled on as the night moved ever closer to approaching morning. She let him just ramble, it was nice hearing his voice, most of it passed her by, but she picked up on little things he said, storing them away for future reference.

They had made excellent progress through the night, and as daylight was fast approaching, Dug pointed out the forest had just come into view on the horizon. As she looked, she could make out a darker smudge in the distance, "Do you think we can make it before daylight is with us"? "I hope so we need the cover of the trees, once in the woods we can travel by day, come on let's hurry", they pushed the horses on as fast as they dared, covering ground much quicker. Just as the sun was rising above the horizon, they made the beginnings of the forest, a few minutes later they were into the trees, where they had to dismount due to the low branches and walk the horses.

Continuing in the westerly direction, they walked a good

distance before coming on a small clearing, surrounded by the trees and low bushes. A small stream was flowing along the edge. It was here they decided to make camp, taking the saddles from the horses and tying them off by the stream so they could drink. Anouk looked through her backpack and came up with two of the apples, which she fed to them, "We are going to have to find some feed for the horses, they can't survive on an apple" she called over her shoulder, either Dug wasn't listening or just didn't answer. She looked over; he was messing around with the saddles and sorting supplies. Anouk shrugged looking around for some dry bracken, finding some, she used two handfuls to wipe the horses down. Happy with her efforts she made her way back to Dug, he was already laying on the ground with his head supported by his saddle, "we should rest for only a short time, we can travel by day here, so we need to be getting on soon".

Anouk agreed and laid down beside him with her head on her saddle. Laying there reminded her of her days in the woods at the farm, smelling the damp woody smell, listening to the birds, and the babble of the stream. All of which lulled her off into a light doze, she awoke with a jerk and looked instinctively over to Dug, he was sitting up eating, "Come on sleepyhead, have something to eat. We should be off soon to make the best use of the day". She sat up, wiped the sleep from her eyes and started eating, around a mouthful of bread and cheese she asked, "How will you know which way is west in here"? "Easy, just look at the tree trunks, find a smooth-barked tree and look about head height to see where the moss is growing, that's north, once you know that, it's easy to find west". "Oh", she replied, "Who taught you that", Dug laughed, "I thought you were a farmers girl, you should know that my Lady". She ignored the little dig at her, "I can plough a field, look after the animals and reap the wheat, I learned what I needed to", she said with a little pout.

They finished eating and after saddling the horses they set off, Dug in front and Anouk following, they still couldn't ride the horses as the trees were too densely packed. They weaved their way further into the forest without talking, as Dug's horse was between them. So she took to looking around as she walked, enjoying the feel of being outside in a wood, loving the colours and smells. Suddenly Anouk spotted movement between the trees, with her heart racing she stopped and stared into the gloomy distance, have we been found again? She thought as she tried harder to make out what was moving. Something brown was walking between the trees, not making any sound, Dug had walked on for a little way before realizing she had stopped.

He now made his way back to her whispering "What's wrong, have you seen something"? Anouk nodded and pointed in the direction of the movement, squatting down they continued watching when a brown animal, smaller than a horse with horns on its head popped into view. The horns were curly and quite large, Dug let out a sigh of relief, "It's ok, only a deer". Anouk had not seen one before, "Are you sure it's ok, it won't attack us will it"? Dug smiled at her and stood up, the deer spotted his movement and disappeared in the opposite direction, "Nope, more scared of us than we are of it, see he's gone now".

They continued further into the forest, as they travelled, the trees started to space out more until it became possible to ride the horses. Breaks in the canopy above started to let sunlight through, Anouk busied herself with watching for animals and listening to the birds chirping their happy songs, the afternoon passed uneventfully. As darkness started to fall Dug called back, "Need to keep an eye out for somewhere to camp soon". A short while later found them in a clearing with a patch of grass, leaving the horses to graze Anouk made her way over to Dug, he had made a small pit which he had surrounded with small stones and was lighting a fire. "Should be safe to have a bit of warmth tonight and the fire will scare off any wild animals that venture our way".

After settling down and eating supper, they talked through the evening; the conversation turned to Regis. Dug described the town, and what he knew of the palace, this led to a conversation about the Royal family. Dug told her of King Uther, his bad temper and violent ways. He was on his second wife, the first Queen, Diana, had died very suddenly and he moved on quickly to his second Queen Amelia. "It is interesting to note that the Latin meaning for Diana is Divine, whereas Amelia means industrious and fertile, which doesn't describe her at all". "So, tell me about Princess Geraldine", Anouk asked.

"Well I don't know a lot about her, she was overshadowed by her brother Harold, him being first in line to the throne. I only saw her two or three times, the last time she must have been about sixteen summers old, growing into a beautiful young Lady. That was the last ball I attended. But everything I have heard since is that she is nothing like her father, kind, sweet and caring for others in a way unknown for the Royal family". "Dug", she paused trying to form the question correctly, "Do you think, there is any chance, that I may be related to them"?

Dug paused with a furrowed brow as he thought the question through, eventually, he spoke, "I know Harold was a bit of a one for the ladies, I had heard tale that not all his conquests were agreeable to his advances. All I can say is if he had taken a fancy to your mother, and she was not in agreement, I don't think it would have stopped him. Anything further than that I cannot say". They both sat in silence for a few minutes, each deep in their thoughts, when a smile crept over Dug's face. "But, if what you are thinking is true, then not only are you a Lady, you are also a Princess too, your highness", the mischief was clear to see on his face now. As his words sank in Anouk scowled at him, picking up her water skin throwing it in a perfect shot for his head, Dug batted it away, "Now, now, that's not very Lady like your highness". Anouk hmphed, laying back crossing her arms over her chest.

They both slept well, taking the chance not to keep watch, as the day was dawning it started to rain, most of it was kept off them by the canopy overhead but gathered droplets started to fall. A particularly big one hit Anouk in the face bringing her to wakefulness, she busied herself sorting the bags and a bit of food for their breakfast. Having eaten and saddled the horses once more they were ready to move on. Dug cleared the campsite removing signs of them being there, before getting on the horses and continuing their journey.

Luckily the two knights had wet weather cloaks packed on the horses, they both had put one on as the rain continued with large droplets hitting them regularly soaking their hair and their legs. Having travelled what seemed a short distance that morning, they came to a track in the forest meeting it on a bend, to their left the track led away to the south and ahead it continued west. Looking around no one could be seen for as far as the eye could see, so using the track they continued their journey west. By midday the rain had stopped allowing them to remove the sodden cloaks, the sun had started to peek in through the canopy above which lightened their mood. Riding along the track they encountered no other person which seemed odd as someone must have made it, but on the plus side it made travel through the forest so much quicker, and they could ride side by side.

As afternoon gave way to evening, they came upon a fork, the track continuing away to the west and the fork leading off to their right and north, "Should be around the right time to start heading north, do you agree", Dug said. Looking up through the gaps in the canopy, she could see there was only a short time until the sun would be gone, "Yes I would agree, and we will have to find somewhere to camp again soon". "Hmm, lets ride for as long as we have light and then find somewhere just off the track to camp", they headed off north.

The following day, around noon they heard the sound of the waterfall, as they followed the track the sound started to move more to their left. So they veered off into the woods and were once again single file weaving through the trees. The sound got louder and louder the closer they got to it, until, about mid-afternoon they came out of the trees in a large dell.

There was plenty of flat grass for the horses, but the most spectacular sight was a waterfall which must have been fifty tall men high, the water cascaded down before crashing into a large lake, where it bubbled and swirled like a large cauldron of boiling water. The shore of the lake was rocky, and over to their right was a big plateau of rock at the back of which an entrance to cave could be seen. Bushes of white flowers grew around the plateau, Anouk immediately fell in love with the serenity of the dell, she couldn't wait to swim in the lake, washing away the grime of the past few days.

Work first, need to get sorted before we can indulge, she told herself. They rode to the plateau and made their way into the cave, it was quite large inside and inhabited on occasions as there was a large fire pit in the centre, under a hole that looked man-made in the roof. Along the back walls were several straw mattress beds and on one wall hung a bow with a quiver of arrows. The sight of these made her shudder thinking back to Pata's untimely end. "Well, may as well make ourselves comfortable, don't know how long we are going to be here, I will go sort the horses, see if you can start a fire with the wood over there", Dug said as he walked back out of the cave.

By the time he returned with the bags and saddles from the horses Anouk had started the fire, she was going through a bag selecting some clothes from the spare sets, "Right, I am going to have a little nap now", Dug announced. Anouk, carrying the clothes headed out of the cave saying over her shoulder, "Ok, I am going to bathe and have a swim in the lake, back soon".

Chapter 10

Princess Geraldine was walking in the Palace gardens, trying to savour the pleasant smells of the many pretty flowers and orange trees, it had been raining that morning but was now a pleasant afternoon with a slight breeze. The gardens were set out in a geometric design with square raised flower beds separated by straight paths running the length and width of the garden. There were several other courtiers also walking, some as couples' arm in arm, others were officials taking air as they discussed their self-important business, each bowed or curtsied as she passed by them. Geraldine hated all the pomp and ceremony but knew she had to keep up the appearance of a Royal Princess. Behind her walked her two handmaidens, at a respectable two paces behind of course, oh how she hated all of this, all she wanted to do was linked arms with them, talk and laugh and enjoy the lovely day. But this day, a dark shadow hung over her heavy heart, her thoughts being occupied with her disgraced handmaid Nesta. Questions kept running through her head, what happened to her? Was she alright? Could she do anything to help? Geraldine made her way over to the side of the gardens where a golden metal bench stood, it was under an arbour adorned with blue hydrangea which had flowered with huge blue sweet-smelling blooms.

She perched herself on the bench with the handmaidens taking up position behind her. Geraldine looked around to make sure no one was listening, or watching before speaking quietly to the two behind her, "Fina, you have a day off tomorrow, are you going to visit you family in town"? Fina didn't look to her but answered quietly, "Yes your highness, I will be visiting with mother and father, unless you require me to stay and attend you"? The speech was stiff and formal between them just in case anyone heard them.

Geraldine nodded, "I will need you to run an errand for me, please go to Nesta's house and find out how she is, and what they did to her. I want every detail, and names if she can remember any". "I will, your highness", she replied. "Thank you Fina, and I will give you ten silver coins to take to the family, which should cover the cost of her lost earnings", this did cause a reaction on both of the handmaid's faces, ten silver coins was a year's wages, They both loved their princess, but once again she had shown how different she was to all the other Royal family members.

The next day Geraldine was sitting in her quarters, this was the day she was to meet the suitor her father had chosen, she wasn't nervous as she had already made up her mind not to like him, whoever it was. Her father and stepmother stopped by before his arrival, sitting on the couch with Amelia, her father was pacing around the room extolling the virtues of the man, and telling her that she should feel happy that such a man would be interested in her at her age. She had stopped listening to him a while ago, the drone of his voice going on and on, suddenly she realized he had stopped talking and looked up, he was staring at her as if waiting for an answer, “Uhm, what was that father?” She said quickly. He moved in front of her, raising his hand with a pointed finger.

Geraldine instinctively recoiled in fear, but he just pointed, “I know you don’t want this, but you will marry this man, even if I have to drag you down the aisle by your hair, you hear me”? “But, father”, she started to say then thought better of it and stayed quiet, “Ahh, you are just impossible, talk some sense into her Amelia. The King left the room, and Amelia took her hand, “Look what your father is saying is true, you are not a spring chicken anymore, because of that anyone marrying you has to be ok with the fact that you may not bear his children. At least when you see him, give him a chance, you never know you may grow to love him”.

Geraldine smiled weakly at her, “Ok, I will meet him and see where it goes, will that satisfy you and father?” Amelia smiled back, “That is all we ask of you, sweetheart, just give it a chance. Now he will be here shortly so I will be gone, just make sure your handmaidens are in the room at all times he is here, you wouldn’t want a scandal starting about you, would you?” She said snidely, sliding off the couch she made her way to the door, “Good luck” she called back as she left.

Geraldine continued to sit on the couch wringing her hands in her lap, but her thoughts were elsewhere, she was thinking about Fina, and whether she had been to Nesta’s home yet, she was desperate to get news about her, the thought of what she must have endured made her sick to her stomach. A knock at the door brought her out of her thoughts, “Mary answer the door please”, Mary entered from the bed chamber and crossed the room. Mary was the youngest of her maids about eighteen summers, of average height and slim build with a young face and blue eyes, her hair was dark and curly, tied back in a plait. She opened the door standing aside so the caller could enter, as Geraldine looked, she let out a sigh "Glitch, what do you want? I didn't call for you".

Glitch continued into the room stopping just before her and taking a knee, he reached for her hand intending to kiss the back of it. Geraldine recoiled in horror, "Whatever do you think you are doing? Have you gone mad? GUARDS", Two guards hastily entered the room and Glitch just looked and waved a hand at them, "You are not needed, go back out will you", he then turned to Geraldine. "I am your suitor, I have asked your father for your hand in marriage, and he has accepted". Geraldine got up and backed away, putting the couch between them, looking at him made her feel sick, he was a horrible, slimy, weasel of a man. The last man, any woman, would want to be near, let alone marry. "Guards, I do not want this man in my quarters, will you kindly remove him".

The guards started to move towards him, but he held up his hand again, "I am here with the Kings blessing so unless you wish to answer to him, I suggest you leave the room, Now". The guards looked at each other, turned and left closing the door. Mary had shrunk back and was now stood in the corner of the room, "And you wench can also leave, get out", Mary looked to the Princess for guidance. "No, she will not leave this room, it is improper for a man and woman to be alone unless they are wed if she leaves then so shall I". Glitch moved towards the Princess placing a knee on the couch and his hands on the back, as he leaned forward coming closer to her. "Know this, your highness, your father has agreed to our union and a wedding will be in the not too distant future, you will be my wife, and you will love me, do you understand?" As he spoke his bad breath washed over her making her want to gag. "I will never marry you, the thought of it disgusts me to my core. If you were the last man in the realm, I would never lower myself to you".

Glitch's hand shot out and grabbed the Princess's wrist pulling her forward against the back of the couch, face to face with him; he spoke in a low menacing growl, "Now listen to me girl, your father has given his blessing, and I want you as my wife, it will happen. So, you had better get used to the idea, and start to treat me with the respect I deserve, or I will knock it into you, understood". His weaselly face close to hers, and the smell of his breath over powering now made her physically gag, without thinking she swung her free hand around as hard as she could, slapping him in the face. Releasing her wrist and moving back he brought his hand up to his face, Geraldine also stepped back, her hand stinging from the contact. He looked at her with fury in his eyes, "When we are wed you are going to regret that woman". Geraldine just stared at him, the red flush of anger still in her cheeks, he turned and made for the door saying, "I will be back tomorrow to see if my future bride is in a more suitable frame of mind", the door closed behind him.

Mary was still stood in the corner of the room, frozen with horror, she stood with her hand to her mouth and tears in her eyes, for her Princess. How could her father do this to her? Marry him! I would rather die; she thought quietly to herself. Snapping herself out of it, she approached the Princess, who was just standing looking at the door, tears beginning to well in her eyes. She reached out, putting her hand on Geraldine's arm, the Princess slowly turned her head to look at Mary, and she could see the hurt and betrayal written across her face. "I am going to have to think on this, this final indignity that my father has subjected me to, please leave me to compose myself", Mary nodded and made her way out of the room.

Later that day Fina arrived back at the Palace after her day away, stopping at her room to drop off a few things she made her way to Mary's room for a catchup on the day's events, just in case she needed to know anything. As she entered her room, she saw Mary sitting in her chair looking out the window, she was obviously deep in thought as she had not heard the knock at the door, or even Fina's entry into the room. "Hi Mary, penny for your thoughts", she said cheerily, Mary jumped a little and turned to look, Fina could see she had been crying. Sitting on the edge of her bed she took her hand, "Whatever is the matter, are you in trouble"? Mary shook her head and after a pause recounted the events of the day, when she had finished Fina just stared at her, not knowing what to say for several minutes. The air hung silent and palpable within the room, Mary in sadness, and Fina in shock. "Ok, I also have bad news, but I think we should go to the Princess before I tell it", Mary nodded, "But she said she wanted to be left alone, I'm not sure it is a good idea to disturb her", "She will want to know what I have found out, so come on wipe your face and let's go" she replied.

Making their way to the Princess's quarters they found her in her bed-chamber, she was laying on her side staring at the wall, a painting of her father hung there, but now there was a hole in the canvas, a smashed vase lay on the dresser top below it. Looking up, first with annoyance at being disturbed which was quickly replaced with relief at seeing Fina. "Come sit with me, I hope you bring good news; I am sorely in need of some", the two girls climbed onto the bed and sat with her. Fina clasped her hands and steeled herself in readiness to impart the news, "I am afraid I only have bad news to tell your highness", the Princess's face fell at her words. "I went straight to Nesta's house after leaving the palace, when I got there her two children were sitting outside, but there was no joy in them. I met her husband and enquired after Nesta; he said she was very unwell and maybe I should return another day, after much insistence he did allow me to see her".

Fina braced herself for what she had to say next. Geraldine and Mary's eyes were fixed upon her, "I found Nesta in her bedroom lying face down on her bed with her back exposed, the sight of which made me feel physically sick, she had been flayed to within an inch of her life. Her back reminded me of raw meat at the butchers. She was sleeping; her husband said the healer had given something to help her, with the pain and to sleep.". She paused and looked at the Princess, her eyes were once again watering, glancing at Mary she saw she was wide-eyed with horror and her face had lost all colour. She pressed on, "I sat and spoke with her husband and asked him to explain what had taken place, he told me she was stripped of all clothing in the palace and paraded naked through the streets to the square, where she was flogged for disrespecting the crown".

Mary was now crying, her hands covering her mouth, the

princess's face had become cold, stone-like, a single tear tracked its way down her cheek. How dare he violate a woman, my friend, like that, he is no longer my father from this day forward she thought. Fina continued, "I thanked him for his time and gave him the coins you sent, I told him that you had no hand in what had happened and you sent your best wishes to them all. He stated quite clearly to me that he knew this, and you were the only one of the Royal family respected within the town. Disquiet has been building over the years, and this latest atrocity had only helped to fuel the fire of discontent among the people".

The Princess studied their faces, and thought to herself this has gone too far for me to deal with, I have to get out of here, I will have to leave the Palace and soon. "I have made my decision", she said looking from one to the other, "I am going to flee the Palace, but first I need your help", both nodded vigorously. "Mary, please secure food and water for me, do it quietly, so no one notices", Mary nodded slowly, "But where will you go"? She asked. "I don't know yet, but it will need to be far from Regis. Fina, I need you to go out on an errand for me tomorrow, purchase some ordinary clothes, a cloak and walking boots for me, do you have anywhere you can hide them outside the Palace?" "Yes, that won't be a problem, but I am coming with you", "Me as well", Mary piped up, "I would rather be with you than here". Geraldine looked lovingly at the pair, "I can't ask you to do that, it may be dangerous, especially for anyone with me if I get caught", "it's a good job you are not asking then, and it is getting dangerous to be in the Palace of late, I'll take my chances with you, your highness". Mary sat nodding, vigorously agreeing with Fina. "But where shall we head to once out of here, we need a plan", Geraldine mused aloud.

Fina coughed lightly drawing their attention, "I may know of a place you could go where it would be hard to find you, it's called Forest town and is a big secret from most people especially the Royals". Geraldine looked at her puzzled, "If it's such a secret how do you know about it?" Fina looked at the two of them, obviously having an internal battle as to whether she should tell them something. "Ok, I will show you, but don't freak out, do you both promise me that", both nodded. Fina stood from the bed, held out her hand and focused on her palm, with a snap a small ball of flame appeared above her hand. It flickered and shimmered reflecting in their eyes, both of them gasped in awe and amazement, Fina then placed her other hand over it to extinguish the ball.

Mary spoke first, "So you are a witch"? Fina smiled at her, "I like to think of myself as special, I don't know where it comes from as neither of my parents has it, but both my younger brother and I do. When I came into my power my parents sent myself and my brother out to the Forest town to live, there are many more people like me there, in hiding. They taught me about my power and how to control it. After, I wanted to return to Regis to be around my parents but my brother, Ben, decided to stay in the Forest, he helps run the place now". "So that will be our destination", Geraldine decided, "On second thoughts, Mary, go with Fina tomorrow morning and purchase food and supplies, whilst she gets the clothing for all three of us, hide it all, and tomorrow afternoon we will make our move".

The next day Geraldine had to endure another visit from Glitch, whom she kept at arm's length eventually getting rid of him by saying her stepmother was due to arrive shortly, it wasn't a lie she did expect her at any moment. During her visit, they exchanged pleasantries, as usual, but it got a bit sticky when she noticed her handmaids were not present. She managed to cover that and was told she would be receiving a new handmaid tomorrow to replace Nesta; she came highly recommended and was specially selected by her father. So, he is trying to put a spy in my camp, good job I won't be here tomorrow, she thought. At lunchtime, she feigned a headache and said she was going to lay down for a while, hoping that would keep people away. When she got back to her quarters, she packed a small bag with a few essentials, gathered up all her coins from the small coffer on her sideboard, placing them in a silk purse. She then sat in her reception room, awaiting the return of Fina and Mary.

As she sat, she began to fret, I hope I gave them enough coin, wonder where they have got to? I do hope they haven't been caught getting the supplies, time passed slowly, but eventually the door opened and the two girls walked in whilst having a banter with the guards outside. Mary came straight to her, "Sorry we took so long, Fina needed to change, so it wouldn't look odd her buying ordinary clothes whilst dressed in her finery. But we got it all, with some coin left over, it's all hidden in a lean-to at the back of my parent's house. So, we are all set, are you sure this is what you want your highness?". Fina stood close by; they both waited for her to answer. "Yes, it is, without doubt, the best thing to do and we have to do it now", she replied, standing up and smoothing her dress. Fina went to get Geraldine's cloak, returning and placing it over her shoulders, she smiled at the two, "Shall we".

They walked to the door, as they stepped out the guards came to attention, Geraldine instructed them, “We are just going for a walk in the grounds, no need for you to come”, they did this often so neither guard questioned it. Making their way down the long hallways and stairs, taking the long way around so as not to meet anyone of importance who might question them, they eventually reached the ground level side door. Pulling up their hoods, Fina stepped out first to check it was clear, the other two followed a few seconds later. It was starting to rain, good, it won’t look odd for us to have our hoods up, she thought. They had come out to the side of the front courtyard, to their left stood a few stables with horses and in front to the right was the main gate.

There were several guards in and around the gateway, “We are never going to get through the gate without them recognizing me”, Geraldine pointed out. “Look you two walk up close to the gate, not too close though, I will cause a distraction and meet you there whilst they are occupied, go now,” Fina told them. The two of them wandered across the courtyard, walking up the centre not directly towards the gate. As they were drawing level with it a shout went up, “Fire, by the stables”, they could hear the horses neighing as they watched all but one of the guards start running for the stables. Glancing back Geraldine could see black smoke billowing from just around the corner by the stables, everyone was running for the fire except the one guard left at the gate, but he was stood to the side watching what was happening, not what was going on at the gate.

Fina arrived by their side a little out of breath, “Quick whilst no one is looking”, the three of them ducked past the back of the guard, and out of the gate. Walking quickly, they put as much distance as they could between them and the gate without running. Entering the town, Mary took the lead meandering through the roads and alleys, within minutes Geraldine was completely lost. But Mary seemed to know exactly where she was going, not stopping even for a second, she led them through the maze of streets until at last, she ducked into the back of a house. Geraldine followed and saw an overgrown garden area and to one side was a lean-to shed on the back of a house.

Mary led them through a side door into the lean-to, inside were crates, bottles, and other oddments of items scattered around. She pulled open a crate lid and lifted bundles of clothes out, handing one to each of them and taking one herself. Helping each other, they stripped away all their fine clothes, jewellery, and hair-pieces, and donned the rough country style clothes and cloaks. Hiding all the fine clothes and items in one of the crates, they pushed the lid on and put it in a pile of other crates. All this was done with the minimum of talking so as not to be discovered. Fina recovered three backpacks from behind the crates, putting one on herself she handed another to Mary, "I will carry yours your highness", she whispered. Geraldine reached out and took it from her, "No you won't I will carry my fair share, and from this point on I am Geraldine, I don't want to hear any reference to highness, lady or Royalty, that will surely get us in trouble, right let's go and get out of the town before I am missed". The three of them stepped out of the garden, Mary taking the lead again. They zig-zagged through the town; eventually they came out into a field. At this point Fina took over, checking her direction, she led them off over the fields and away from Regis.

Chapter 11

Anouk and Dug had been at the waterfall for six days, there had been no sight or sound of anyone else in that time, and they had fallen into a bit of a routine. Anouk cleaned the cave each morning and looked after the horses, whilst Dug scavenged for firewood, collected water from the lake, and generally got under her feet. They had become firm friends over the days, with some banter at times. Dug teasing her about being a lady and she, in turn, teasing him about being a ne'er-do-well thief and pickpocket. Dug enjoyed taking a nap in the afternoons, "I'll just have forty winks" he would say, settling on his bed. Anouk knew that meant at least half the afternoon, she would use this time to swim and bathe in the lake. Today she had finished her swim and was sunning herself on the rocks watching the two horses. Anouk had decided on names for them, hers was a chestnut mare with a black mane and tail. She had two white socks on her rear legs and a wide white blaze down the middle of her face. She had shown her personality over the days too, being very aloof and expecting things done for her at certain times, for this reason she called her Lady. Dug's horse was more of a golden sort of colour with dark brown fetlocks, tail, and mane; she was far more laid back, like Dug, taking things as they came, she had named her Goldie due to her colour. As she continued sunning herself, she mused quietly, Lady and Goldie, thank god you came along, or I would surely have gotten sore feet before getting here.

Suddenly she spotted a movement just into the tree line behind the horses, darting off the rock she scrambled to pull on her clothes whilst peeking over the top of the rock. As she watched a young man, about twenty summers, came out of the trees, he was tall with sandy brown short hair and dressed in rough farmers style clothing. In his hand he carried a walking staff almost as long as he was tall. The man stopped to look at the horses, after a short pause he turned and started walking towards the plateau, Anouk started to panic, oh god, Dug is asleep in there, he won't know he is coming. Anouk waited for the man to get to the plateau before she stood and shouted in her loudest voice, "STOP, who are you"?

He stopped, slowly turning around until he was facing her, looking her up and down he remained silent, "Well, who are you"? Anouk repeated, a voice behind the man came, "The lady asked you a question, I think it only polite to answer her, don't you"? Dug was standing behind him, bow in hand and an arrow nocked ready to fire, he swivelled around to look at Dug before returning his gaze to Anouk, he still remained silent as if he were sizing them up. Anouk studied his face; he was actually quite handsome in looks with a strong square jaw and piercing blue eyes, he looked strong as well with broad shoulders and slim build. Looks like he can handle himself, she thought quietly to herself, "Well"? Anouk repeated. Finally, he spoke with slow, careful words, "I, am Ben, and you are in our camp", as he said this, he swept his arm out towards the tree line, and several more people stepped out of the trees, most carrying bows with arrows nocked.

She looked back to Ben, he was now smiling, "Your turn, who are you and what are you doing here"? "I, am Anouk and the man behind you is Dug, we are travellers, and a good friend of ours said we should come here, so here we are". Ben continued to stare at her, taking no notice of Dug behind him, his expression calm but unreadable, "Anouk from Belcher"? The statement scared her, how does he know where I come from, is he one of those sent to kill me? Panic and fear rose in her stomach, the power manifesting itself into a ball. Raising her hands in defence, ready to let go at any moment, "Yes, why"?

A relieved look crossed his face, "We have been looking for you, we got word of what was happening and sent people to help, but they got there too late. How did you find this place"? His words settled her a bit allowing the power to reduce slightly, "Well, we were helped by a knight of Belcher, called Shan, he directed us to travel here, he said we would be met by someone who could help". A big smile crept over Ben's face, "And so you have my Lady" he said sweeping into a courteous bow". Confusion swept over her, the power dissipated and she looked to Dug blushing deeply. He stood grinning from ear to ear with a look of 'I told you so' on his face.

After the others made their way from the tree line, they all sat on the plateau in a circle. Ben sat opposite Anouk and Dug sat by her side, the others making up the circle. Ben explained how word had got to them about her impending execution; unfortunately, they had not arrived until the afternoon of that day, all they could gather was the town was in an uproar, and she had escaped. As no one knew how or where she had gone, they returned empty-handed. "We continued to search for you, but all we found were soldiers and knights everywhere, that was worrying but also comforting because if they were still looking, they obviously didn't have you". He paused before continuing, "Yesterday one of our scouts reported seeing smoke coming from here, hence our arrival today".

Ben waited for them to process what he had said, "So, Anouk, please tell us your story", she cleared her throat and started from the day her foster parents were killed, deliberately skipping over the jail and what happened there. She told of Shan's help and how he was stabbed in the back, their flight from the town and their travels to get to the waterfall. Dug noticed she neglected to include anything about her gift but kept silent. Ben had a worried look on his face, "Please tell me what you know about Shan's injuries, will he be alright"? Anouk smiled, "Yes, it was a single stab to the back, the healer said it had missed his vital organs, he just needed rest to let the wound heal". Ben looked relieved, "I hope the coward gets caught and dealt with for his crime", "Oh, he doesn't need to be caught, he's deader than dead, ouch", Dug exclaimed as Anouk hit his ribs with the point of her elbow. "Don't", she said, looking at him sideways with a warning in her voice.

Ben looked on watching the interaction between the two, "I think you are not telling us every detail, so to put your mind at rest, I will show you something". He held out his hand, a small orb of fire sputtered into existence, hovering over his palm slowly rotating, one of the others picked up a small rock which he held in his outstretched hand. As Anouk watched the rock crumbled into dust then rose up to form an erect pillar above his palm, which then shifted into a miniature bust of her face, by now she was wide-eyed with wonder. One of the women, Cheryl, raised a hand above her head, palm facing the lake, a small amount of water rose and formed a ball before hovering over to her, where she played with it, making it jump from one hand to the other, perfectly in control. Dug was completely in awe of this but still managed to joke, "Where were you when I had to lug all that water around", the woman smiled and with a flick of her hand the ball of water floated over Dug's head before dropping, bursting on his head soaking his hair. "Ah, careful", he exclaimed, Anouk laughed out loud, "The first bath he has had in days, you needed that". Anouk looked back to Ben who was also smiling, "So you see, you are not alone, you can talk freely with us. What power do you have"? She thought for a second, "I don't know, just when I get angry I feel this thing grow inside me, one time it got so big I couldn't keep hold of it.

I remember floating off the ground before it exploded out of me, blowing the roof and door off the building I was in and all my clothes leaving me naked". She blushed whilst wringing her hands, thinking back to the jail and the fact she had killed someone. She realized everyone was quiet; they must think I am a monster, looking up, she saw everyone was looking at her with wide eyes, no one spoke. Eventually, Ben leaned forward and took her hand opening it palm side up, cupping her hand in his. "I want you to close your eyes and picture something that will cause the feeling to start, don't let it build too much, and hold the power, do you have it"? Anouk nodded, "Now slowly open your eyes and focus on your palm", Dug was sitting forward now totally immersed in what was happening. Ben continued, “Now let some of the power travel down your arm, not too much though”, Slowly the air began to move above her hand, starting too take the shape of a funnel, the air swirling around and around until it formed a miniature tornado dancing on her palm. Ben stared for some time at the tornado before looking to the others of his group; they were all captivated by what they were seeing.

Anouk sensing the quietness of the group looked up to Ben, the miniature tornado reacted immediately leaping from her palm in Ben’s direction, bowling him over and off the plateau. The tornado travelled over the grass before hitting a large tree; a shiver ran up the whole of the tree releasing a shower of leaves which came cascading down. Ben jumped back up onto the plateau, “My fault, I should have warned you about controlling it”, he rejoined the circle. The other four of his group were all muttering between themselves, Anouk was starting to feel quite the outsider again, just when she had started to feel included by them.

She got up and walked away sulkily to the lake, sitting down on her rock she gazed at the waterfall watching all the colours in the water illuminated by the sunlight. Ben followed shortly after, sitting himself down next to her, “You know it wasn’t your fault don’t you, I should have warned you about the control before getting you to do that”. She looked at him, “But I do feel bad, and now they are all whispering about me, I feel I am on the outside looking in again”. Ben laughed softly causing Anouk more irritation. “Look, let me tell you about us, I mean the people who have the power. There are four main types; the most common are the fire and water like myself and Cheryl, we cannot cross over because water puts out fire, and if the fire is too hot then it will turn water to steam, so they cancel themselves. The third type, and less common, is earth, like Benji. Now he cannot cross over anyone either because his soil will extinguish flame and water will wash away his earth or rock, so although the gifts are powerful, they do have their limitations". He let her think on that, "But you said there are four main types"?

Ben nodded, "Well done, you are listening. The fourth type is you, the gift of air which is not only very powerful on its own but can cross over with all the other gifts. The gift you have is extremely rare, only four or five people every hundred summers are born with it, you may never meet another like you. So, you see we are not excluding you; we are in awe of you, to actually meet an air gift is an incredible honour in its self". Anouk's head was spinning with all this information, but one question did pop up. "When we first met you called me 'My Lady' and bowed, why did you do that?" Ben shifted slightly clearing his throat, "That is not my story to tell, tomorrow we will travel to Forest town. When we get there, I will introduce you to someone who can answer all your questions, deal?" Anouk was disappointed but replied "deal".

The night passed uneventfully, and by early morning they all set out for the town. Walking single file through the trees with Dug and Anouk at the rear leading the horses, they travelled for a short time before reaching the track they had followed to get to the waterfall. Once on the track Dug mounted his horse, but Anouk decided to walk, and Ben joined her, she was enjoying the fresh morning air, and the woodland smells, it was good to be doing something other than just sitting around. Ben's voice cut into her thoughts, "When we get there, you will see the town is quite large, we do have a lot of people living there, but not all have the gift. Some families of the gifted ones all moved to Forest Town, as they did not want to be separated, but needed to keep their children safe. Anyway, your arrival will cause a bit of a stir, Dom has gone ahead to let them know you are safe. Just stay close to me, and I will guide you through".

Anouk looked at him, he was smiling and had a look in his eyes, what was that look? She thought to herself, respect, pity, or, was it adoration! Love? She looked away hastily, blushing, trying to think of a question to ask. "Who is this person I have to meet to get my answers"? "Ah that would be Gretta, she is the oldest resident of the town and the head of the council, she doesn't go out much nowadays, but she hears everything that goes on". They were approaching the bend where the track turned south, Cheryl was up ahead of the group looking around the bend, she turned and made a sign in the air with her hand. They all reacted immediately; Ben turned to Anouk whispering "Knights are coming we need to get off the track, quickly follow me", they all darted into the tree line. But unfortunately, the horses were not very good at being quiet with branches snapping and one neighed loudly at being dragged back into the forest. As the knights drew level they stopped, the leader shouting, "Who's there? Come out where we can see you". Ben made an arm movement telling Anouk and Dug to stay put, taking the reins of Anouk's horse he and the others stepped out of the trees, "What were you doing in there"? The big leader asked, "Sir, we are just travellers walking through this wonderful forest, we only tried to hide as your presence scares us, and hoped you would just ride on by", Ben replied. The knight laughed looking back at the two behind him, "Seems we scare the locals", he directed his comment to his companions making them chuckle. Turning back to Ben, "We are searching for a slim young girl about eighteen summers old with long blonde hair, have you seen anyone like that on your travels"? Ben pretended to think for a few seconds, "No, can't say we have, what are we to do if we come across her"? "Well the king has put a price on her head of fifty gold coins, dead or alive, so if you do, I'd suggest you collect, either way".

Ben nodded thoughtfully, "Ok Sir, rest assured we will be keeping our eyes out for her, that is surely a lot of money". The knight nodded and kicked his horse forward, the two behind him did the same, as the back two were passing Ben one pulled up sharply, staring at the horse Ben was holding. "Wait a minute, that's Stefan's horse", he jumped from his saddle striding over to the horse, grabbing the reins out of Ben's hands, turning the horse sideways for a better look. "Yes, there look", he pointed at a feint scare on the horse's stomach, "That's where the boar got her, I would know this horse anywhere", he spun around approaching Ben menacingly. "Where did you get this horse? And where is Stefan? Talk man, quickly", Ben shrugged. "We just found her wondering, no one was with her, and I don't know this Stefan you speak of", the knight lashed out his gauntleted hand hitting Ben aside his head causing him to fall to the ground. The knight began drawing his sword, "Speak quickly or those will be the last words you utter".

Anouk, hiding in the trees watched all this unfold, panic

for Ben's safety gripped her, then the anger at the violence these men lived for, she saw the other two knights' getting off their horses and thought, this is bad and going to get worse. With the power growing inside her also grew courage, stepping out of the trees into full view of the knights'.

The power continued to grow almost becoming a living thing within her, remembering what Ben had said she raised her hands, her hair broke free, whipping around her head and her eyes began to glow. "Begone knights', or you shall feel the full force of my anger", they exchanged anxious glances between them before starting to advance on her. She could tell by the look on their faces they were intent on slaughter. Letting the power travel down her arm, it broke free from her palm in a precise tornado of air, striking the big knight in the breastplate which instantly crumpled inwards. The power was so great it lifted him clean off the ground throwing him back into his horse's flank, he and the horse continued backwards eventually colliding with a tree, both man and horse remained pinned there. The second knight who had attacked Ben, now had his sword drawn, and was charging Anouk, his sword high ready for a fatal downward blow. Anouk allowed her power to travel down her other arm and released it against the second knight, again the armour imploded with the power of the air throwing him backwards off the track into the trees the other side. Anouk released the power, and as it drained away she felt exhaustion creeping over her. But the third knight had not given up and with a yell flew across the grass at her, sword ready to strike her down, "Oh god he is going to kill me, I am too tired to summon the power again" she thought. Dropping to her knees, accepting her fate, she waited for the final blow, as the knight rounded on her ready to strike. As he passed by Ben still laying on the floor, Ben's hand shot out and grabbed his ankle, flame sprouted up his trousers and quickly ran up his body, his jerkin catching fire under his armour. Within seconds he was alight, screaming and dropping his sword, he ran past Anouk a short distance before falling to the ground. Within seconds all three were dead as well as one of the horses.

Ben got up and immediately started to organize them, "We need to get this cleaned up before anyone else comes along", two of the knights were stripped of their weapons and anything of value, no one wanted to check the third burnt one. Benji went into the trees a short distance and opened a pit for the bodies, which they all helped to get there. The horse was more of a problem, but between the six of them, they managed to drag it over and roll it into the pit. Then with a few words for their souls, Benji closed the earth over and pressed it down flat again. As they now had four horses, they decided to ride the rest of the way, much to Anouk's relief as she was way too tired to walk for a while. Anouk shared her horse with Ben and Dug shared with Cheryl, the other two grabbed the spare horses, and they set off down the track at a fast trot.

It was mid-afternoon when Ben led them off the track heading into the trees and west again, threading their way through the trees. Anouk didn't mind as she had recovered some of her energy on the ride here, Ben had sat behind her with his arms around her waist, whilst chatting away about the power and ways to control it. She had felt his hot breath on her ear and neck, and on several occasions, his lips would graze her ear sending a tingling feeling down her neck into her chest, it was a good job she had been facing away from him as it had caused quite a few deep blushes.

As they walked, they had to push through patches of dense foliage; they came across several deep troughs in the ground which they had to coax the horses through gently, Anouk was starting to feel the strain, her legs and back had started to hurt. She was thinking of asking for a break when the trees began to get wider apart making walking easier, Ben looked back at her, "Not far to go now, be able to rest soon" he said with a smile. "Humph, almost as if he is reading my mind," she thought quietly.

As they came out of the trees Anouk stood at the top of a slope; she saw a huge clearing roughly in a circle with forest on all sides, and a river down to the left flowing into the town that stood before her. There were far too many houses to count, which were surrounded by a tall palisade made from tree trunks, each of which had been sharpened into a point. The palisade ran completely around the town keeping it contained and safe, dotted around the town were plumes of smoke from many cooking fires She could make out numerous people walking around living their daily lives. To the north of the town was a larger building than all the rest, must be where the council sits, she thought. "Welcome to Forest Town" announced Ben, "It's bigger than I thought it would be", she stated, "How do we get in"? Ben smiled, "There are gates North, South, West and East, you will see it when we get closer". They all headed off down the slope, as they got closer Anouk marvelled at how tall the palisade was. "They must have been full-grown trees, however did you get them there"? "Easy when you have the power", he answered. Anouk could make out the gate now, as they headed for it a shout went up from the top of the palisade, the gate cracked and started to swing open.

Chapter 12

King Uther and Amelia were seated in the banquet hall, supper having been served, and they were discussing state matters as they ate. The banquet hall by its very nature was a vast room, with white walls decorated with shields and weapons down one side. Paintings of past and present monarchs adorned the opposite wall, and oak beams stretched across the ceiling. The floor was of dark oak as was the banquet table and chairs, the table seating at least fifty people. A large fireplace stood at the end of the hall. Uther was sitting at the head of the table with Amelia to his left, to his right, the chair stood empty and the place settings unused. "What is going on with that girl? Why is she so late for supper"? Uther said looking to Amelia for an answer. "The last I saw of her she said she had a headache and was going to lay down for a while, maybe she is still asleep".

"Humph, damned insolent girl", the King clicked his fingers. The head server scurried over bowing low when he got there, "Send someone to find out why the Princess is so late for supper and tell her that her father demands her presence". "Yes, your highness, immediately", the server replied bowing deeply before scurrying off to send someone. It was only a matter of minutes before a breathless runner returned to the door of the banquet hall. A hushed discussion took place between the runner and the head server before the server returned to the King bowing deeply once more, waiting respectfully until the King indicated he could speak. Hesitantly the server announced, "The Princess is not in her quarters, and neither are her handmaids, it would appear no one knows where they are, your highness". "What, she can't just have disappeared, get all the servants and guards searching the Palace, I want her found, and get me, my advisor, now". Bowing deeply once more he rushed off to do the King's bidding. Uther looked to Amelia who had stopped eating and was sitting with a thoughtful look on her face. "What are you thinking now", he asked bad-temperedly, "Well I was thinking maybe we have pushed her too far, sacking and flogging her maid, replacing that maid with one of our own, and forcing her to marry Glitch.

Not to mention the regularity that you strike her my love, these are all things that would hurt her deeply, maybe she couldn't take anymore". "What you are thinking? She has run away! Preposterous, she couldn't survive a day without all her finery and soft cushions, and Glitch would make a good husband for her, he would know how to keep her inline". The door to the hall opened, and Glitch slinked in walking over to them, bowing deeply, "You sent for me your highness", he glanced at Amelia who sat with a look of disdain on her face, as if she had caught a bad smell of something. "Glitch, your betrothed has disappeared with her maids, do you know where they may be?" the king asked. Glitch stood with a look of complete surprise on his face, "No your highness; this is news to me, I've been in a meeting all afternoon, when was she last seen"? Amelia sneered, "I saw her about mid-day when she said she was going for a lay down". The King was getting increasingly angry, slamming his fist on the table making everyone jump, "GO AND FIND HER GLITCH, LEAVE NO ROOM UNSEARCHED", Glitch bowed, "At once your highness".

A hue and cry went up through the whole Palace with servants and guards scurrying everywhere; every room meticulously searched. As time stretched on it was becoming increasingly evident, she and the maids were no longer in the Palace. Glitch was standing in the Princess's bed-chamber, looking around, everything seemed in order. Her gowns were hanging in the wardrobe, her personal belongings spread over furniture, his eyes fixed on the small coffer on the dressing table, opening it he noted it was empty. A Princess with no coin? He mused to himself, scanning the tabletop he saw there were several items present, but more significant were the gaps. No hairbrush, comb, or hand mirror? This is looking more like she has run-a-way, than been abducted, and of course the two missing maids, they would go with her, wouldn't they? Having come to a conclusion he headed out to speak with the King. He is not going to like this, was I too forceful with her? Or was the King?

Either way, there is going to be a lot of fallout with this, the thought filled him with dread. As he entered the throne room the King was seated on his throne dealing with a local lord, something about his land; he didn't take too much notice as he was more concerned with his own problem and Uther's reaction to the news. Glitch waited off to one side letting several others go before him; finally, the King motioned for him to approach. Glitch did so where he swept into a deep bow before the King. "So, Glitch, what news of my daughter"? Glitch gulped, "The Palace has been searched twice over, revealing no sign of her your Highness", the King listened, his eyes fixed on Glitch. "So, you are telling me you cannot find her, have you any theories as to where she may have gone?

Glitch started to panic, this next bit is going to really upset him, "I have a theory your Highness, bearing in mind her two handmaids are also missing, and a check of the Princess's room revealed coin and personal grooming items were missing", he gulped, "I think she may have run-a-way your Highness". The King slowly rose from the throne and walked down the few steps, grabbing the front of Glitch's robes pulling him close. Speaking directly into his face, he said slowly and with grave menace, "Extend the search to the town and after that the realm, I want my daughter back, or you will lose your head, do-you-understand-me"? Glitch felt his legs go weak and his stomach turn but managed to say, "It will be done your Highness, I will see to it personally", the King released his robes and smoothed them out, "I know you will, your head depends on it, go".

Glitch bowed and scuttled out of the throne room heading for the barracks, finding the Squire of the garrison, he gave instructions for them to move out and search the town for the Princess. "Let it be known that anyone who has knowledge of her where-a-bouts, or information that leads to her return will receive a reward of 100 gold coins". The Squire's jaw dropped at the size of the reward, and immediately scrambled to get his soldiers out looking for the Princess; the search continued late into the night when word of a discovery reached Glitch.

He made his way down into the town to an unassuming townhouse which was surrounded by soldiers, the Squire was waiting and indicated he should follow him into the rear garden. Looking around Glitch could see the garden was quite unkept with a small lean-to at the back of the house, the Squire led him into the lean-to and indicated a crate which had been separated from the others. Inside were a pile of very fine dresses, reaching in he pulled one out. He recognized the dress as the one the Princess had been wearing earlier, raising it to his nose he breathed in deeply, "I would recognize that scent anywhere, this is the Princess's dress, the rest of this must be the Maids clothes", he said to the Squire without turning. He continued to breathe in the scent of Geraldine, "Who's house is this"? He asked. The Squire replied, "It belongs to the family of Mary, one of her handmaids, we have the parents and her siblings detained in the house". Dropping the dress back in the crate Glitch started for the door, "I will speak with them, have someone take the crate back to the Palace".

Glitch spoke quietly with the Squire before he made his way into the house, it was obviously one owned by poor lower-class people; there were few furnishings and bare floors. In the centre of the room stood a table with four chairs, and four people were sitting along the back wall on the floor, with several soldier's guarding them. Glitch pulled out a chair turning it towards them, taking a seat he studied them one by one using the hardest stare he could muster, the whole family looked terrified. "I have a problem; I am hoping you are going to solve that problem for me, Princess Geraldine is missing, and so are her maids, now one of those maids is your daughter, Mary. In your shed outback is a crate of their palace clothes which proves they were here", he paused for that to sink in. "So, here is my question, where have they gone after leaving here"?

Glitch looked to the father, "Consider your answer very carefully as the wrong one will have severe consequences". "I don't know, I didn't even know they had been here, I rarely go out back" he replied. Glitch sat shaking his head, "Wrong answer", looking to the guards, "Take the boy out the back and execute him", the mother screamed, all of them tried to rise, but the guards forced them back down. Two guards grabbed the boy and dragged him from the house, after a short time a dull thwack, like an axe hitting a log, could be heard. Glitch just stared at them with uncaring eyes; the father was now having to be physically restrained, the mother was hugging her daughter, all were crying. "So, my question once again, where have they gone after leaving here"? The father shouted his reply, "I DON'T KNOW", Glitch sat nodding, "Take the girl out the back and execute her", guards pulled the daughter from her mother and dragged her outside, once again the dull thwack could be heard. The fight was leaving the father who was now openly sobbing, his wife clinging to him, "Maybe you can get it right to save your wife, where have they gone after leaving here"? Again, he could not answer, and his wife was taken outside, the familiar dull thwack was heard, the man was broken hanging limply from the guards. "So, are you still saying you don't know even though it is your head next", the man hung from the guards nodding his head not bothering to speak.

The Squire approached Glitch, "He is broken my lord, he would have said something by now if he knew", Glitch nodded in agreement, "Take him to the dungeons the King can decide his fate" he ordered. As the man was dragged from his house, he hung his head with his eyes closed, completely desolate at having lost his family. The gate to the prison wagon clanged open, and he was thrown in. As he lay on the floor, he heard one word, "Father". Looking up and saw his family huddled at the back of the cage, scrambling to them, they all hugged and cried. The sound of the axe had been just that, the sound of an axe hitting a log.

Travelling for some time from the town the girls decided it was better to hide somewhere until nightfall; Fina knew of an old disused cottage a short distance ahead, so they made for that. Once inside, they hunkered down in a corner waiting for the dark to come. Mary asked, "Do you think we got away with no one seeing us"? Fina replied, "I think so, if anyone had, then we would have had a lot of Knight's and soldiers chasing us. I've been keeping an eye out, and I haven't seen anyone following us yet. Ok, you two try and get some sleep, we will be walking all night tonight". The two snuggled into their cloaks whilst Fina detached herself from the group and found herself a good spot to keep watch. Settling into her watch, she thought, "Luckily I don't need much sleep", she looked across the room at the two snuggled up, worrying about the Princess, "This is going to be much tougher than she thinks, the next five days are going to be hard on her".

As darkness was creeping its way across the land, Fina awakened the two-sleeping beauty's with gentle shoves, "We should have something to eat now before we shove off, by the time we have eaten it will be fully dark". They agreed and shared food out of the packs, having finished eating they slipped out of the old cottage, Fina checked the stars for direction and led the group off across the dark expanse. The wind had come up from the north, without the sun it was cold and cut through the cheap clothing they had on, pulling their cloaks close round them and putting up their hoods they travelled on. There was no talking whilst they walked, they were all concentrating on the ground not wanting to trip in the dark hurting themselves. As the night wore on towards midnight Geraldine started thinking about what she was going to do in the future. Yes, she had about twenty gold coins, but that would only last her a few years, and that was if she didn't pay Fina and Mary.

She was good at sewing and embroidery, maybe she would become a seamstress, maybe get married, to someone she chose, and have a family. The wind started to blow a little harder, and spots of rain began to fall, "Great that's all we need right now", Fina called out, they trudged on as the rain got heavier. The ever-present wind was whipping the rain into their faces and clothes, before long they were soaked and shivering. Fina was slightly ahead and called back, "Keep moving, your effort walking will keep you warmer than if you stop". Mary stayed by Geraldine's side, helping her keep up, the two of them just kept putting one foot in front of the other willing themselves on.

After a while, the rain stopped, but the wind continued to blow, Geraldine was feeling particularly low. The new boots were hurting her feet, her shoulders were burning where the straps rubbed, the cheap clothes itched, and she was wet, cold and miserable. She was sobbing quietly to herself, thinking, what have I done? What have I got us into? A big shiver ran through her body causing her to catch her breath and cough, Mary looked at her and could see she was in a lot of discomfort, calling ahead to Fina who was five steps or so in front of them. "It's starting to get light Fina; we should be looking for somewhere to stop for the day". Fina stopped, letting them catch up, "Yes I noticed that and I can just see a copse of trees ahead, thought we could get in amongst them and lay low there, not far now". She looked at Geraldine and saw the angst written all over her face. Trying to make light conversation she told her, "Come on, we will be resting soon". By the time they got to the trees Geraldine was limping quite badly, they both helped her into the copse making their way to the centre where Mary and Fina made camp.

Helping Geraldine get the wet cloak and pack off, the Princess groaned with relief from the burden, Mary sorted some spare clothing from the packs whilst Fina helped Geraldine remove her wet dress. Fina noticed the sore and chaffed skin of her shoulders, getting some salve from out of her pack she said, "Here let me see to that it's a good job I packed some of this", holding up the vial of salve for her to see. As Fina smeared it over her skin there was an almost immediate relief. "You two must think I am an absolute wimp; it's only been one night's walk" Geraldine stated.

The two of them replied together, "No". Mary continued, "We have been brought up in a very different manner to you, having to work at chores around the home and out to work at an early age. Our bodies may look similar, but they are not, ours are more accustomed to this way of life", they had got her into her spare dress as Mary talked. Sitting next to a small fire Fina had started, Mary continued whilst removing her boots, "You have to let us help you more until your body starts to build its outdoor strength. Fina, can you come look at her feet, they are going to need some of your tender care". Fina had just finished changing, Mary and Fina changed places so Mary could get changed. Having taken care of themselves they sorted some food and sat by the small fire to eat.

Geraldine voiced her fears, "I am sorry I have got you into this mess, I thought it would be so much easier than it is, can you forgive me"? Fina replied around a mouthful of bread, "What's to forgive? We both knew better than you what this would be like. It was our decision to come with you, not yours, and I personally wouldn't have it any other way". Mary was nodding to this, "Yes, my feelings exactly, so stop beating yourself up, you are not responsible for us or our decisions". Geraldine started to feel quite emotional, "You do know I think of you as my best friends in all the realm, don't you"? This caused them to smile widely, Fina leant over shoulder bumping her, "We are your only friends in all the realm it seems, sisters unite", she said fist-pumping the air causing them all to giggle.

It was decided they should keep a lookout whilst they slept, Mary took the first watch, Fina the second and Geraldine would watch last. Mary watched as they snuggled down together, sharing body warmth, they had each noticed Geraldine was still shivering. Once they were settled, Mary went about the task of hanging the wet clothes and cloaks out on the low branches. The sun had risen quite a bit, and the wind had become warmer, should dry them out nicely, turning her attention to the packs. Mary emptied all three and started sorting the items by weight, all the heavier ones went in hers, and Fina's while all the lighter items went in Geraldine's, that should help her a lot over the coming nights she thought to herself. The rest of the morning passed slowly; nobody came anywhere near the copse although she did see some rider's way off in the distance at one point, they were travelling away from them so didn't worry her at all.

When the sun was high in the sky, she woke Fina from her slumber, who slipped away from the Princess, in quiet whispers she told her of the riders, but nothing else of note had happened. She explained what she had done with the packs; Fina was in full agreement that it was a good idea. She then slipped into the spot Fina had vacated, putting her arm around Geraldine, she quickly fell asleep. As Fina didn't need a lot of sleep, she let the two of them sleep on. It was late afternoon with the sun low in the sky when Geraldine awoke, she slipped away from Mary and looked for Fina finding her on the edge of the copse. "You should have woken me for my watch" she protested, "It's ok, I don't need a lot of sleep, and you needed the rest, come on help me pack up the camp before we eat". Between them they collected all the clothes, which were now dry and folded them into the packs before laying out some food. Having eaten, they donned their still damp cloaks and packs, before heading out the copse into the night for another night's walking.

Chapter 13

As Anouk approached the gate to the town, which had now swung fully open, she could see people gathering along the long straight road which led into the town. Ben had slipped off the back of the horse and was now leading Lady with one hand on her bridle. The road had houses and alleyways on either side which people were coming out of and lining the road. As they passed by, the watchers bowed and curtsied, all eyes were on her. Anouk started to feel very uncomfortable. She leaned forward speaking to Ben, "Why are they doing that"? Ben smiled up at her, "Like I said, not my story to tell, just go with it". Sitting back in her saddle she looked back to Dug; he was watching her with a massive grin on his face, he winked at her with the hidden meaning of 'I told you so', turning back she felt the embarrassment grow, colouring her cheeks with a subtle rosy glow. This continued for a while until a man stepped out into the middle of the road, the man was short and stocky with messy black hair, dressed in the clothes of a farmer. He was smiling at Ben, who brought her horse to a stop before walking up to the man, the two clasped each other in a friendly hug and spoke quietly.

Anouk couldn't hear the conversation, but the man pointed to a house to her left whilst talking, Ben nodded before returning to her. "Right come on down, Tom has arranged for you and Dug to use this house", he reached up taking Anouk by the waist easing her to the ground, as she met the hard-packed road, she became acutely aware how close they were standing to each other, his hands still on her waist. Anouk felt a tingling sensation in her body and a fluttering in her stomach, looking up into Ben's face she realized she was blushing again.

Ben quickly removed his hands and took a half step back, "I'm sorry, let me show you the house", he also had colour in his cheeks. "Wait, I need to tend to Lady and Goldie first, where are the stables?" she asked, "You don't have to worry about that, we have people here who look after the horses". Ben took her arm and started to lead her to the front of the house, "But they need to be fed, and Lady will need to be wiped down, I should really go and see to her". Ben smiled and shook his head, "You really don't have to worry yourself about her, we have excellent stable boys, and it is their job to care for the horses, they are in good hands", secretly he thought how humble she was to care about the animals.

Entering the house, Anouk found herself in a front room; there was a fireplace which already had a smouldering fire in the grate, two couches on either wall with a rug spread out between them, a low table stood on the rug. "You should be comfortable here", Ben said, taking her arm, "Come on I will show you the rest". He led her through into a kitchen which had a large table and chairs, and down a corridor into a bed-chamber at the back of the house, as she entered, she saw there was a large bed nicely made and a bathtub stood over by the window, it was full of steaming water.

A girl stood by the tub, and when Anouk entered, she

curtsied, the girl was about Anouk's age with black hair tied back in a bun, dressed not in farmers clothes, but what looked like her best dress. She was about Anouk's age with a slim hourglass figure and a beautiful face, almost perfect features with deep blue eyes, high cheekbones and soft rosy lips. As she stood with her hands clasped together in front of her, Anouk looked to Ben, "Ah, I will take my leave and let you freshen up", Ben turned disappearing out of the room closing the door behind him. Anouk looked back to the girl who had now approached her and was reaching out for the buttons on her top; she stepped back from her. "What are you doing"? The girl looked at her in puzzlement, "My lady will need to disrobe before getting in the bath", she replied. Anouk thought to herself, has the world gone mad, before replying, "I am not a lady, and I am quite sure I am capable of undressing myself, now please go".

The girl looked crestfallen, as she headed to the door Anouk saw a tear rolling down her cheek, "Stop", the girl stopped and turned to her, "Why are you getting upset? I didn't intend to be mean to you". The girl stood wringing her hands looking to the floor, "I was chosen to be your maid, it will be a great dishonour to my family to be rejected by you, and I will be severely scolded, my lady". Anouk stood and considered what she had said, I don't want her to get in trouble, and I suppose I can live with this charade for a while. Her mind made up she asked, "What is your name"? "I am Anita, my lady" she replied, "Ok Anita, you can stay, but I would like to refer to you as my companion, not my maid, and stop calling me 'my lady', my name is Anouk, agreed?" Anita nodded vigorously, "I will, Anouk, but I will have to show respect when we have company, so please don't scold me when I call you 'my lady' when others are around".

Anouk disrobed and slipped into the hot water; she had never had a hot bath in her life, usually bathing in lakes. She laid back feeling the aches in her muscles fade away and closing her eyes she started to dose, whilst dozing her mind relived the events on the holding, seeing Pata's body all over again. The dash to the house and finding Katcha with her throat cut, she awoke suddenly sitting up in a rush of water shouting "NO". Anita who had been busying herself in the room jumped, looking across at her sat up in the tub, quickly going to her and kneeling by the side, she took her hand, "Are you ok"? She asked full of concern. Anouk turned to her with a faraway look in her eyes, but quickly she composed herself, "Yes, yes, I was just seeing...., never mind, I'm ok, tell me about you, Anita". She smiled, "Well, I have lived here most of my life, I was three when we came here, and I live in the house next door to this one. My father is Tom, my mother died when I was two, and I have an older brother, Kam. Shortly after mother's death, father moved us here, Kam has the gift, he can control water. I have many friends in the town, and they are all jealous that I get to spend time with you. I would just like to say it is an honour to be your maid, Uhm, companion and I hope you will be pleased with me". Anouk smiled thinking, who do these people think I am? It must be because I have the gift of air, she told herself.

Having bathed she quickly put on a lovely light blue dress, Anita had laid out on the bed for her, all the time Anita was fussing around her trying to help, God this is going to take some getting used to, she thought. She was directed to a chair which was in front of a small table, sitting in the chair Anouk saw there were several items on the table one of which was a comb, Anita picked it up and started to comb out her wet hair. Ooh, now this I could get used to, she thought happily. Anita started talking while working on the knots, "I always wished I had blonde hair, much prettier than black, I think". "Don't wish for things you can't change Anita, and anyway you really are a pretty girl as you are", Anita blushed, "Thank you My...., Anouk".

After finishing with her hair, the two walked back through the house to the front room, Dug was sitting on a couch, and Ben was stood leaning on the fireplace, talking. Stopping mid-sentence, and getting up "Now there is My lady, looking as pretty as a picture, I must say". Anouk rolled her eyes and sniffed loudly, "So why haven't you bathed, Dug"? "Why, do you think I need to then"? He made a show of sniffing his armpits, "Yes, you do, you smell of horse and other things, please go bathe and change your clothes". "Ok", he replied with a cheeky look on his face, "Maybe your pretty maid can come to help me", he winked at Anita. Anouk looked back at her and saw the horrified look in her wide eyes, turning back she saw Ben was giggling. "I have a better idea, maybe Ben can assist you and wash your back, as you are so in need of help". It was his turn to look horrified standing there shaking his head. "Bah, I'm off to have that bath", Dug said as he stomped out of the room. Anouk looked back to Anita and whispered, "Don't worry, I've got your back". Anita grinned, not only at her comment but also at the horrified look still hanging on Ben's face.

As Anouk sat down on the couch, Anita slipped off into the kitchen, giving them some privacy. Ben turned to her, "Gretta has requested to see you as soon as possible, are you up to it now? We could leave it to tomorrow morning, if you are too tired", "No, I would love to see her, and maybe get some answers". Ben started for the front door, "Ok, let's go then", Anouk let Anita know they were off out before following Ben to the door. They stepped out onto the road and started walking in a northerly direction up the road; she looked around as they walked, taking in the sights and sounds of the town. Children were playing in the side alleys, their gleeful shouts echoing around, traders shouting for people to look at their wares. She could hear the sound of metal ringing as a blacksmith hammered, a woman just across the road from them was sitting outside her door singing, the song was a mournful one but very melodious. As she studied her, she realized she must be blind as although she looked around, it was obvious her eyes did not see, Anouk stopped to listen to her. "That's old Peggy, she lost her sight by the hands of Knights from Regis, they put a hot dagger point in each eye trying to get information from her, but she didn't say a thing to them". Anouk looked to her feet where a small pot sat, "Ben, could you lend me a coin please". Ben fished a copper from his purse and handed it to her, thanking him she made her way over and dropped the coin in the pot, the older woman stopped singing and held out her hand. Anouk took her hand and squatted down beside her; they spoke for a brief time before she returned to Ben, the woman was smiling in their direction. "What did you say to her?", Ben asked, "That's between her and I", she replied with a glint in her eye.

As they walked away, she started singing again, a happy, cheerful song. Ben looked at Anouk with admiration.

Eventually, they reached an older looking dwelling with a front porch; Ben approached the front door, pausing, he turned to Anouk, "Wait here and let me announce you, she's a bit old fashioned like that". Anouk waited as Ben disappeared through the door, she saw several people had stopped to look at her, she tried not to make eye contact looking to her boots. Ben returned quickly, "She is ready to see you, she has asked I not stay, so I'll pop back later for you". Ben held the door open for her as she entered, closing it behind her. Well here goes girl, she told herself as she stepped into the next room.

The room wasn't well lit, but it was light enough to see, it was a large room with furniture dotted around, in the corner to her right she could see a bed tucked behind a curtain. Several pictures hung on the walls, and there was a large fireplace to her left which was lit, in front of this were two chairs, one either side. The one to her right was occupied by an old lady; she was wrapped in a shawl and had a blanket over her legs. Her hair was white and patchy, her face was wrinkled with age, she must be at least seventy summers, she thought. "Hello Gretta, I am Anouk, you asked for me to come and see you", "Anouk my dear girl, come closer so that I may look upon you", she said in an old croaky voice.

Anouk moved forward and stood in front of her, watery eyes travelled up her body to her face, which she studied for some time, all the time shaking her head, "Oh my, it is as if your mother is once again standing in front of me, you have so much of her in you". Anouk was shocked by this statement, dropping to her knee's she took the old ladies' hand in hers, "Did you know my mother? What was her name? What was she like?" Questions tumbled out of her as her mind whirled with the comprehension that she might finally get to know where she came from. “Hush girl, let an old lady get a word in edgewise”, she raised her free hand up to her cheek, her thumb stroking her cheekbone. Leaning forward she looked deep into her eyes, “Oh, you have grown into a beautiful woman, your mother would have been so proud, sit and I will tell you all that I know”. Anouk backed into the chair opposite sitting forward expectantly.

Gretta settled herself back in her chair, “I met your mother, Anya, some thirty summers ago when they happened upon this town, we became firm friends very quickly, she was a lively, vivacious woman who could see no wrong in anyone. She lit up a room just by entering and many a man envied her husband Terry. They became regular visitors here, feeling at home due to their particular gifts”, she stopped to take a sip of water. Anouk's mind was racing 'So they were coming here not going to Regis as Shan had said, and my mother was called Anya, I have so wanted to know her name'. “Anyway, Terry was summoned to attend the royal court, and your mother went with him to Regis, your mother told me after they had been to the Palace, where they met the King and his son, they got lodgings at an inn in the town. Later they received visitors, it was Noble's from the Palace who invited Terry out for drinks and business discussions, he wasn't going to go, but your mother told him to as she would have an early night.

After they departed Prince Harold arrived at the room, and insisted she let him in; he was the Prince she couldn't really say no. Once in the room, he made advances to your mother, when she rejected him, he raped her. Terry returned early that night and caught the prince in the room after the fact, he was so incensed he attacked the Prince and between the two of them, using their gifts, killed him. They fled the town and came straight here, your mother stayed with me for a week to compose herself, they then returned to Belcher". She stopped for another sip of water, Anouk noticed it was getting dark outside but wanted to hear everything, "Is that all you know or is there more"? The old lady smiled at her, "Oh, there is more. A few months went by before they returned here, this time she was heavy with child, she told me there was no doubt in her mind that it was the Prince's baby. They remained here until the birth, in fact, she gave birth in that very bed over there, that was your birth, and I helped her to deliver you. She wanted to give you away before you were born, but she took one look at you after the birth, and instantly fell in love with you".

Gretta pointed to a shape by the wall covered in a blanket, "Sweetheart, I have something for you, and I think it is the right time for you to have it. Remove the blanket and open that up, it is what your mother left here the last time I saw her". Anouk knelt by the chest pulling the lid up, inside were several items laying on some clothing. She was drawn immediately to an oval-shaped pendant on a chain made of shiny metal; it was intricately carved on both sides; a small button was evident at the edge. Pressing the button, it sprang open revealing small drawn pictures of two people, a man and a woman. "Who are they"? She asked looking up to Gretta, "They are your parents, Terry and Anya, they had those drawn in Regis by a street artist, and very good likeness's they are too". Anouk stared at the pictures, tears welling up in her eyes, her mother was beautiful, with a proud soft face. Her father handsome with strong features, "Oh my, I never dreamt I would ever see what they looked like, this will be my most treasured possession, they were a handsome couple". Gretta sat nodding agreement, letting her savour the moment. Anouk put the chain over her head letting the pendant drop down to her chest, "I will treasure this for the rest of my life".

Anything else was now secondary to the pendant, but wiping the moisture from her eyes, she set about looking at the rest of the contents. There was a large hairbrush, a small hand mirror and an ornate dagger, the metal of which was golden and a large red stone was set at the end of the handle. Picking it up she found it was attached to a brown leather belt, drawing the dagger from the scabbard it was of shiny steel and looked extremely sharp on both sides, culminating at a deadly point. Oh, nasty looking she thought, replacing the dagger back in the scabbard, she turned to the clothing. Lifting it up, she saw it was a long fitted black leather dress, laced down the front to just above the waist; it was open at the lower part for the legs. Two brown stripes ran vertically down the front. The leather was soft but heavy and well made, putting it aside, the other piece of clothing in the chest was a pair of black leather trousers of the same quality, holding them to her she could see they were the right size. "These must have cost a fortune," she thought out loud. "They did, and your mother looked stunning in them as I am sure you will do", Gretta replied.

Anouk sat back in her chair clutching the pendant in her hand, stunned by all the information she had finally been given, thinking so they did kill the Prince, for raping mother. "Wait a minute, if the Prince is my father through rape, does that make me Royalty"? She mused out loud. Gretta chuckled, "I am afraid so, you are the Princess daughter of Prince Harold, King Uther is your Grandfather and Queen Amelia your step Grandmother, oh, and you have an Aunt, Princess Geraldine". "So that's why everyone has been acting like that around me, well I am not a Princess, never have and never will be", Gretta could see she was getting upset, "That is enough news for one day, but please think on this, the Royal family is rotten to the core, except maybe Geraldine, and the people are getting fed up with them. You are one step removed, but still, of Royal blood, you may be the only chance this realm has of becoming good again. Now go and rest child, we can talk more tomorrow". Anouk rose from the chair, collecting the other items from the chest, then walked to the bed in the corner. Looking at it she thought, my mother was here, I was born here, how crazy this day has become, "Ok, I will go now, but I will be back tomorrow", as she passed through the door Gretta called after her, "I am counting on it".

Leaving the house, she found Ben waiting outside, not speaking, she walked past him and set off back to the house deep in thought. Ben could see she was troubled by what she had learnt, so he just fell in beside her, walking silently down the road. Anouk didn't speak the whole way, Royalty, me royalty, a princess. It can't be true I don't feel any different, I wonder what they are like? Do I look like any of them? I have an Aunty, I wonder what is she like?

Entering the house, she couldn't even remember the walk back, just Gretta's words rushing around her brain. The smell of food wafted in from the kitchen, and her stomach growled, she had forgotten about food but now realized how hungry she was. In the kitchen she found Anita had laid the table with all manner of food, bread, cheese, meat, fruit and was spooning a hot broth into a bowl. "Perfect timing My lady, please sit here", she said as she placed the bowl of broth at the head of the table. Dug was already sat slurping at his bowl, "Hmm, yes you should this is excellent broth", Anouk gave him a mischievous look, "Isn't it customary to stand when a Lady enters the room"? Dug shot her a pointed look whilst raising his backside slightly from the chair, broth still around his lips. "It is, but as you keep reminding me, you ain't no lady", she laughed and sat in the chair offered as Ben sat in one of the other two.

They all tucked into the broth as Anita moved back to a corner in the kitchen, suddenly realizing she hadn't sat down with them Anouk looked over, "What are you doing, come sit and eat, there is more than enough for everyone here", everyone's eyes turned to her, blushing she replied, "Well it wouldn't be proper for me to sit and eat with you, My Lady". "Nonsense, you are part of this group, and we all eat together, come, sit down and eat". Ben and Dug muttered in agreement. Ben got up pulling the spare chair out, in a flourish indicated for Anita to sit, embarrassing the girl even more.

After having eaten their fill, they all helped clear the table, taking their seats again with a jug of ale and one of water on the table. Anouk sat back in her chair holding her belly, "I haven't eaten that much in weeks, thank you Anita, for such a lovely spread, now to business". She looked around the table, "I don't want anything I say now to go beyond these four walls, does everyone understand"? She waited for each to confirm they understood before telling them all about the conversation with Gretta. When she had finished, everyone sat silent for a long moment. "I knew it, I just knew it, didn't I tell you there was more to you than meets the eye, Your Highness", Dug blurted out. Anouk was looking at Anita who didn't seem at all surprised by the news, "What, we all know the story of your birth and who your father was", she said with a shrug of her shoulders.

"Well actually", Ben started, he looked at Anouk, "I knew only a small part of that, but you might be interested in knowing I have an elder sister called Fina". She looked at him with a puzzled expression, "That's nice Ben, but why would I be interested, as you put it"? "Well my sister lived here for some time before returning to live with my parents in Regis, she is employed in the Palace as one of Princess Geraldine's handmaidens". Anouk fell back in her chair, this just keeps getting better she thought to herself, "Have you spoken with your sister about the Princess at all"? Ben nodded with a concerned look on his face, "I have, and the Princess, your Aunt, is an extremely unhappy woman. Fina said she is a very beautiful lady who is compassionate to all around her, but she is ruled over by her father the King with almost an iron fist, controlling where she goes and who she sees. Fina has witnessed the King striking her on several occasions and had to cover the bruises with powder many more times. Her mother Queen Diana died when she was young, now she has a stepmother Queen Amelia. Who Fina doesn't trust one bit, she describes her as a self-important person with her own hidden agenda. The Princess is almost a prisoner in the Palace".

Dug, who was on his second mug of ale said, “If it’s that bad for her why doesn’t she get out of there”? Ben looked at him shaking his head, “The guards that keep people out also keep people in, she can’t escape, she is trapped there”. Anouk stayed silent thinking about her, poor woman, imagine having to put up with that, certainly not what a Princess’s life should be. Suddenly she was taken over by a massive yawn, “Well, I am absolutely shattered, so I am off to bed, good night gentlemen I will see you tomorrow”, she got up and headed for the bedchamber with Anita following close behind her, “Good night”, she heard them call after her. “Oh, your training starts tomorrow, and you have me as a trainer”, Ben called out. Anouk stopped in her tracks, “Training, what training”? “You have to learn how to use your gift properly, without knocking people over of course”, he said with a sly grin”. Anouk raised her arms, “Ha-ha, you said that was your fault, and a poor teacher always blames his students, good night”.

Chapter 14

Anouk awoke in the morning having had the best night's sleep in days. It had taken her a while to drift off having so much to think about, but when she did, it was into a deep relaxing slumber. Looking around the room, it was bright with sunlight, the birds singing their happy tunes; could be heard outside the window. Anouk stretched, she felt loathe to leave the warmth and comfort of the bed, "Good morning My Lady", Anita stepped to the side of the bed where she could see her. "Hmm, good morning, why are you up so early"? she replied rubbing her eyes, "Early" Anita replied, "It is mid-morning My Lady, I have prepared a bath for you". Anouk scrambled out the bed, "Mid-morning! I have never slept that late in my life". Looking across to the bathtub, "Another bath, are you trying to wash me away"? Anita stood back, fidgeting, "No My Lady, I just thought you would like to start the day fresh is all, I am sorry if I have offended you". Anouk walked over and took her hands in hers, "No, I am sorry, I'm not used to all this. It may be new to you looking after me, but it's just as new to me too".

They smiled at each other as Anouk announced in a posh voice, "I am now ready to bathe, would you be a darling and wash my back", both of them giggled as she removed her nightgown, slipping into the bath. Having bathed and dressed she walked through to the kitchen, Ben and

Dug were sitting at the table. As she entered, they both got up and swept into a respectful bow chorusing, "Good morning Your Highness", Anita watched with a sheepish grin whilst Anouk looked at them with distaste, "Looks like you two have been practising that. As you have had your fun, can I have breakfast in peace"?

Later that morning, Ben walked her down to an area by the river; there was a cleared semi-circle on each side with the water running through the centre. Several people were standing along the river bank, using their gift to manipulate the fluid. Balls of water hovered in the air dancing in the sunlight, like small silver globes, a spiral of water whirling as a whirlpool rose out of the river. As it reached the height of three men, it curved over and descended back to the river, making an arch of whirling water sparkling in the daylight. Whilst the arch stood across the river, the globes started to chase each other through it, some going around the side pillar and some over the top.

Anouk was mesmerized with the beauty of it, the control these people have is fantastic, she thought. "That's the water people and over here are the earth people", Ben said taking her by the arm leading her away. Two people were practising, one she recognized as Benji, he was making a large cube of earth, twisting it one way then the other. He looked over and saw who was watching, letting the cube go it crashed to the ground in a massive pile of earth. He winked at Ben, turned back to the mound and started to raise it again, only this time as it rose it formed a model of a palace. With towers, ramparts, and courtyards in such detail it was unbelievable. "I present a palace for Your Highness", Benji announced, Anouk placed her hand on his shoulder, "Why thank you, Benji, that was most thoughtful of you". Looking at her smiling, "Are you here to train"? "Yes, I am going to take her over to the fire side to start with", Ben answered for her. Taking her arm, he led her off towards the river, over a small foot-bridge to the other semi-circle. "This is where the fire gifts train, we don't have an area for Air as we haven't had anyone who could do that, until you of course". Anouk looked around, the ground had scorch marks in several places, three tree trunks were set upright in one area and several boulders in another, all were scorched by fire. "Ok, the first lesson of how to use your gift effectively".

Anouk turned to face Ben, "The power you have is inside you, hidden away until you call upon it, your body is the power, but your mind is what control's it". Ben held out his hand, "I am building my power and focusing on my finger, thinking of a small flickering flame", as he said this a small flame appeared above his fingertip. "Now I am focusing on my palm and thinking of a bigger flame", the little flame reacted, travelling down his finger to his palm, growing in size until it settled in the centre of his hand, dancing and flickering, she could feel the heat from the flame. "And now I am thinking of a ball of flame about the size of an apple", the flame transformed in a ball of fire, the heat immediately increased radiating out around it. Anouk had to step back, but couldn't take her eyes off it. The ball rotated above his palm, the centre a boiling mass of fire, he didn't seem to be affected by the heat, but she was beginning to feel quite uncomfortable, sweat breaking out on her brow. "Watch the centre tree trunk over by the river; I will send the ball to it". Anouk turned as the ball flew out of Ben's hand, straight as an arrow to the trunk, where it exploded against it setting the bark on fire. A large column of water leapt from the river hitting the tree putting the flames out; Ben waved to one of the water gift people shouting, "Thank you, Simon".

She turned back to Ben with wide eyes, "That was amazing, but it scares me using my gift, people tend to get hurt. And why was it when I was in jail that I went off like that? It was so bad I lost all my clothes"; she asked a little embarrassed. "Well, as I said your body holds the power, you were not ready for that, whatever happened in there caused you to explode, literally. But it's possible to direct the power to any part of your body". Shocked Anouk said, "Any part"? "Yup, once I thought it would be funny to see if I could shoot a fireball from my backside, turns out it was, I burned a hole right through the seat of my pants, my sister wasn't amused though".

Anouk started to giggle, looking up to Ben's face, it was a picture of embarrassment, which made her laugh all the more. "Right, your turn, now remember your power will react to your mind, so keep it clear what you want it to do", Ben moved around behind her taking her right wrist, raising her arm with her palm upwards. "Now summon your power, let it build a little and focus on your hand", the air shimmered starting to stir, "Good, now think of a mini-tornado as you did before", the tornado took shape in her hand, spinning wildly. "Excellent, now picture in your head a tall tornado with a long tail", the air changed shape, and the tornado grew taller, the tail stretching longer. "Ok, now I want you to picture a cyclone with no tail, just the top whirling around", the spout seemed to suck up into the top, and she was left with a vortex of air spinning in concentric circles above her hand, it started growing larger and larger. "I think you need to think about a soft breeze blowing over the fields", Anouk did so and the cyclone dissipated into a gentle breeze wafting over her hand, looking up to the boulder the breeze wafted away in the afternoon air. "So, you see from that you can control your gift, you just need to use your mind and concentrate on what it is you want to do. Don't allow it to get too big whilst training, because if it gets away from you in the town, well we don't want to see that eh!". "I'm amazed I could do that, thank you Ben, but I am feeling quite tired now". Ben nodded, "You will because using the gift takes energy, bigger the use the more it takes. But practice regularly, and you will get stronger".

Anouk took note of what he had said storing it away for later, "I need to go over to Gretta's now, she will be expecting me, thank you for your help today, I promise I will practice". As she made her way from the training ground up to Gretta's house, meandering her way through the alleys and roads, men kept bowing and the women curtsying. She was getting used to it, no matter how much she asked for them not to do it, they just carried on, so now she would politely nod as she passed. On arrival at Gretta's house, she met a woman of about thirty summers leaving with a small girl clinging to her hand; the woman curtsied before passing her on the path. As Anouk headed for the door, she felt a tug on her dress, looking down she saw the little girl looking up at her whilst holding her dress. Anouk squatted down to speak to her, "Hello, what's your name"? The girl just stared at her with big round eyes, "I am sorry Your Highness, her name is Sarah" the mother replied. She then found her voice saying in a soft childish voice, "Are you really a Princess"? Anouk smiled, "Yes, I suppose I am, but all little girls are princesses, and you are a particularly beautiful one", she beamed with a lovely smile, "Thank you". Anouk watched as her mother led her away, waving to her.

Stepping into Gretta's front room, she saw her sitting in her favourite chair, "Hello Gretta, here as promised, hope you are well"? She turned in her chair, peering at her, "Come child, sit with me. I hope you've had time to come to terms with what we spoke about yesterday"? Anouk sat, looking at her, she seemed tired, more aged than yesterday with a worried frown across her brow. "I have, and I've come to the conclusion that I cannot change the past, so I have to accept the future in whatever form it takes. But I will never live in a palace or become one of the royal family", Gretta sat watching her intently. "That is good child, but sometimes the best rulers are those that don't really want the job, as opposed to those that crave it". Anouk nodded, "I hear what you are saying, but I am a simple farm girl, I grew up on hard work, feeding the animals or helping on the land. I didn't have splendid clothes or people waiting on me hand and foot in a palace. I wouldn't be any good with all of that, and I don't know the first thing about ruling anyone".

Gretta reached out placing a hand on her knee, "I know my child, but these things can be learnt if only the person is willing. Apart from that I have had news from my sources which is very worrying, Princess Geraldine has gone missing". Stunned, Anouk just looked at the old lady, she continued, "It would appear the town of Regis is in turmoil, no one in the palace or the town has a clue what has happened to her. It appears she and her handmaids just disappeared". "In a heavily guarded palace, how is that possible? Someone must know something", Anouk thought out loud. Gretta nodded, "My thoughts exactly, either her father had a hand in this, in which case she and the handmaids will never be seen again, or she did manage to escape the Palace, in which case they could be headed here. I have doubled the guard and sent lookouts into the forest". Anouk sat back in her chair thinking, "Ok, so why would the Princess run to here? How would she know of this place"? "Ahh", Gretta responded, "One of her handmaids comes from here, she sends regular updates to me about what is going on in the Palace, she would recommend they head this way if they did run".

Sudden realization crept over Anouk, "Oh my god, Ben's sister, someone needs to tell him what is going on". Anouk jumped out of the chair and headed for the door, "Slow down my child, I have already sent word to him, I expect he will be here shortly, sit back down". Anouk slowly made her way back to the seat, "I wanted to tell you more about your mother, what she was like and how she lived", Anouk nodded, half-listening as Gretta started a long description of her mother, she heard most of it, but part of her waited for the sound of the front door opening. A long while later, Gretta was still talking when a loud knock sounded from the front door followed by the sound of the door opening.

Anouk flew out the chair heading towards the door, as Ben walked in she took him in her arms giving him a big hug, whispering in his ear, "I am so sorry Ben, I am sure she will be ok, she will make her way here, won't she"? Ben didn't speak, shocked at the sudden closeness of Anouk, enjoying the feeling of her pressed against him, her warm breath on his ear and neck. His arms instinctively wrapped around her waist, holding her closer, they stood for long seconds in their embrace. Gretta finally spoke, "If you two love birds are finished, we need to speak about what is to be done", they broke apart, both blushing a little. Ben spoke, "Gretta, do you think it's possible they escaped from the palace? And if they do make their way here, they might be tracked by the soldiers, that would really mess up the secrecy of this town".

Anouk sat back in her chair, and Ben stood by the fireplace in front of Gretta, "That is why I have doubled the guard and sent additional lookouts into the forest, Ben you need to gather all the gifted and explain what could be coming, make sure they all double their practice time". Ben nodded, "I will get on to that as soon as possible, can I then go out into the forest to help watch"? Gretta shook her head, "No you are needed in the town, organize the practice sessions and set up a defence plan should we be attacked", she gave Ben an anxious look, "you have to remember if your sister does make for us, not only will we be harbouring the Princess, we also have Anouk, whom the King has ordered to be killed, a double reason to send his soldiers". Ben's face fell, Anouk felt sorry for him knowing it would be hell just waiting in town, not knowing what has happened to his sister. "So, what should I be doing Gretta? As I am part of the problem here". Gretta reached out rubbing her hand, "Never feel you are a problem, you were born here, and that makes this your home. I want you to double your efforts with practising your gift. I feel sure we will have need of it soon".

Later that evening, Anouk was sitting in her nightgown

having her hair brushed by Anita, the bed-chamber was warm and cosy, letting her relax and enjoy the feeling of her hair being brushed. Anita was humming a pretty tune as she worked on the tangles, it acted like a lullaby would for a baby, making her sleepy. "Thank you, Anita," she said, getting up and making her way to the bed, "Think I will sleep well tonight even though many things are rattling around in my head". Slipping in between the sheets, she curled up in a fetal position facing Anita; an enormous yawn escaped as she settled her head into the pillow. "See you in the morning," she said smiling up at her, "Good night Anouk, sweet dreams", Anita replied as she headed off across the room, blowing out the candle before settling into her cot in the opposite corner.

Anouk drifted off almost immediately. She dreamed about running through the fields of the holding, brushing the ears of the corn with her hands, the day was bright and sunny, warm from the sun washing over her as she ran. What a wonderful day when all was right with her life, she was grateful for what she had and the love she received from Pata and Katcha, what more could a girl ask for. As she approached the ploughed field, she could see a mound at the back of the plough. Her mind started to scream, don't go there, stay away. But her legs continued to carry her forward; she felt powerless to stop them, drawing her closer to the mound. She could see it was Pata now, laying on his back, arrows sticking from his chest, blood staining his shirt front, sightless eyes staring up at the sky. She stood silently over his body, looking down, unable to tear her eyes away as his head started to turn towards her, ever so slowly. His sightless eyes looking deep into her, his words boomed in her head, but his lips did not move, "Stay safe girl, trust only those worthy of it, they will come for you, they will be coming, and they will kill you as they have me". The vision changed; she was standing in a burning kitchen, the kitchen of their house, Katcha lay on the floor with her throat cut. Her sightless eyes bored into her; the fire was leaping all around, beams falling to the floor in a shower of sparks, burning thatch drifting down like fireflies floating through the air. Katcha's voice sounded in her head, "My sweet love, live your life as you want to, but be careful, not everyone is as they seem, there is a viper in the nest!" The fire started to consume her body, clothing being burned away, her hair catching fire. Anouk tried to look away but could not, as if she was being forced to watch her beloved Katcha being consumed by the fire, she started to scream, "No, leave her alone, haven't you done enough".

Anita felt as if she had only just closed her eyes when she awoke suddenly, not sure of why she had awoken. Looking around the room, it was dark with faint shadows of the furniture visible, but all seemed quiet. Laying quietly, she listened for anything out of the ordinary, nothing except for the sound of Anouk moving about in her bed, suddenly Anouk shouted, "No", Anita leapt from her bed quickly lighting a candle and rushing to her side. The bedclothes were awry, and Anouk thrashed about in the bed, "Leave her alone", she shouted. Anita placed her hand on her shoulder shaking her gently whilst calling her name softly. Anouk started to awake just as the door to the bed-chamber burst open, Dug stood in the doorway, bare-chested with a knife in his hand. "What's going on"? He asked, looking at the two of them, "Just a bad dream, we are ok, thank you Dug", "Humph, well if you are sure I will leave you ladies to it", Dug replied whilst scanning around for the second time.

When they were alone again Anita looked down at her face; she could see tears had rolled down her cheeks, smoothing her hair out of her eyes she could see they were wide with fear staring up at her. “Do you want to talk about it”, she asked, Anouk shook her head whilst clutching her arms around her and rolling on her side, Anita sat looking at her back for a few moments, “Ok, try to get some sleep now, the dreams shouldn’t return tonight”. As she stood from the bed, Anouk spoke, “Anita, would you hold me, please”, her voice was pleading almost like a little girl. “Of course,” she replied, sliding into the bed behind her, as she put her arm around her Anouk grabbed it, pulling it tight while snuggling back against her. They both laid quietly just listening to each other’s breathing, Anouk slowly raised Anita’s hand to her breast holding it there, she didn’t pull away so Anouk moved her hand away to see if she’d keep it there, she did.

For long moments they lay together, Anita gently caressing her, both were feeling the excitement of the closeness they had discovered, both overcome by the physical bond they were creating. Turning slowly, Anouk faced Anita, moving her hair from her face she looked into her eyes, she could see excitement, joy, love and lust there, as she was sure there was in her own. Moving closer, she brushed her lips with her own; the feeling was electric, sending shivers down her spine. Her chest felt like it would explode with the excitement, barely able to breathe, her body shaking with the passion Anita brought out in her. Their lips locked, and they fell hopelessly into each other’s embrace.

During the next few days, Ben busied himself with organizing the gifted ones, making sure all practised twice a day. He walked the walls of the town looking for weak spots, anywhere outside the walls that could be an advantage to attackers. He got the earth people to level off any small mounds and fill all the ditches, several of them he put to work widening and cutting new courses for the river to flow around the town, creating a moat. It wasn't a large moat; the idea was to put water in reach of the people with the water gift where ever they were on the walls. The water people were tasked with filling all water butts, troughs and barrels they could find and placing them strategically about the town. The fire people had been tasked with scorching all vegetation between the trees and the town, when they were finished nothing taller than a blade of grass stood in the circle. As Ben walked through the town checking the preparations, he could feel the atmosphere of the town had changed; people were walking around silently with an air of doom about them. Children huddled together in small groups, not laughing or playing as children do; they just sat talking in hushed tones. Ben stopped, watching three children playing with stones in the dust, "they look so sad as if the end was coming", he thought quietly. "I need to speak with Gretta about the effect it is having on the town", he decided.

As he walked across town, he passed by the practice grounds. Anouk was standing in the semi-circle, sitting a little bit away from her was Anita watching her. Ben had noticed the two of them had been a lot closer of late which was good as she needed a close female friend. Anouk's arms were outstretched shaking a little; she was focused on the boulder in front of her. Ben thought for a second his eyes were deceiving him; the boulder was slowly rising from the ground, he stood riveted to the spot. "That boulder must weigh as much as fifty horses"! Ben turned to find Benji stood next to him, he was staring ahead with wide eyes, he looked back, and the boulder had now lifted as high as a man. "I know, how did she learn to do that"! As they watched, she released the boulder which crashed back down hitting the ground with a loud thump. Ben could feel the shock waves of the impact through his feet. Ben approached Anouk, "How did you manage that"? He asked, "I just thought it would be fun to pick it up, so I tried. I can do all sorts of things now, Tornado's, light winds, gales, I can even make a wall of air and throw it in any direction, do you want to see"? Ben smiled, "Well done, but not now I need to go see Gretta, keep practising though you are getting better than I thought possible". Anouk smiled at him as he walked off in the direction of Gretta's house.

Chapter 15

Geraldine was feeling very sorry for herself; the past three nights had gone without incident for them, but the travelling was getting harder each night. Her feet blistered in several places because of the new boots, her back hurt from the pack, her shoulders were rubbed raw by the straps. She felt sure the other two knew she was suffering, but Geraldine had decided she would suffer in silence, after all, it was her idea to do this. Thankfully the packs were getting lighter as the food and water were used, but this brought other worries of when or where were they going to be able to replenish them. This was the start of the fourth night, and they only had enough food for the morning meal, voicing her thoughts she asked, "Fina how much further is it? As we are going to run out of food tomorrow". Fina was kneeling packing items into her pack, "Well we should see the forest by morning, if we can keep up a good pace, we can eat once we are there, and it will be about a day through the forest. So that should put us in the town for the evening if we keep going". Mary squatted down, putting her arm around her shoulders, "Nearly there, we should be ok to get to the town, you have done so well". Geraldine looked at her, smiling, "Thank you, Mary, you are both such good friends, I could never have been able to do this without you". The three stood, nodded to each other and set off into the night once more.

As they made their way through the night, with Fina navigating by the stars, they chatted quietly, hummed tunes and joked about Fina's and Mary's past boyfriends. Anything to keep Geraldine's mind off the pain she was feeling, it worked a bit, but she was limping again, and she knew she was slowing them down. Gritting her teeth, she forged on telling herself, I will do this, I am going to make it to the town. This thought raised a question in her mind, "Fina tell me about the town"? Fina moved to her side putting her arm through the Princess's and matching her pace, "Well the town is built in a circle shape with a river running through the south part, there is a large wall of tree trunks which runs all around the outside". Geraldine interrupted her, "No, tell me of the people, what are they like? Do they care for the royal family"?

Fina thought for a second, "You have to remember that most fled the other towns in fear of their children's or their own lives, the royal family was the reason for that", Geraldine's face fell, "Oh, so they will hate me"? Fina shook her head, "Let me finish, all the people I have spoken to hate the royal family, yes, but there has always been one who they all loved and felt a little sorry for. I have heard on many occasions; now she would be a Queen worthy of the title, and that person is you, your highness". "But how is that possible? My father and his queen have always overshadowed me, how could they possibly know who I am or what I am like"? Mary laughed, "Because you have the best handmaids in the realm, every time you gave to the poor, or helped someone with their problems and stood up for the people, we were there to tell it how it is. You are famous with the people for your compassion, generosity and fairness. You thought you were doing it anonymously, but we made sure everyone knew what a special person you are".

Fina suddenly dropped to the ground pulling the Princess with her, Mary quickly following, when all three were laying on the grass Fina whispered, "Shh, someone's coming, cover yourselves with your cloaks and stay down". Geraldine squirmed into the smallest form she could make, checking her cloak was covering everything. Laying still, Fina one side and Mary on her other, she strained her hearing for any sound; she could feel her heart racing, fear gripping her insides. Slowly the sound of a horse walking and several pairs of feet following reached her ears, a gruff voice suddenly spoke, "I don't know why they sent us out this way, nothing but fields and grass, bloody waste of time if you ask me". A second male voice answered, "Aw shut your yap Jez; we do what they tell us. If they say patrol out here then that's what we do, no use moaning about it", a third voice joined the conversation, "So what are we supposed to do with them if we catch them"? The voices were getting closer, by the sound, Geraldine guessed they would pass them a short distance in front. The second voice spoke again, "Well they said we have to get the Princess back unharmed, but the two handmaids are not needed, so I guess we can have a bit of fun with them before we deal with them, get my meaning Jez". There followed a dirty laugh closely followed by several more. The one they called Jez replied, "Yeah, I get your meaning, I want first go with one if we catch them, been a while since I laid with a woman", a fourth voice spoke, "Have you ever laid with a woman Jez? Bet you wouldn't know what to do". The group starting laughing whilst Jez tried to protest his prowess with women. Geraldine reached out her hands, taking Fina and Mary's in hers, squeezing them gently to show her support for them.

The group were now passing in front of them, they could make out the silhouettes of a knight atop a horse, and several soldiers walking behind him. The clink of metal on metal could be heard from the armour and weapons they carried, a much more noble voice sounded out over them, "Shut up you lot, you're making enough noise to raise the dead. Sergeant, we will go a little further before we make camp for the night". The group had moved over to their left and was getting out of earshot before the Sergeant answered. "Yes, My Lord, may I suggest we camp down now, it's blacker than the inside of a cauldron out here, we can't see anything until morning". "Yes ok, make camp here then, set a guard and the rest can source a fire" the noble answered.

Fina slipped closer to Geraldine and whispered, "We've got to go, as soon as they start a fire the glow could give us away, pass on to Mary start crawling away from the soldiers, but stay low!" After she passed the message, Mary immediately started crawling away in the direction the soldiers had come from, Geraldine and Fina following close behind. They had been crawling for what seemed ages to Geraldine, crossing several muddy puddles which had covered them with slime and mud, soaking their clothes. The cold of the water instantly chilling them, pushing on fueled by fear until Fina whispered "Hold up", Geraldine looked back and could see Fina staring at the men's camp, a glow had started in that direction indicating they had got their fire going. "We can wait here a few minutes we are far enough away, let them get used to the light from the fire which will ruin their night vision". The three waited huddled together, all now shivering from their wet, muddy clothes. "Right that should be enough time, keep low and follow me", moving in a stooped posture they set off in their original direction. Geraldine moved quickly, her feet, back and shoulders still hurt, but fear and adrenaline numbed the pain giving her more energy.

After a long while, they had started walking normally again, always keeping an ear out for any sounds of pursuit, but none came. The sky was beginning to brighten with a red glow rising over the horizon, "Red sky in the morning, witches warning", Mary mused aloud, she stopped herself blushing deeply, "I am sorry Fina, I didn't mean, well you know"? Fina just smiled back at her, "No problem, I don't think of myself as a witch anyway, I am just gifted. Look I can see the forest up ahead, we are closer than I thought we would be, we have nearly made it".

She spun around facing them with a beaming smile, which quickly disappeared as the sounds of baying hounds floated in on the wind, "Oh god, RUN, we have to run the last part, their hounds have found us". They all started to run, fear and panic once again knotting their stomachs, each taking one of Geraldine's arms they ran pulling her as fast as she could go. As they closed the gap to the forest, so the hounds started to close the gap on them, the baying getting louder and louder, none of them daring to look back fixing their sight on the tree line. Geraldine's feet, legs and back were screaming in pain, tears started to roll down her cheeks, all of a sudden, her legs gave out, and she tumbled to the ground taking Fina and Mary with her, they all landed in a heap. Looking back, Fina could see the hounds on the horizon, small blobs tearing towards them baying their delight of getting to their quarry. "Get her up, get her up NOW!" she screamed to Mary, between them they dragged the Princess to her feet continuing to the forest, "Leave me, leave me, save yourselves", Geraldine protested, but they ignored her forcing her closer and closer to the forest. They were nearly there, and the hounds almost upon them. The howling of the hounds had become deafening, suddenly several people stepped out of the tree line in front of them, all three now totally exhausted fell to the ground just short of the trees. As they looked back, they saw the ground begin to churn in front of the hounds, Geraldine noticed they were large, powerful animals, wearing long spiked collars around their necks, and soulless black eyes staring at their quarry. The ground churned more violently as the hounds entered, quickly sinking into soil, the howling of joy at getting their prey, changed to a howling of fear and panic as they got sucked into the vortex beneath their feet. Like a patch of quicksand, the hounds quickly disappeared into the earth, their howls slowly silenced one by one, until they were gone. The dog handlers were still some distance off, small blobs slowly getting bigger as they raced to catch up with the hounds. Several people helped lift the three of them from the ground and take them into the forest, one of them stepped forward and manipulated the freshly turned soil, changing it back to hard level ground before slipping back into the woods.

Geraldine and Mary were quickly bundled on to a horse, Fina going on the second, they all headed into the forest.

Following tracks which were well known to the group, they quickly put distance between them and the edge of the woods. Geraldine had now managed to catch her breath; eternally thankful she didn't have to walk, she looked around at the group who had saved them. There were several men and two women all dressed in rough farmer type clothes. Looking back to Fina, she saw one of the young men walking alongside her horse holding her hand, they were speaking quietly. He released her hand and stepped away coming to the side of her horse, "Your Highness, my name is Tom, a friend of Fina's. You are in safe hands now, we will get you back to Forest Town by nightfall, so just try and rest as much as you can on the horse".

She looked down at his sincere face and saw only kindness and concern for her, causing her to choke a little, a single tear travelled down her cheek cutting through the dirt smeared on it. "Thank you, Tom, for saving and helping us, we would have been caught if you hadn't come along", "My pleasure Your Highness, never saved an actual Princess before", he beamed a toothy grin up to her before making his way to the front of the column. The morning passed slowly as they all made their way through the forest, Geraldine took the time to look around as they moved through the trees, it was full daylight and beams of sunlight made its way through the forest canopy. The forest was full of wildlife, animals skittering through the branches whilst larger animals foraged through the undergrowth; occasionally lifting their heads to watch them pass by. The motion of the horse rocking her as it plodded along its way started to lull her to sleep, her eyelids growing heavy as she leaned back against Mary, realizing what was happening she put her arms around the Princess, holding her so she could sleep.

Just after mid-day, they stopped in a clearing next to a stream for lunch, the three ladies sat together and shared out the last of the food from the packs, sitting quietly whilst they ate. As they were finishing Tom came over to sit with them, "Not far from the town now, Ben's there sorting the defences, he will be really happy to see you, Fina". "As I will be to see him, Tom, how is Gretta? I hope she is well", Tom nodded, "Yes she is well just a bit older, oh and she has a guest, would you believe an air gifted girl"! Fina looked up sharply with a shocked look on her face, "Wow an air gift! That is so rare, where did she come from"? "Well apparently Shan sent her from Belcher, she was to be executed for something or other, so he got her out, and gave her directions to us. I think Ben's more than a little taken with her, well, she is rather beautiful so I get that", Fina smiled knowingly, "He always did have an eye for the ladies". Turning to Geraldine and Mary, "You two better watch out because he can be quite the charmer", Mary grinned, but Geraldine seemed not to hear her.

Geraldine's mind was racing, who is this girl? Due to be executed, could this be my niece? How is it possible we could end up in the same place? Fate, misfortune or just dumb luck! Mary shoulder bumped her bringing her back from her thoughts, looking around all eyes were on her, feeling she should say something she looked at Tom, "Thank you for saving us Tom, those hounds were terrifying". Tom smiled back at her, "And again, it was my pleasure. When we get to the town can you ladies put your hoods up, we will get you to Gretta's house straight away, but there is no point in announcing your presence to the town immediately". They all nodded in agreement.

As dusk started to creep in, they broke free from the trees; Forest town stood before them, Geraldine was amazed that such a place could exist in secrecy as she looked down the hill into the town. She saw a river moat surrounding a huge palisade wall with a complete town contained inside, all surrounded by the forest; it was a beautiful and very welcome sight after the horrendous days of travel they had endured. As the small group made their way down to the town, Geraldine thoughts went back to the questions she had been secretly asking herself all afternoon. Who is this girl? Will I finally be able to meet my niece? I wonder what she will be like, will she even like me?

Chapter 16

Anouk was sitting at the kitchen table feeling a little light-headed for the wine she had drunk. Anita had brought it over, saying it was a gift from her father, and she had found it far more palatable than the ale the men were drinking. Dug and Benji were sitting together, Benji was playing the lute and Dug playing a small flute, the tunes they played were light and airy creating a party atmosphere.

Ben had talked Anita into dancing with him, as he twirled her around the room Anouk noticed Dug making eyes at Cheryl, who was obviously receptive to this. She smiled thinking it's good he has found someone. The music ended, and she noticed Benji and Dug whispering, Benji nodded and started to strum his lute and sing a soft love song. Whilst Dug put down the flute he was holding and made his way over to Cheryl. The two began a slow dance swaying in each other's arms, Anouk suddenly realized Ben was at her side, hand outstretched inviting her to dance. She smiled up at him taking his hand and rose unsteadily from the chair, phew that wine must be quite strong, her legs felt a little shaky and the room started to spin a little. Letting Ben walk her around the table he swept her into his arms holding her close, as he held her gently but firmly against him, he started to sway in time to the song. Anouk matched his swaying looking up into his face. Ben's eyes were closed with a rosy glow to his cheeks, was that from the ale he had drunk or was he enjoying holding her too much she thought to herself. Don't be silly; he is almost like a brother to me now. I'm sure it is the ale, she let the music and Benji's melodic voice take her as she lay her head on Ben's shoulder.

Suddenly she became aware everything had gone quiet and Ben had stopped moving, all in the room had stopped and was staring to the front room doorway. Which Ben had his back to, looking over his shoulder Anouk saw a large man standing in the door. It took her a few seconds to recognize who it was, "SHAN, you made it here", she pulled away from Ben stepping quickly over to him, throwing her arms around him hugging tightly. Shan grimaced but hugged her back, "Careful my lady, my back is still pretty sore you know". Anouk smiled up at him, "It is so good to see you, how did you get here? What's happening back home? Did they suspect you at all? You have to tell me everything".

Taking her by the shoulders, Shan moved her back to arm's length so he could look at her, his face betraying his relief at finding her in such good health. "I will answer all your questions, but first I need to wash up and get something to eat, it has been a long day's travelling and longer since I ate". Anouk smiled up at him, "Of course, there is a spare bed in Dug's room and facilities to wash, Dug will you show you where it is, and Anita could you prepare some food for him". Anita curtsied, "Of course, my lady." She hurried off to prepare food as Dug took Shan through to the bed-chamber.

When Shan returned, he found an assortment of food laid on the table for him which he quickly tucked into; all eyes were on him. Anouk sat at the head of the table and couldn't contain herself anymore, "So, what's happening back in Belcher"? Shan took a long swig of ale before answering, "Well, after you left, the town was in an uproar for several days, most everybody was set to searching for you but couldn't understand how you had gotten away. A girl came to me, Minit was her name, desperate for any information saying she was your best friend, I told her you were ok but could not say any more than that. I hope that is alright with you, my lady"? Anouk gasped, "Yes, yes, oh poor Minit, and I do hope to see her again one day". Shan ate a few more mouthfuls before speaking again, "I also found out how the Royal family has been getting all its information, appears Dard is in their pocket passing all goings-on in Belcher back to them. Life has returned to pretty much normal in the town. I waited for my injuries to settle to a dull ache before leaving, but I did pick up an interesting bit of information before I left. Princess Geraldine has disappeared from the palace with her two handmaids, some are saying they had kidnapped her". "WHAT, THAT IS SLANDEROUS LIES", Ben shouted as he jumped up from his chair sending it crashing across the room, "I WILL NOT HEAR SUCH THINGS UTTERED HERE".

Ben was standing with his chest puffed out and his hands clenched glaring around the room. Anouk quickly went to his side speaking softly whilst holding his arm, "Ben, we know these are lies probably sent out from the Royal family, none of us here believe it". Reaching up and placing her hand on his cheek she directed him to look at her. Looking into his eyes, she could see the hurt displayed there, "I am sure Fina is helping her not kidnapping her, as everyone here thinks too". Looking around the room everyone was nodding adding agreement to what she was saying. She saw the anger and hurt start to slide away from his face, and his body began to relax. Turning to Shan, "Ben's sister, Fina, is one of the handmaids which makes this doubly worrying. Where do you think they may have gone? Gretta thinks they may head here".

Shan continued to eat his meal whilst everyone else sat quietly pondering the implications of what he had said. It was Dug who broke the silence, stroking his chin and thinking out loud, "Well, if the Princess is heading here and the King gets to hear of this place, he will have two reasons to send all his forces against us. That is a lot of soldiers and knights; we will need to be prepared to meet this attack". Anouk looked at him with a quizzical expression, "What do you mean two reasons"? Dug shrugged, "You are here, and if the princess comes, that's two reasons by my calculation", "So if she comes here, I should leave, maybe set up a distraction and lead them off someplace else". The room filled with a chorus of dissent at her remark, all shaking their heads.

Anita stepped to her side placing a hand on her arm and whispering in her ear, "I don't think your friends will let you do that, and I for one would be heartbroken if you did". Anouk looked to her seeing the concern etched across her face, "Thank you, Anita, you are a special friend", Anita blushed, feeling the deep connection between them tighten.

Whenever she was this close to Anouk, she always started to feel tingly, butterflies dancing in her stomach, is this really what love feels like she asked herself quietly. Dug continued, "That is not an option my lady, we all need to steel ourselves to the task of dealing with whatever the King throws at us. Shan, would any of the knights follow you"? Shan was washing down the last of the food with his ale, looking over at Dug he pulled a quizzical face. "Well, I hadn't thought of that, I have heard whispers from my friends that not all the knights are happy with the Kings tyrannical reign. But even so, there would only be a handful at best who would turn".

Dug looked into his empty mug swishing the dregs around as he thought, "A handful is better than none I suppose, and that means it is a handful less for us to fight. Shan, I don't know how the knights communicate but get word to the handful as soon as you can. Also, can you consult with Ben, he has been preparing the defences of the town, help him with the tactics they might employ to attack". Shan sat nodding in agreement as Dug continued whilst looking around the room, "Those of you with the gift should continue with your practice, those that don't should help out where possible. A storm is coming, and we need to be ready". Anouk was sitting back in her chair, Anita's hand on her shoulder.

She was studying Dug whilst listening, "My, you have certainly come out of your shell Dug, quite the leader has sprung forth". Dug's eyes softened as he looked at her, "It is because of you, My Lady, ever since that day I found you in that jail, I have sworn to myself that no harm will ever come to you whilst I still draw breath". Anouk reached out across the table taking his hand in hers, squeezing it tightly, "Thank you Dug, I don't know what I ever did to receive such a good friend as you". She looked around the room at the faces of everyone, her other hand going to her shoulder holding Anita's hand, "In fact thank you, to you all for standing by a poor farm girl who has been thrown into a life of chaos. You all mean the world to me", she gave an extra squeeze to Anita's hand as she said it.

A young lad burst into the room, gasping for breath from running; Ben looked over at him, "Sean, what are you here for"? Still gasping and trying to get his words out around the breaths he looked at Anouk, "Gretta... huff... would like you... puff... to go to her now, puff... it is huff... important, puff... Your Highness". Anouk considered this whilst going to the boy and squatting down to his level. Taking his hand she instructed him, "Sean, take some deep breaths and settle down a bit", she waited for him to get his breathing under control before asking, "Now, what is so important that it cannot wait until the morning". The lad replied, "I cannot say, she just said to get you as fast as I could, you should hurry, Your Highness".

Anouk looked to the others, most of which were shrugging indicating they didn't know either, "Anita, will you walk with me over to Gretta's", Anita's face lit up as she hurried off to get their capes whilst saying "Of course, My Lady". Dug looked at the expression on Anita's face then to Anouk; she was looking at him, doesn't he miss anything she thought to herself, out loud Anouk announced, "We will need to get back to this when I return from Gretta's, Dug, please continue with your excellent leadership". Dug smiled, nodding knowingly, "Sean, lead the way if you would", the three set out across the town towards Gretta's house.

Stepping into the front room Anouk paused to survey who was there, Gretta was sitting in her usual chair, and the fire was burning bright in the grate and sat on the rug at Gretta's feet were two women. Studying the women, she could see they were a little older than her, one with black hair the other was a blonde, both were wearing simple farm clothes. She looked over to where the bed was and saw the curtain drawn; a candle flickered behind it silhouetting a person moving around. Curious she thought, "Hello Gretta, you sent for me", Gretta looked over, "Yes child, please come over and say hello to my guests".

As Anouk approached Gretta announced, "This is Mary and Fina, handmaids to Princess Geraldine. Fina, Mary, this is Princess Anouk, daughter of Harold and niece to Princess Geraldine". The two women stood immediately and curtsied chorusing "Pleased to meet you, Your Highness", Fina continued, "We have heard so little about you and would love to get to know you". Anouk nodded, "Uhm, well, that was a little embarrassing, thank you Gretta. Let me introduce my handmaid, although I prefer to call her my companion, Anita", Anita stepped forward. She greeted them warmly although a little awkwardly.

Anouk moved to Fina taking her hands in hers, "Fina, you are Ben's sister, I have heard a lot about you, we must let Ben know you are safe, he has been so worried about you". Fina's eyes widened, a mildly shocked look on her face as she looked at the beautiful Princess standing before her. Gretta giggled, "You will have to get used to our resident Princess, Fina, she is not one for convention or ceremony. I have told you where he is, go put his mind at rest. Mary, you go with her. Geraldine is safe here with us, and we have Anita to be a 'companion' if needed".

Anita stood blushing at the loaded remark as the two

ladies took their leave and left the room. Gretta turned to Anouk smiling as a grandmother would at her beautiful granddaughter, “Now is the time for you to meet your Aunt, forgive me if I do not get up, my old bones are weary. Anita come sit with me whilst they get acquainted”. Anouk turned and took a tentative step towards the curtain, her mind running riot with all the thoughts she had had over the past days, since knowing about her past. What if she doesn’t like me? What if she thinks I am some sort of threat to her? Will I even like her? Oh god, this is really happening. She had reached the curtain, looking back to Anita, who was now seated in the other chair and watching her closely. Anita smiled an encouraging smile which bolstered her resolve, reaching out with a shaking hand she slowly started to pull it to one side.

As she entered, she saw a woman lying on the bed wearing the clothes of a farmer, her long black hair splayed out across the pillow, eyes closed and wincing in pain. She was taken with her beauty, flawless features accented by the darkness of her hair, strong, but feminine jawline and long slender neck. Her skin was like alabaster, no porcelain, moulded by the gods. Realizing she was staring she looked to the person at the foot of the bed, it was Susie, a healer from the town, who was tending to some nasty blisters on her feet. She was focused on her feet and hadn’t even looked up. Anouk moved to the side of the bed, “Ahem”, she said, clearing her throat, Geraldine opened her eyes and looked up at her, they were piercing deep blue. “I don’t know the correct way for me to address a senior royal, for which I apologize, never having met one before, should I curtsy? Your Highness”, she rambled whilst scratching the back of her head in embarrassment. Geraldine continued to study her without speaking; she seemed to be drinking in every feature of her face, studying her. As Anouk looked down, she saw the moistness spring into her eyes, collecting at the corners before spilling over, running down the sides of her face. Finally, Geraldine spoke, "So it is true, you are Harold's daughter, I see so much of him in you", sitting up she pulled Anouk to her wrapping her arms around her neck, hugging her whilst weeping. "I never thought I would get to meet you, my niece, my brother's daughter, I can't believe it". Geraldine was shaking as Anouk put her arms around her, also holding her tight, emotions were running rife through her as well, my Aunt, my family, what I always wanted, she thought. The two sat and hugged for what seemed ages.

When they finally pulled apart, they continued to study each other, Anouk could only see beauty and kindness in her face. "Tell me about you, Anouk, tell me of your life, have you been happy? Is there someone special? I want to know everything; I have your whole life to catch up on". The two sat and talked for hours about the farm holding she grew up on, her foster parents, the animals she so loved caring for, her friends and the town of Belcher. Skipping the hard to express events of recent times and focusing on the happier times.

Geraldine was fascinated with her life, almost envying the simplicity of it, jealous of the love she had experienced growing up. Realizing it was getting late, how long have I been here Anouk thought quietly, "I have taken up enough of your time, Your Highness" she announced, "I should leave you to get some rest". Geraldine looked a little sad at this but admitted she was tired, "But please don't call me that, my name is Geraldine, we are equals here. Promise me you will come again tomorrow; I am so looking forward to spending as much time with you as possible". Anouk smiled, "I will Geraldine, wild horses couldn't keep me away", Geraldine's face lit up with a huge smile, "Until tomorrow, good night, My niece". As she said her goodbyes Anouk stepped outside the curtain, the room was silent, in the glow from the fire she could see Gretta fast asleep in her chair, and Anita curled up asleep in the other. Tiptoeing over to Anita, she quietly awakened her, indicating they should leave.

Later, Anouk and Anita lay naked and breathless in each other's arms, savouring the touch of their bodies, the closeness of their souls. Anouk knew she was falling hopelessly in love with her, hating when they were apart, feeling whole when they were together. Anita propped herself up on an elbow looking down at her, "Where do you see us after all this is over"? "Well, our love is forbidden by law, but I would like to go far away and start a farm holding with many animals. Grow crops and enjoy nature, and grow old with you at my side". Anita smiled, "Mmm, I would like that too. We could feed the animals, tend the crops and make such a special life for ourselves. Go for picnics on summer days, keep each other warm on cold nights, Anouk, I love you". Anouk took a moment to soak that in, beaming with the biggest smile, she looked deep into her eyes, "I love you too Anita, you are the world to me".

Chapter 17

King Uther stood in his war room, a large table in front of him on which he had a map spread out showing the realm. His attention was being held by an area of wooded land some days ride from Regis, stabbing his chubby finger into the centre of the woods his voice boomed, "So this is where my daughter has run to, why would she go to these woods"? His eyes were now fixed on his Lord Commander who was standing the other side of the table; Lord Commander Alfonse was a tall man of fifty-six summers, his short hair was grey which framed a brown weather-worn face. He had been a soldier all his life working his way up through the ranks; he was battle-hardened and an excellent commander. "Your Highness, we know little of the woods except they cover a vast expanse of land, patrols do randomly travel through, but there has never been anything of note there. We cannot understand any reason for her to travel there other than being kidnapped and forced to".

King Uther now lost his temper again, slamming his fist down on the desk, "NO, there has got to be something there, whether she ran away or was kidnapped, it makes no sense to run to a wood, we need a thorough search of those woods to find what is going on there". The Lord Commander stepped back from the table and saluted his King, "I will send several patrols to the area at once Your

Highness, if there is anything there, we will find it". As he strode towards the door Glitch appeared and seemed to be in a hurry, "Your Highness, Your Highness" he repeated making his way to the table. "Lord Commander you will need to hear this as well, I have just received word from one of my spies", he waited for the Lord Commander to return. "Well, spit it out Glitch we haven't got all day", Uther ordered. "The woods you are looking at Sire are not just woods, in the center a town has been secretly built and inhabited by the witches", both the King and the Lord Commander gasped. "And that's not all Your Highness, a while ago a young girl arrived at the town known as Anouk, the very same as the one who ran from Belcher, the bastard daughter of Harold".

Silence settled over the room as they processed the new information, the King spoke first, slowly and deliberately, "What else do you know of this town? Are there any defences"? Glitch nodded, "It is built in the centre of the forest, Forest Town they call it. The town is quite large within a cleared area and has a huge palisade wooden wall surrounding it; anyone approaching can be seen for some time before reaching the wall". "Hmm", the Lord Commander picked up a small round coaster and placed it on the map in the centre of the forest, "Our forces will need to travel through the forest to reach it, which will slow us providing ample opportunity for an ambush, and will give them plenty of warning of our approach".

Deep in thought, his military mind analyzing the problem, "Do they have soldiers? Dedicated defenders of the town"? Glitch realized that was directed at him, "No, none that I was made aware of". "So", the Lord Commander continued, “Apart from the slow approach and possible ambush, we will only be up against civilians with pitchforks, maybe the occasional bow”. Glitch nodded, “Uh, don’t forget the witches”, “Hah, the knights have dealt with those devils before, let them throw their fire and water around. When they see a full-on charge, they will be too busy running”.

King Uther turned and walked to the huge fireplace, standing close warming his hands. “Lord Commander, muster every available soldier and knight, you have two days to prepare after which you will lead my army to the woods”. Uther turned with his back to the fire now looking directly at the Lord Commander, “Any soldier or knight that cannot make it here in that time will have to catch you up, when you get there you are to unleash hell on that town, I want it razed to the ground and all the occupants dead, do you understand me?” The Lord Commander nodded, “But, your daughter was tracked to those woods, she may well be in that town, what of her safety, Your Highness”? “Lord Commander you have your orders, she made her choice when she ran from the palace, if she has chosen to live with dogs then she can die with them”. The Lord Commander grimaced, “As you wish Your Highness, I will beg your leave to start preparations”, Uther waved his hand in dismissal as the Lord Commander disappeared through the door. Glitch continued to stand by the table looking at the map, his thoughts all over the place, although he didn’t love the princess, he was very fond of her, and she was supposed to be his way to wrangle a seat on the throne. This will send all his plans up in smoke, what can I do to change his mind, think, Glitch, think.

Uther was studying Glitch as he stood there, "Something on your mind, Glitch, have you any more to say"? "Ah-hem, I just thought that the princess is very popular with the people; if she should die at the hands of our forces, it could seed more discontent. Would it not be more pertinent to order the Lord Commander to return her to the palace if at all possible"? "No Glitch, I understand she is your betrothed, she is also my daughter. However, she committed treason when she ran and joined the witches, for the offence of treason there is only one sentence, as you well know". Glitch nodded to this and turned towards the King, "But as yet we still do not know if she ran or was kidnapped, if it was the latter, then she had no choice and therefore could not have committed treason". The King threw his arms up in exasperation and started walking to the door.

"Ran, Kidnapped, all the same, if she is there she will be treated the same as any other there, now shut up Glitch, I will hear no more of it", Uther stomped out of the room leaving Glitch to his thoughts. As he continued to stare down at the coaster on the map, he became aware of the palace becoming alive with shouts, boots stamping as soldiers started to rally, orders being barked by the officers. So, a new war begins, well the end of an old war, I suppose, he thought to himself. Just have to ride this out and see what else I can come up with when it is all over, I usually find a way around the obstacle's life throws at me. I wonder if my spy can get more info for me?

Uther stomped down the corridors of the palace with his personal guards surrounding him, reaching the door to Amelia's rooms he walked in without knocking. Amelia was sitting at her desk working on some paperwork or other; her handmaids were sitting around the room quietly sewing. "Leave us", he ordered, all three scuttled off into an adjoining room closing the door. "And what brings my husband to me at this hour of the day" Amelia enquired with a gracious smile putting down her quill. Uther paced the room as he detailed the new information and the course of action he had put in place. He wasn't looking for her approval, after all, he was the King, and he didn't need anyone's approval, he was just curious whether she would think of something he hadn't. Amelia listened attentively and after he was finished pondered for a short while, "Well you seem to have everything under control, are you sure you want your daughter dealt with the same as all other residents of this town"? Uther continued to pace, not answering, "I only ask as once it is done, it cannot be undone", secretly thinking well that will remove one of my problems and it will not be of my doing.

Uther stopped and fixed her with a stare, "I cannot be seen to treat her differently to anyone else, but I was wondering if you could think of a way out"? Amelia rose from the desk and walked to Uther taking his hands in hers, "I can not my love, this is going to be a challenge for you of massive proportions, but you must rise to it, show yourself to be a right and just King". Uther stood looking into her eyes, "You are right, I feel I knew that anyway, thank you for your council". "Uther, who is to lead the army against this town"? "I have given the task to Lord Commander Alfonse, he will be taking every available soldier and Knight, the task shouldn't take too long".

Amelia considered this, "But surely something as important as this should be led by you, it would do you good to get out of the palace, and your army will see you are as committed as they are". Uther let go of her hands and started to pace again, "But, I have responsibilities here, I can't just up and leave". Amelia stopped him pacing, taking hold of his hands again, "I am here, I can run things whilst you are gone, and you said yourself it won't take too long to deal with". Uther actually broke out a smile, "You are right once again, I will lead the army and get this done once and for all". Leaning forward he kissed Amelia before heading for the door, as he disappeared from view Amelia could hear him shouting, "Get me Lord Commander Alfonse".

Amelia sat back at her desk, this is better than I could have imagined, that whiny daughter of his, and bastard daughter of Harold's will be killed in the town, and my assassin should be able to dispense with Uther during the battle. With them all gone, I will be the only option left to rule the realm. She immediately set about writing a coded message to her assassin.

Glitch entered his offices, walking slowly over to his desk, which was piled high with official paperwork. He was deep in thought about the events that had just transpired in the war room, stopping by his desk, he looked out the window, the grounds were already a hive of military activity. "You called for me", a deep rough voice sounded from a dark corner of the room, Glitch almost jumped out his skin, "Don't you people ever knock and come through doors"?

The man stepped forward into the light; he was short, stocky and muscley wearing all black clothes, a hood pulled over his head hiding his face. Two leather belts hung from his shoulders crossing in the centre of his chest, each carrying three throwing knives, a cruel-looking curved sword hung from his waist. Ignoring the question, he asked, “What is it you need this time, Glitch”? Turning to face him Glitch couldn’t see his face just his stubbly chin, the rest was in the shadow of the hood. “I need you to go to the forest NE from here, in the centre of the forest is a town with a large palisade wall. In that town are two people, the first is the bastard daughter of Harold, called Anouk, Kill her. The second is Princess Geraldine. You need to capture her and return her to the Palace”.

The man stood pondering this for a second whilst rubbing his fingers over his stubble, “The army is mobilizing to attack that town, we will need to be in and out quick, and as it is two people you need to be dealt with, it will be double the price.” Glitch glared at him, “I don’t care about the price, in fact, get this done and I will pay three times the usual price”, “So be it, I will leave immediately”, the man spun and disappeared through the door without making a sound.

Over the next two days, the palace was a hive of activity, weapons being cleaned and sharpened, armour prepared and polished, wagons readied with food and supplies for the travelling army. More and more soldiers poured in from the outlying towns and outposts, there was a real buzz to the air of expectation. Lord Commander Alfonse walked through the barracks parade square; a young Squire matched his stride alongside him. “Well the preparations seem to be going well Night”, the young Squires name was a constant source of amusement among his subordinates, who continually pointed out if he were to be promoted, he would be Knight Night. In fact, it had gotten so stale that anyone pointing it out now ended up doing fifty laps of the parade ground in full gear. "Yes, provisions are pouring in, so the food wagons are nearly full, the armourers have serviced all weaponry and armour, and the siege engines have been readied, Sir". "Good, good, have we enough horses"? "Yes sir, the knights have their own obviously, and we have enough to pull the wagons and sieges". Alfonse turned to the Squire, "Well done, I will make sure you get a mention for your leadership and organization, make sure everyone is mustered and ready to move out first thing tomorrow". The Squire threw up a smart salute, "I will Sir", Alfonse returned the salute before striding off to meet with the King.

Alfonse found the King in the war room looking over the map, "All ready for the off first thing tomorrow, Your Highness". Uther, looked up watching the Lord Commander walk across the room, "So what do you propose when we get to the forest Lord Commander"? "Well, I thought we should divide our forces into two, a half-day from the forest, one force enters from the north and the second from the west. Both forces should travel through the forest at the same pace and so come upon the town at the same time. We can co-ordinate the attack, so we hit the town from two sides at the same time, which will split whatever defenders they have". Uther nodded agreement throughout the Lord Commander's plan, "Excellent, well thought out Lord Commander. I will lead one of the forces so, just leaves us to get a good night's sleep tonight before the fun starts, eh!" Uther was starting to feel the thrill of battle course through his body; it had been many years since he had felt this way. It's going to be a glorious victory, finally able to wipe out those witches and sorcerer's and that infernal girl, he thought.

The next morning Uther stepped out of the palace just as the sun was rising, dressed in full armour. The armour he wore was golden in colour intricately decorated with horses standing on hind legs, one either side of his chest. Holding his helmet under his arm, he strode out onto the gathering ground to a chorus of cheers from his soldiers. His army was arrayed in front of him, to his left a hundred knights sat quietly on their horses, armour and weapons glinting in the rising sun. To his right were the soldiers, five hundred at last count, standing proud in ranks, halberds sprouting up from their bodies, the axe blades and spear points also glinting in the morning sun. An army fit for a King he thought as he approached his waiting horse, Alfonse was stood next to it waiting for the King. As he approached Alfonse bowed, "Your army awaits and is ready to move out as soon as you wish, Your Highness", Uther handed his helmet to him and proceeded to get on his horse, "Thank you Lord Commander, instruct the vanguard to proceed, we need to get this done".

As the army moved out of the palace and through the town of Regis, Uther noted there weren't many locals out to see them off, what few there were, sparsely scattered along the route were silent, watching the procession of the army. Turning to Alfonse, who rode beside him, "Where are all my subjects? Don't they realize we are going to end the scourge of the realm"?. Alfonse looked around before replying, "It is probably too early for most of them, Your Highness, still tucked up in their beds I don't doubt", but in reality, they all hate you and couldn't give a damn about your war or your reign, he must be the most unpopular ruler in the history of this realm, he thought quietly.

Dard paced around his front room, occasionally kicking the couch as he passed by, his fists clenched and a look of fury covered his face. Word had reached him that the King had found the young witch in a forest some days ride from Belcher. He had mobilized the army and knights, which he was leading personally. "Ahh" he shouted to the empty room, "How am I going to ingratiate myself with the King if he has done all the work, this has all gone wrong". Continuing to pace about the room, he desperately tried to find a plan which would return him to the King's good graces. There has got to be something he hasn't thought of, some way to assist him with his goal, Dard continued pacing getting more and more frustrated at his lack of vision. A loud double knock sounded from his back door, breaking off from his train of thought he went to answer it. A man called Ron stood outside, he was a smallish man with a wiry build which belied his strength, "Quick come in before anyone sees you". Ron darted through the door with Dard closing it behind him, they both made their way into the front room.

Dard started to pace again, "We have a problem, the King has found where the witch is hiding and is sorting it out personally, we need a way to get back in his favour, and I am coming up with nothing", he stopped pacing and stared at Ron, "Can you think of anything"? Ron took a seat on the sofa thinking for a few moments, "Yes, there is a girl, here in the town called Minit". Dard threw his arm's in the air, "How is that supposed to help us, there are a lot of girls in the town you idiot", Ron chuckled quietly, he knew, as he had gotten to know a lot of them, personally. "No, this one is different, she is, or was the best friend of the witch. They practically grew up together, we can use her to get leverage on the witch, and so making it easier for the King".

He sat back on the sofa smiling as he watched Dard working through what he had said. "Ok, ok, so we grab the girl and take her to the forest where we meet up with the King and his army, present the girl to him as a gift, he gets to take the witch quietly, and we are back in good favour. I like it, well done". Ron was sat cleaning the dirt from his nails with the tip of his dagger, he liked to watch people as they caught on and realized where his thoughts were going. "Minit works at one of the house Inn's up the road, after she finishes and is on her way home, I will grab her. But we will have to leave for the forest immediately, so we don't get caught". Dard smashed his fist into his open palm, "Right, I will ready the horses, and when you have her, meet me at the back of the sheds. We can head off immediately". With their plan made, they headed off in different directions to complete their assigned tasks.

Ron sat quiet as a mouse waiting for the silhouette of Minit to approach; he had selected a particularly dark area for the kidnap, in his pockets were a gag and rope and held in his right hand was a small cosh. After a short while he made out the form of female walking towards his spot, moving back into the shadows he pulled up his face mask and lowered his hat, don't want anyone recognizing me if they see what's happening, he thought.

As Minit approached Ron readied himself, coiled like a spring and ready to pounce, the hunter and the hunted, he chuckled quietly. As she passed him, he launched himself out of the shadows swinging his right hand and cosh, the cosh connected with the back of her head, causing the girl to collapse silently to the ground. Got to work quickly now, he told himself as he dragged the unconscious girl back to the deeper shadows. Moving as quickly as he was able, he gagged and tied her.

Suddenly a male shouted, "Hey, what are you doing, who's there"? Looking up, Ron spotted a person who was rapidly closing on him, not speaking and remaining perfectly still; he allowed him to get closer. When he was almost upon him, Ron spoke, "Hey, I just found this girl laying here, I think she might be hurt". The male dropped to one knee leaning forward to look at the prone girl, "Minit! Oh god what happened to you"? Chandra looked up just as the cosh fell striking him a glancing blow to the side of the head, causing him to fall back, the shadow advanced towards him. Now the full realization that he was under attack sunk in he lashed out with both feet towards the shadow, one of his feet connected, drawing a yelp from the shadow. Just a man, he thought, now you have a fight on your hand's you bastard, leaping to his feet Chandra lashed out with his fist but the shadow avoided it with ease. Chandra moved closer lashing out again, aiming for the head of the shadow, his arm was brushed aside, causing his body to continue forward with the power of the punch. The shadow calmly stepped in close plunging a dagger deep into Chandra's chest, within the blink of an eye the dagger was withdrawn and plunged in a second time, this time piercing his heart, he was dead before hitting the ground.

Ron stood over the body of the man, damn, that wasn't supposed to happen, messy, well couldn't be helped I suppose, he quickly dragged the body into the deepest shadows and covered it with anything he could find. Standing back, he studied his efforts, satisfied it was the best he could do he turned, picked up the unconscious Minit throwing her over his shoulder. Dodging through the shadows, he made his way to the back of the sheds where he found Dard; he was already mounted on his horse with a second stood close by. "Good you are here at last, and you have the girl, what took so long, any trouble"? Ron lifted Minit over his horse in front of the saddle, "None that I couldn't handle, shall we get going"? Dard watched as he settled himself into his saddle and secured his passenger, "Ok, let's go, we need to be there before anything starts for this to work". The two set off at a canter across the fields towards the forest.

Chapter 18

Anouk slowly opened her eyes, it was morning again, looking across the room she could see by the light coming through the window, it was well after dawn. Snuggling back under the covers in a cocoon of warmth, she closed her eyes, thinking back to the days she had awoken in her little bed in the farmhouse. How she would lay there and listen to the animals outside, muffled voices of Pata and Katcha coming from the kitchen, she could almost smell the breakfast which was always ready for her each day. It all seemed so far away now, never to be a part of my life again, she thought sadly. A little moan sounded behind her, followed by Anita shifting in the bed. A smile crept onto her face, well I suppose some things come to an end, and others begin, you have to find the beauty in life as you live it, as I have found the love in mine, she told herself. Turning over she found Anita's back was towards her, putting her arm around her she snuggled in squeezing herself to her. The thrill of being close to her ran through her body, Anita's scent filled her nose, making her lust for her all the more. "Good morning Your Highness, I trust you had a good night", Anita said sleepily, Anouk laughed, "You are incorrigible, know that young lady". "Ah, would that be incorrigible or insatiable, never did know the difference", Anita giggled, whilst wiggling her backside against

Anouk, which set both off into a giggling fit.

Anita rolled onto her back and gazed up at Anouk, a look of pure adoration passed between the two, over the last few weeks they had been inseparable, except when Anouk had been to see Geraldine. The subject of her love had still not been discussed, as she didn't know how the Princess would take that revelation, but she had resolved to broach that very subject with her today. She didn't want to hide her love for Anita when out of the bed-chamber anymore. She wanted to shout it from the rooftops and damn anyone who disapproved, it was hers and Anita's love to give, it was their love. "You look troubled this morning my love, is there anything I can help with", Anita asked, concern etched in her voice. "No, no trouble, just something I have to do today, I need to go and see Geraldine as there is something we need to discuss". Anita showed a little pout, "Oh, ok", Anouk reached out moving a stray strand of hair from her face, "I know I have spent quite a bit of time with her of late, but we have had a lifetime to catch up on. But I promise you after today things will be a bit different, ok"? Anita brightened at her words, pulling her down so their lips could meet, their bodies melded together as Anita pulled the blanket up over their heads.

Later that day Anouk strolled across town heading for the house Geraldine had been given, the breeze felt cool with the first touch of the autumn season approaching, looking up the sky was a paler kind of blue with big white fluffy clouds heading off to the west. She noticed to the east the clouds look dark and heavy, rain coming and looks as though it will be quite the downpour, she mused. Tugging her cloak tighter around her she picked up her pace; small raindrops were spattering down as she approached the green-painted house, she had become to know so well just lately. Knocking on the door she huddled under the small porch roof as the rain started to get heavier. Fina opened the door, "Oh, we weren't expecting you today Your Highness", she said with a curtsy. "Can I come in as I am getting a bit wet out here, Fina"? Fina glanced over her shoulder, "Uh, yes, of course", opening the door wider for her to enter. As Fina took her cloak and turned to hang it up, Anouk walked over to the front room door, which was closed, odd she thought. Opening the door stepping into the room, she stopped short, frozen with shock, sitting on the couch were Geraldine and Shan, kissing. "Oh, oh my god, I am so sorry, I would have knocked if I had known. Should I leave? I'll leave," her cheeks cherry red with embarrassment as she spun to leave the room. Geraldine replied, "Anouk, don't be silly please stay, come sit with us, we should talk". Anouk looked to both of them, "Ok, if you are sure", both nodded in agreement, so she walked to the other couch and sat looking first to Geraldine and then Shan.

Geraldine spoke first, "Shan and I have a past, when he was a newly appointed knight we met at the palace", she turned to Shan taking his hand whilst looking lovingly at him, "He was my first kiss, my first love. But Shan wasn't of noble birth, having worked his way up to being a knight". Looking back at Anouk, she wore a look of hope for acceptance from her, "My father deemed him unworthy of me and sent him away, forbidding us to see each other again. I never lost my love for him, and maybe that is why I have never married, so you see he is very special to me, and I to him. Please say you understand". Anouk smiled at them both, "What is there to understand, the heart wants what it wants, as long as you make each other happy, then I am happy for you".

Anouk clasped her hands in her lap looking down at them, now is the time to come clean with her. Still, I am so very afraid she won't be so understanding, she thought to herself. "Anouk, is something troubling you"? She looked up to find them both studying her, "Ah, um, well, I have something to tell you, I hope you can be as understanding and accepting of me", a puzzled look passed over both their faces but they kept quiet seeing that Anouk was struggling. "I, um, I don't like boys; men, well not in that way. I am however in a relationship which people may not like or understand. But it is our lives, and we should be able to love whomever we want, shouldn't we"? She now saw the puzzlement change to smiles which left her completely confused, "Anouk, we know, we just decided not to say anything until you decided to confide in us". Anouk was stunned, looking between the two of them, "What do you know"? Geraldine moved to her couch sitting next to her and taking her hand, "We know you and Anita are in love, we would have to be blind not to see it, we are all happy for you both".

Well, this wasn't exactly how I saw this conversation going she thought, "How do you know? And what do you mean, We"? "Sweetheart, when someone falls hopelessly in love it shows when one or other of you walk into a room, the reaction of the other is obvious, the little looks and quiet comments and smiles between you, it's as easy to read as a book. The 'we' I used means anyone close to you knows. We all decided to give you your privacy until you and Anita wanted to share the news". Well, she thought, that was easier than I thought it was going to be, "Geraldine, you won't judge me for my decision, will you? Because I know it isn't a conventional relationship, do you think anything less of me"?

Geraldine squeezed her hand tighter, with a large smile she shook her head, "No, you are my niece and always will be, who you love is your affair, not mine. I will accept Anita as I would accept any partner you chose, after all, I can see, *no*. We can see how happy you make each other, and that is what is important". Anouk looked to Shan who was sitting watching them, nodding in agreement, "You are a special lady your highness, and I only wish to see you happy. However, I do have to point out that whilst we are accepting of your choice, outside this town will be another matter. The King has ruled such relationships illegal; anyone caught would be stoned to death." Anouk laughed out loud, "Where have I heard that before". "Should I ever get to the throne", Geraldine said, "I will make sure that is one of the first things to be abolished, along with victimizing gifted people and the barbaric act of stoning".

Shan stood from his couch, "I have a few things to do so will leave you ladies to talk", as he made his way to the door, he looked back winking at Geraldine, "Oh we have set up a meeting at your house this evening, Anouk. We have to plan our strategy if and when the attack comes, hope you don't mind"? Shan left the room not waiting for an answer; the two women sat for the next couple of hours talking about their new partners and how happy they were, finally. Geraldine looked out the window noticing it was getting a little dark, "Oh dear, don't you have a meeting you have to get to"?

A loud thud sounded from the rear of the house; the two looked at each other surprised when suddenly the door from the kitchen flew open. Stood in the doorway was a short man dressed all in black wearing a hood, a sword hung from his waist, and several knives glinted on his chest. Geraldine screamed as the man threw a knife at Anouk, leaping off the couch away from him the knife almost missed, slicing across the side of her head cutting her scalp before sticking in the wall behind her. As she hit the floor, she could hear Geraldine screaming from behind the couch, who is he? He wants to kill me; she thought scooting back across the floor away from him. The man started to approach her, Anouk was aware of two more shadowy figures entering the room through the door, making their way to Geraldine. The man in black had reached her, grabbing for her, his hand gripping her around the neck. Lifting her from the floor and slamming her back against the wall.

Anouk felt panic and fear grip her and the now-familiar ball blossoming in her stomach, the man's hand tightened its grip on her throat, she couldn't breathe as he leaned in towards her. He spoke in a low hissing voice, "You are going to die now, nothing personal, but you are a witch, and you are vermin, needing to be put down". He had completely cut off her airway, her lungs crying out for air as sparkles danced before her eyes and blackness started to creep into the edge of her sight.

Time seemed to slow down for Anouk, his free hand moving to the knives on his chest, she was aware that Geraldine had gone silent and the other two shadows were carrying her out through the kitchen door. The man's hand was almost on another knife; you have to act now girl, or you are dead, she thought, summoning the power she placed her hands on the man's chest. The power had built, so she released it down her arms to her hands, summoning strong winds in both palms, the man flew across the room hitting the opposite wall with a loud oomph. Anouk slid down the wall gasping for breath, gulping like a fish out of water, her sight slowly returning to normal. The man slowly stood at the other side of the room, as she watched he drew another knife, raising his arm preparing to throw it at her. Anouk again summoned the power, as the knife left the man's hand, she released a wall of wind at him. The two met in the middle of the room, the knife stopped, turned, and flew back towards the man faster than any man could throw it. The knife hitting him in the neck, driving deep with the point piercing his spine; his eyes flew open in total surprise before he collapsed to the floor, choking on his own blood.

Anouk scrambled her way over to the kitchen, as she entered, she saw the back door was wide open, there was no sign of Geraldine but Mary was laid on the floor. First checking Mary to make sure she was breathing, she was. She went to the open door, grabbing the lantern hanging outside, she looked around but couldn't see anyone. Swinging the lantern, she shouted, "Help, help, we are under attack, someone help, they have got the Princess. Please will someone help!" Almost immediately a hue and cry began from the guards on the wall; soon it was being repeated all around the town, lanterns and people began crowding the streets. Anouk fell to her knees on the grass, they have taken Geraldine, oh my god what will they do with her? Who were those men? As she sat there, she became aware of the stinging on the side of her head, putting her hand up she felt the warm stickiness of her own blood which was still running down.

Fina got to her first as she sat horrified with what had happened, dimly aware of her shouting for more to come. Friendly hands helped her to her feet and took her back inside the kitchen, sitting her in a chair; everything was a blur to her. As if it were happening to someone else, as if she was on the outside looking in. Suddenly a friendly voice broke through her shock, it was Shan, "Anouk, what happened here? Who did this to you? Where is Geraldine"? Anouk looked into his concerned face, "I don't know, they just burst in and attacked us, they took her, Shan they took her".

Shan's face hardened, "The dead man in there, was that you"? Anouk nodded, "Yes, he was trying to kill me, there were two more though, they took her whilst I was fighting him, I'm so sorry Shan, it was all so quick". Shan leaned forward giving her a hug, "Not your fault my lady, you did what you could", as he released her, he spoke with a woman who was now at her side, "Look after her please, she is a very special and brave lady". The woman was Susie, the healer, who immediately began fussing with the wound on her head.

Shan moved to the front room to look at the body of the man, Dug and Ben were there already. "What have you found out about this one so far"? He asked. Dug was squatted down looking closely at him, "Well, this here is one of the King's special hitmen, actually the top one. So, A, they are going to be pretty peeved he has been killed, and B, you can be sure the King sent them". Dug looked between the two seeing his words sink in, "Also from what happened here we can surmise they were sent to kill Anouk and get the Princess back. So, my best guess is they are on their way back to the palace with her now". "Also, if the King sent them, we must assume the King knows about Forest town, and Anouk's and the Princess's presence here. We may have a spy in our midst who will have passed a lot more information than that", Ben stated. Shan stood quietly considering all that had been said, "Well, we will have to assume Princess Geraldine is ok, just being returned to the palace, although god only knows what her father is going to do to her. We need to double the guard on the walls tonight".

Later, Shan, Dug and Ben escorted Anouk back to her house, Anouk's head was bandaged with a little blood oozing through the cloth. "Are you sure you feel ok"? Shan asked as they approached her front door, "I am fine Shan, just a little scratch. I just wish I could have stopped them from taking her". Shan stopped her, turning to face her, "You did all you could, My Lady, it was three against one, we both know Geraldine isn't a fighter. You took down the King's top assassin, which was no mean feat. Please don't blame yourself for what has happened, I know I don't". Anouk hugged him tightly, with her face buried in his chest her words muffled, "I don't blame myself, I am just so scared for Geraldine, what will her father do to her now"?

Stepping through the door, Anita jumped up from the couch rushing over to her, "Anouk, I was so scared I was going to lose you", immediately putting her arms around her neck hugging her tightly, a little tear trickled down her cheek. Anouk put her arms around Anita's waist and hugged her just as tight, "You will never lose me, Sweetheart". Anita gasped moving back, her face was a picture of confusion and concern, “Wha, What”? Anouk laughed, “They all know Anita, we thought we were being discrete, but they all know about us anyway”. As Shan and Dug passed by the two of them, Dug whispered, “The walls aren’t as thick as you might think ladies”. The two blushed with embarrassment, Anita particularly looking mortified, to cover the embarrassment they continued to hug whilst the men walked out into the kitchen.

Dug’s voice floated back, “Have we got anything to eat, I’m starved”. Anita reached up turning her head so she could look at the bandaged part, “Does it hurt? Are you sure you are ok”? Anouk smiled, “Yes I am fine, just a small cut”, the urge to kiss her was too big to ignore, leaning in, their lips locked in a loving, sensual kiss. It only lasted seconds, but to Anouk, it felt like minutes, once again the closeness of their bodies and the electric passion of the kiss, set her body trembling with desire for her girlfriend. Dug’s voice floated in from the kitchen once more, “When you love birds are finished, there are hungry men out here, where’s the food Anita”? Breaking apart Anita looked lovingly at her, in a whisper she told her, “I love you Anouk”, Anouk replied, “I love you too Anita, you are my world”. Anita beamed a massive smile as she turned to the kitchen, “Coming, I will sort you all a meal, and Dug get your mitts off the ale jug”. A sheepish Dug’s voice floated back, “Hey, how do you do that, you ain’t even in the room”. Anouk followed Anita towards the kitchen, laughing out loud, “She’s got you sussed Dug, watch out”.

Having eaten and cleared the table, everyone took their seats again in order to start the meeting; several others had arrived at the house for this purpose. Anouk, sat at the head of the table looking around. First to Anita sat at her right, then slowly around the expectant faces of Shan, Ben, Fina, Mary, Dug, Cheryl and Benji. "Ok, first things first I will address the boulder in the room, Anita and I are a couple. We did not look for it, but we found each other", reaching out she took Anita's hand in hers, "We are very much in love, and she means the world to me, I am not asking for acceptance or disagreement from you, I am merely stating a fact. Anita is my equal here, not a maid or servant", now Anouk looked directly at Dug, he harrumphed quietly looking down at the table, "And so she shall have a voice at these meetings as much as anyone else, Ok"? The group nodded in agreement; Shan spoke, "We are glad you and Anita found each other, speaking for everyone here we are happy you brighten each other's day, but we do have more pressing matters to discuss".

Anouk thanked him for his comments and turned to Ben, "How are the defence plans going for the town"? Ben outlined all the tasks he had completed and that the town was as ready as it would ever be for an attack, "So unless anyone can think of anything I haven't, we are ready". Dug spoke next, "The assassins at the Princess's house were the King's own, so we can be very sure that he knows about this town and will send his forces against it. It would be my assumption we have a spy in our midst; after all, they knew how to get in and went straight to her house. That said we should assume he knows everything about the town including the defences, we need to double-check everything before he gets here". "Let him come, I will put a fireball up his ass", Ben said slapping the table. Dug shook his head at the naivety of youth, "When he comes, he will be behind at least a hundred knights and five hundred soldiers, you will need to get through them before you can light him up".

Anouk looked to Shan, "Did you manage to get word to the knights, Shan"? Shan nodded, "Yes I did, and I have received a reply from my closest friend. He said the King was mustering all his forces and leading them himself, we can assume here. There are indeed a hundred or so knights", he said nodding to Dug. "But at least half are not in agreement with the King or his methods; my friend has indicated when the King orders a charge they will turn away from the battle". Ben looked hopeful, "So they will fight for us then"? Shan shook his head, "No, they may turn away, but they will not take up arms against him, the best we can hope for is we only have half the knights to contend with". "Ok, so we know we have a fight coming to us, and it's not going to be easy, Shan how do you expect the King to attack us"?

Shan sat back in his chair and considered the question for a moment; all eyes in the room were on him. "Well, if I were him considering the town is made of wood as is the palisade, he will start by raining fire arrows on the town. When there is enough on fire to draw defenders from their posts, he will start with the siege catapults to break a hole in the palisade or gates. When the palisade wall is breached, he would order a full charge by the knights closely followed by the soldiers". Anouk's brain was working double time working out a plan, "Ben, make sure all the water gifted are on fire patrol throughout the town, along with anyone old enough to carry a bucket, we will need all fire and earth gifts up on the walls along with anyone who has a bow. Then we will have to deal as best we can with anything they throw at us from there", Ben nodded in agreement.

The meeting continued late into the night, each getting their own assignments for the coming battle, slowly people drifted away until eventually only Shan, Dug, Anita and Anouk were left sitting in the kitchen. Anouk was watching Shan as he sat fingering the side of the table deep in thought with a faraway look in his eyes, reaching out she took his hand, squeezing it. "She will be ok Shan; they took her alive because her father wants her back. She may not be a fighter, but she is strong in other ways, and she has you to look forward to getting back to". Shan gave her a weak smile, "I know, I am just so worried about what her father will do to her when he gets her back, but thank you Anouk. I am off to bed now; we will see what the new day brings". He made his way to his room, followed shortly by Dug leaving Anouk and Anita alone at the table. Looking lovingly at Anita, "Shall we retire as well, been a long day for us both and we don't know what tomorrow will bring". Anita looked at her bandage with tired eyes, "Come on then; I just want to hug you and keep you safe, my love".

Chapter 19

Anouk lay curled up with her back to Anita who was cuddled in close holding her, Anouk was sleeping but another night of bad dreams had plagued her. Anita had comforted her on two occasions during the night, she still didn't know what caused her such night terrors but knew it was something to do with her foster parents. On both occasions she had been saying their names, Pata and Katcha, Anouk never spoke of the dreams, but she knew it had to be about their deaths. Maybe one day I will be able to get her to talk about it, she thought, then the dreams might stop bothering her.

A loud banging sounded from the door, Dug's voice came next, urgency sounded within it. "Anouk, Anita, get up, the Kingsmen have been sighted and are headed straight for us". Anita called back, "Ok, getting up", Anouk stirred in her arms turning towards her, "What's all the row about"? She asked in a sleepy voice. "The King and his men have been sighted heading here, looks like today is the day". Anouk was awake now but remained calm, "Well, it will take them a while to get here, so I think you and I", she pulled her down to kiss her and continued speaking out the side of her mouth, "Should have a little loving before he messes things up". Their lips locked together, bodies entwined, they lost themselves in each other passion for the moment.

A little while later Anouk strode into the kitchen, Ben, Shan and Dug were leaning over the kitchen table looking at a map of the town and surrounding area. All three looked up at her as she entered, all three adopted a look of amazement, mouths hanging open. Anouk stood in front of them dressed in her mother's leathers, the jacket fitted to the waist accentuating her womanly figure, with the tail of the jacket hanging to just above her ankles at the back and sides. It was open at the front showing the figure-hugging leather trousers and boots, around her waist was a belt carrying a gold-coloured dagger with a large red stone, and her hair was tied back in a ponytail. Ben spoke first, "Whoa, you look like you mean business, where did you get that outfit from"? Anouk smiled, "It was my mothers, so you can all put your eyes back into your heads and get on with the preparations". Grabbing some bread and cheese, she returned to the table to look at the map; Shan pointed to a location on the edge of the forest, "One of the Kings columns entered here, travelling straight through the forest they will come out on our north wall, the second column entered here".

He moved his finger over the map, "So, they will come out on our west wall, clever, but I would never have thought he would divide his forces like this". "So, they are going to hit us from two sides", Anouk said whilst nibbling on a chunk of cheese, "Does that mean we can reduce the defenders on the other two walls"? "Yes, we still need people on them but, Ben move every second and third defender from those walls to the ones they will hit. We can reassess when it starts, one things for sure, when the battle starts, plans tend to go out the window. We will need to react".

Anouk left the men pondering over the map and battle plans and headed outside with Anita at her side. The town was a hive of activity, townsfolk moving quickly around preparing for the attack. She noticed there was no panic in their actions, they were all just being quick, methodical and calm, "Isn't it amazing how they are all so calm considering what is coming"? She said linking arms with Anita. "It is, I am really scared, why do you think the king is so set on doing us harm"? Anouk looked at her whilst they walked, she looked a little paler than usual, and she could feel her arm shaking. Pulling her closer, "He is a horrible king, and he doesn't care for anyone different to him. Don't worry, I will keep you safe, my love". They had arrived at the largest house in the centre of the town, Sarah and a group of other healers were hurriedly making it into an infirmary, ready for the wounded who were undoubtedly going to come. Sarah stopped and dropped a quick curtsy, "Your Highness, are you here to help"? "I am not Sarah, but you can have use of Anita as an extra pair of hands", turning to Anita, "I hope you don't mind, but this is the safest place for you to be and you can help a lot". Anita smiled first at Anouk then at Sarah, "Of course not, what would you have me do Sarah"? As Anouk made her way from the infirmary, she saw Sarah pairing Anita with Mary before setting them to work.

The day passed quickly with Anouk rushing around checking on what was being prepared, with regular trips up to the North wall walkway to see if anything was happening. On her last visit she met a young man standing lookout, as she approached, he bowed, "Your Highness, do you really think we can hold out against all of the king's men"? She gave him her best smile, "I think he has picked a fight he can't win; I have seen you down the practice ground, haven't I? You have the fire gift"? He nodded, "I have practised as much as possible, I don't want to let you down". Anouk placed her hand on his arm, "You won't let anyone down I am sure, now have you seen anything"? Shaking his head, "Nope, just some of the outer lookouts making their way in. One said the King would be here early evening, well, soon now".

Looking around Anouk noticed more and more people making their way up onto the North and West walls, "The word is out it seems, good luck to you, my friend". Anouk moved further along the wall where she stood watching the forest tree line for any movement. Just as dusk started to creep in, she was joined by Ben and Shan who stood either side of her. Shan asked, "Anything yet"? Anouk shook her head but kept her eyes fixed on the trees, "Not yet, maybe they are being slowed by the forest", as she was finishing her reply she spotted movement at the edge of the trees, "Ah spoke too soon".

As Anouk watched, soldiers marched out of the forest, the column split heading East and West, finally stopping three ranks deep and thirty men wide. "Ok, that doesn't look like too many to deal with", Anouk commented, Shan laughed, "That's just the vanguard, the King will be just in the trees over there, and the rest of his army behind him". Anouk pulled a sad face and jabbed her elbow in his ribs, "You really know how to cheer a girl up don't you Shan", he didn't reply, he was too focused on what was happening across the clearing. The soldiers stood still for a short time with no sign of attack; a shout went up from the West wall, they had also sighted soldiers on their side who had also taken up a position just outside the trees.

As Anouk watched in the growing gloom, she saw the soldier's part in the centre, and three horsemen rode out from the trees towards the town. As they got closer, she could see two were knights, dressed in full armour, one wearing a predominantly blue tabard, the other red and white. They flanked the third rider who was wearing ordinary wealthy person's clothes, carrying a long spear with a white flag attached. The riders stopped a short distance from the wall; the third rider shouted up, "I am here in the King's name and would ask to parley with the leader of this town". Shan whispered to Ben, "You can be the spokesman, they will recognize my voice".

Ben nodded, then called down, "I am here; what is it you wish to talk about when you lead your army against us"? "I am Sir Richard Longsleeves, to whom am I talking"? Shan again whispered in Ben's ear, "Don't give any names, just find out what he wants". Ben shouted back, "Names are of no consequence, just say your piece and be gone". "So be it", the man shouted back, "You have two people we want in your town, Princess Geraldine and a young witch called Anouk. If you hand these two over, we will go and leave your town untouched, if not then we will raise it to the ground with everyone in it. You have until first light tomorrow to make up your minds". Not waiting for an answer, the three horsemen turned and made their way back to the forest.

Ben, Shan, and Anouk turned to each other, "What the hell", Shan blurted out, "Why is he asking for Geraldine when he already has her"? None knew the answer, "We need to go talk to Dug and see if he can shed some light on this" Anouk stated. Shan left orders for some to stand down from the wall and the rest to maintain a watch throughout the night. They headed off back to the house, as they entered the kitchen Dug was sat at the table eating, whilst Mary and Anita fussed over preparing a meal for the rest of them. "You can always trust Dug to be the first to a meal, doesn't anything put you off eating"? Anouk asked, laughing at him, "Nope, as long as you have a full tummy you can face anything, that's what my mum used to say anyway". Anita skipped over to Anouk giving her a big hug, "It's good to see you again", she whispered in her ear, "I said Mary could come to stay with us, Fina is with Gretta, and she didn't want to go back to an empty house, is that ok"? Anouk gave her a squeeze, "Of course, now let's eat, I am starved".

Everyone sat down and tucked in, but Shan couldn't wait any longer to ask, "Dug, the king's mouthpiece, Sir Richard, said we were to hand over Princess Geraldine by first light. If he already has her, why is he asking for her"? Dug considered the question for a moment, "The men who attacked Anouk and took the Princess, were, without doubt, the King's assassins, now if we assume the King has no knowledge of this, there is only one other that can order the assassins". "Who? Who would do that"? Shan blurted out, "Well if he is still there, that would be a man called Glitch, the King's advisor". A sharp intake of breath drew everybody's attention; all were now looking at Mary, who was sat with her hand to her mouth, her eyes darting around the table. Anouk spoke first, "Mary, do you know anything"? Mary nodded, "Princess Geraldine never looked for suitors, and those that did make their intentions known were turned away. She once told me she had fallen for someone and nobody could ever live up to him, so she had no interest in marrying. Her father, the King, wasn't happy with this and announced a while ago he had given his consent for Glitch to marry her. I think it was that which finally pushed her over the edge and caused her to run away from the palace". Shan looked horrified, "Dammit, I remember that greasy weasel of a man, as soon as this is over, I will have to ride for the Palace. I will not let him get his hands on her; rather, he will feel my hands about his neck". Shan's face was red with anger, his hands bunched in fists. Anouk looked on and felt real fear for his enemy; she had never seen him so incensed, the fury exuded out of him as he sat and fumed. She got up and moved to him, putting her arms about his neck and speaking in his ear, "You and I both Shan, we will see that she is free from him, I promise".

Nobody really slept that night, many of them making frequent trips up on to the palisade walkways to check what the Kingsmen were doing. No attack came during the night, true to their word, all that could be seen were the many campfires the soldiers had lit at the edge of the trees. Anouk was stood on the North wall as dawn began to lighten the night, by the time Ben got to her, it was fully light, and she could see the soldiers moving, preparing for the battle. "And so, the day has come when we all will have to look for our strength, many may fall, sacrifices will be made. But hopefully, we will win out over the unjust King and his pawns; God bless us all". Anouk said quietly, staring at the three mounted riders as they approached the wall once more. "Amen", Ben replied, also watching their approach, Sir Richard shouted up to the wall again, "Have you made your decision, will you send them out to us"? Anouk put her hand on Ben's arm, stopping him as he opened his mouth to reply. Instead, she shouted down, "You will not be getting anyone from within these walls, and if your army values their lives, they will all leave and let us live in peace. Tell that to your so-called pumped-up King". The three whirled on their horses and made off back to the forest at a trot. "Humph, no answer I see", she looked at Ben, he had a big grin on his face whilst looking at her. "Well, you sure know how to pick a fight, Your Highness", "I think the fight was already picked, don't you"?

Trumpets began to blare which were picked up and echoed on the west side; soldiers emptied out of the woods, forming rank upon rank away from the trees. The town defenders all raced for the walkways, readying themselves for the fight to come. Anouk moved along the wall speaking to as many as possible in an attempt to calm their fears; she, however, could feel the ball of fear growing inside her, looking for Ben again, "Ben, where is Anita"? Ben replied after speaking to some of the men, "She and Mary took off to the infirmary a short time ago, I saw them running there". Good, she will be as safe as anyone can be there, she thought. The soldiers were all now stood in ranks ready, Anouk could see the glint of armour, in the early sun, just inside the forest. "Ok people, we just have to see what their first move is going to be, rest yourselves, you will need all your strength to use your gift. When the arrows come, as surely, they will, get down and hug the wall, ARE WE READY?" A resounding shout replied, "READY".

They all stood waiting for what seemed ages and nothing happened, suddenly a shout was heard "ARROWS". Anouk looked up and saw a dark swarm sailing up from the edge of the forest, as she watched they rose high in the sky like a cloud of angry birds, the defenders got low and hugged the walls. But Anouk stood defiantly watching them reach their peak, before slowly starting to drop towards the town, fear churned in her stomach, summoning her power. Building it as much as she dared, she raised her arms, palms towards the arrows; she pictured a massive gust of wind before allowing the power to travel down to her hands. Throwing her hands forward a wall of wind left her, travelling towards the arrows. As they met, the arrows stopped, turned, and flew back towards where they had come from. The wind wall hadn't been wide enough with some getting through, but most were now flying back at the soldiers. She saw them drop hiding behind their shields as best they could, but many were hit in the arms or legs, quite a few were killed. Several groups of soldiers started running towards the town, each group carrying a long ladder. Ben, watching over the wall, shouted, "Fire people to the front we have ladders in coming, wait for my order then hit the ladders, wait for them to get closer". Anouk saw another cloud of arrows rise from the forest, ok we will do it again as you didn't learn the first time, she thought. As she was releasing another wind wall, she heard Ben shout, "NOW", all the fire people let loose with fireballs, burning orbs flew down at the men and ladders, exploding in an inferno as they stuck their target, instantly setting fire to the ladders and men alike. The arrows now turned were raining down on the soldiers once more, many more fell to the ground, the rest started retreating into the trees. In a few short minutes, the ground was littered with the bodies of soldiers, isolated fires burning where the fire orbs had struck, and the smell of burnt flesh wafted up over the palisade wall. Anouk looked out at the forest, all but a few soldiers had taken refuge in the forest, "I am going to check on the west wall", she shouted to Ben who nodded his agreement.

She turned and started running around the walkway, as she approached, the sight of what was happening appalled her; townspeople were laying down all along the wall, many with arrows in them. Without me to turn the arrows, so many had suffered and died, oh god I am sorry, she thought. Seeing Shan mid-way along the wall she made for him, just as she reached him, she saw another black cloud of arrows rise from the forest, summoning her winds, she once again sent out a blast towards them. Turning the arrows, she sent them back at the soldiers stood at the edge of the trees, not having happened to them before the soldiers were slow to respond. As the arrows struck home many soldiers crumpled, falling to the ground, "Sorry I couldn't get here sooner Shan, been rather busy at the other wall". Shan nodded, "Just glad you could make it now". Anouk stepped to the wall and looked over, "Be ready fire people, they tried to use ladders on the other wall", she called out.

Dug stepped up to her side, "Glad to see you could make it to our side, you been slacking girl"? Anouk laughed, "Only you could joke in the middle of a battle, how about you do some work", "Oh, I have, I've been getting the injured down to Anita and Mary, they're ok by the way". Anouk's smile quickly vanished when she saw another cloud of arrows rise from the forest, this time they looked like a swarm of fireflies, each with a small black tail of smoke. "Dear God, FIRE ARROWS", she shouted, sending out her wind wall once more to turn them. Anouk realized she was getting extremely tired, all this use of my powers is really taking it out of me, she thought quietly. But she was pushing harder this time to try and get the arrows to the forest's edge. Most of them turned and descended back into the forest setting light to the bracken, and undergrowth, some struck the tops of the trees, setting fire to the foliage and branches dropping embers on anyone below. Smoke billowed in a large cloud above the soldiers, and their urgent cries could be heard wafting back on the wind.

A few of the arrows had got past her and dropped into the town; small fires were ignited where they fell, she could hear the shouts of the people below, as they struggled to put them out. Looking around at the dead and injured, the organized panic of the defending townspeople. She thought, is this what war is? Why would someone want this carnage and death?

King Uther sat astride his horse just inside the edge of the forest, watching events unfold with Sir Richard sat next to him. “How have they got so many archers in that town Longsleeves”? Sir Richard looked away from the retreating soldiers to his King, “Uh, actually, those are our arrows sire, they are sending them back somehow”. “Damn witches, never a fair fight with them, send in the ladders”, Sir Richard moved forward to command the soldiers, within moments several groups began running towards the town, each carrying a large siege ladder. The King watched as they approached the palisade thinking, as soon as the ladders are up, we can swarm them on top that cursed wall. He smiled to himself, oh yes this will be easy, should be done by evening he thought smugly.

Suddenly a volley of glowing spheres cascaded down from the wall, each exploding into an inferno where they hit. Men and ladders were instantly set on fire, as he continued to watch; he saw the attempt collapse into turmoil, what few soldiers that hadn't been hit, turned tail and ran back for the forest. "Sir Richard, move the siege catapults forward, we will smash the wall down if we can't go over it, and move the knights up ready for a charge once it's down". Sir Richard gave the order, and soldiers sprang into action pushing the three large siege engines forward to the edge of the trees, locking them in place as they started cranking back the buckets.

As the knights began their move forward, taking up a position just behind the catapults, had the King bothered to look behind him, he would have seen at least half of them turn away. The knights disappeared through the trees heading back to the forest road, "Hey Bez", one called to the leader of the group, "You know if he wins this, he will want our heads on a spike, don't you"? The leader twisted in his saddle to look back at him. "Kai, he isn't going to win that, he is up against people with powers, a whole town full. In any case, Shan said they are decent folk, and I for one will not take part in any slaughter, which would include two Princesses".

The knights reached the road, heading south away from the battle and back to Regis, the sound of battle slowly diminishing the further they went. Bez noticed two horseback riders travelling towards them at speed, stopping, the knights formed a row across the road preventing passage. As the riders reached them, he could see they were both male and were not soldiers; the rearmost rider had a person bound and slung over the horse in front of him. Bez held up his hand, "Halt riders", he waited for them to pull up in front of him, "What is your business and where are you going"? The older of the two riders answered, "We are on King's business knight, so I suggest you move and let us pass".

Bez turned to Kai with a quizzical look before turning back to the riders, "I ask you again, there will not be a third time, what is your business here and where are you going"? The old man looked exasperated at the questioning, "All I can say is we are here to see the King before the battle starts, we have a gift for him, so please move". Bez urged his horse forward passing the older man so he could better look at the second rider, a scoundrel if ever I saw one, he thought. Pointing at the person laying on the horse, he asked the rider, "And who is this"? The person began struggling at his words, Ron placed a hand on her back pressing her down, "That is of no concern to you knight", Dard called back. As Bez continued to watch, the person managed to lift their head, turning frightened, terrified eyes to him. It quickly dawned on him this was a woman, hands bound and mouth gagged, reaching over to pull the gag down Ron and Dard went for their swords. Their blades half-drawn Dard warned, "I wouldn't do that knight, if you interfere, we will inform the King of your meddling when we speak". Two things passed through Bez's mind, if they talk to the king, they will surely inform him of the knights riding away from the battle, and secondly, why would they be taking a woman on to a battlefield? "As you wish, sir, but I will speak with this woman before you pass", Bez pulled the gag from the woman's mouth. Ron and Dard finished unsheathing their swords, Dard swung back towards Bez, hitting him in the backplate of his armour with a clang, Ron swung down and across at him striking the top of his helm. The blade skidded off before coming to a stop atop his right shoulder, the pauldron preventing any harm. Two things happened in quick succession, Bez pulled his dagger and swept it into the man's chest, years of fighting and training, guiding his aim in one deep, fatal blow to the heart. Kai, who had been carrying a long spear, lunged forward burying it deep into the older man's chest. Both riders fell from their horses, Ron dead and Dard slowly dying, now lay on the ground.

"Well, that was a bit stupid on their part", Bez called back to his friends. Turning his attention to Minit, who was now straining her neck to look up at him, terror was etched all over her face. "So, what did those two want with you, young lady"? Minit shook her head stuttering trying to get her words out, "I... I... don't know, they... they kidnapped me from my village, they wouldn't tell me anything. But I overheard the old one saying it was to get the king's favour". Bez leaned forward, using his dagger he cut the bindings from her wrists, "Can you ride"? Minit moved herself to the saddle, rubbing her wrists whilst looking at Bez, he was about her father's age and had a kind face, she thought she could see concern for her in his eyes. "Yes, my best friend taught me how on her farm, thank you so much for rescuing me", Bez smiled, "No problem at all young lady, you had better ride with us for safety, we are headed for Regis, and on the way, you can tell us your story".

Anouk stood resting during the brief respite whilst the soldiers reorganized, sitting on a small crate she watched the forest for any sign of arrows heading their way, her mind strayed to Anita, turning she looked down into the town trying to see her. God, I hope she is ok, please keep safe and come back to me, she prayed silently. For long moments she scanned the town for a glimpse of her, trying to see through the thick smoke rising in different parts, but there was no sign. Suddenly a massive vibration reverberated through the wall closely followed by a massive thud, "What the hell was that she shouted to no one in particular". Shan was standing looking down to the north wall, "Uh oh, they have catapults shooting at the north side, trying to smash the wall no doubt". Anouk took off running for that side of the wall, thinking they can't be allowed to smash the wall. As she approached, she saw Ben throwing out a fireball, looking over the wall, she could see three catapults positioned just out of the tree line, each firing boulders.

As the boulders struck with a massive thump wooden splinters flew in all directions. Ben's fireball landed considerably short of them having no effect; the catapults fired altogether, three huge boulders sailed through the air towards them. Anouk instinctively knew the wind wall would not work against boulders, so she picked one and sent a spiral column of air towards it, the boulder slowed, but she couldn't push it back at them. As she watched, the boulder dropped out of the air, hitting the field and sinking into it. Well at least it didn't hit the wall, she thought; however, the other two did, one after the other. Thump, thump, the whole wall shook and groaned, splinters of wood flew in all directions, one catching her on the side of her forehead just missing her eye, cutting her the blood flowing down almost instantly.

Ignoring the wound, she shouted, "Earth people, see if you can change the boulders as they approach, ignore the middle one, I will deal with that one". The three catapults launched their boulders once more, sending out her spiral wind she hit the middle one, again dropping it to the ground, looking to her left she saw Benji, arms outstretched towards the boulder headed his way. The strain on his face showed as he used all his power to manipulate the boulder, suddenly the boulder exploded into gravel which rattled harmlessly of the wall. He looked to Anouk, "We are going to have to stop the catapults, I don't know how many I can do like that, and I don't think the wall will be able to take much more". Anouk moved along to Ben, "I have an idea, create a fireball and hold out your hands, don't throw it, just hold it out". Ben did as he was asked forming a fireball and holding it steady, he looked to Anouk nodding when ready, she focused on the fireball whilst building her power, letting loose a spiral blast aimed at the fireball, it soared out across the battlefield. The ball of flame missed the catapult but hit a tree directly behind it; the explosion blew back over the catapult setting fire to the soldiers stood there. "Ben again", she ordered, this time the fireball soared out and with her adjustment of power, struck the catapult full-on, turning it into an instant bonfire.

Cheers sounded along the wall, "One down, two to go", Anouk announced. Whilst celebrating their success they didn't notice the two remaining catapults had fired again, two huge boulders sailed across the expanse hitting the wall with enormous force, the whole wall felt as if it was going to collapse, as it was shaken to its roots. A loud cracking sound could be heard above the noise of the battle, slowly a single tree trunk buckled and tipped away from the town, leaving a gap like a missing tooth. Anouk looked to Ben, for the first time feeling genuinely panicked, "Ben another, quick". The fireball took out the second catapult whilst Benji dealt with the boulder from the third. Soon, between them, they had destroyed all the siege machines with the combination of Ben's fire and Anouk's wind. Ben sat down on a crate, "Time to take a breather, starting to feel exhausted from all this use of the gift, how are you doing Anouk"? She wasn't listening, but watching the tree line she saw a line of knights appear looking as if they were getting ready to charge. More soldiers with ladders came out of the forest behind them, "Looks like they are getting ready to charge again", she shouted to all that could hear.

Shan and Dug were doing all they could to hold the west wall, once again the arrows had started causing everybody to take cover, each time a cloud of them were seen climbing up out of the forest line. Shan had found a war bow, dropped by an injured archer, in between their arrows coming over he would jump up and send a few back along with the other archers. This really isn't enough, he thought, the only reason they aren't at the wall is because of the fire people. Shan felt more than useless as he looked out, he was used to getting up close, hand to hand fighting, not this sitting on top of a wall like an easy target. Dug trotted past dropping off a handful of the enemies' arrows, "Send them back Shan, nothing like killing the enemy with their own arrows eh", he grinned at him before carrying on down the wall dropping off extra arrows to the other archer's. Shan watched him as he went shaking his head, only he could find something to grin about during a battle, he thought chuckling to himself. Turning his attention back to outside, he caught sight of two siege catapults being wheeled out of the tree line; now we've got trouble, he realized.

Anita had been rushing around all day; the wounded just kept coming into the infirmary. Her apron and hands were covered in blood, and she had smears on her forehead, none was hers, thank god. Finishing the bandaging she was doing on a young man's leg she turned to look around, Sarah and Mary were working on a woman who had been hit with an arrow, all the other patients were being well tended for by the other healers, none were waiting to be seen. Anita decided to go and look around outside for any injured that couldn't make it to the infirmary, picking up a bag of bandages; she made her way to the door. Looking out for the first time in what seemed ages, she was astounded by the damage that had been caused; everywhere she looked arrows stood erect from the soil like corn stalks, buildings looked like hedgehogs with their quills standing proud. Seeing this, she realized the danger of being outside, so she moved quickly from building to building, taking shelter as often as she could. Soon she found herself near the west wall; a man was sitting against the wall of a house with an arrow in his leg. Running over to him, "Stay there, I will have a look at your wound", she announced as she got to him. The arrow was in a fleshy part of his leg but was bleeding quite heavily, taking a bandage she tied it off above the wound and pulled it tight. "That should slow the bleeding, for now, I will try and find someone to help you to the infirmary", the man thanked her for her kindness whilst giving her a strained smile.

"ANITA", she heard her name being shouted, but looking around she couldn't see anyone calling her. Suddenly a loud thump sounded against the wall, she could feel the vibrations of it in the ground she knelt on, almost straight away she felt another, this time she saw the wall quiver with the impact. "ANITA, UP HERE", looking up she saw Shan looking down at her, his face was bloody, and he was on his knees staring down. "Shan, do you need my help up there"? He shook his head calling back, "No, I need you to run and get Anouk from the North wall, quickly before they knock this bloody wall down"! Anita took off running as fast as she could, keeping close to the edge of the wall, she reasoned there were no arrows stuck in the ground here, so should be safe as can be. Reaching the sloped access to the walkway she ran up, at the top, she quickly scanned along the wall where she spotted Anouk and Ben. Ben was producing fireballs and Anouk was shooting them out. Good teamwork she thought as she ran towards them, "ANOUK, ANOUK, SHAN NEEDS YOU ON......", she stopped mid-sentence as an arrow sailed in from above hitting her squarely in the chest, knocking the breath from her and stopping her on the spot. Anita sank to her knees, staring down at the arrow shaft, odd it doesn't seem to hurt, maybe it's not that bad, she mused.

Anouk and Ben were working harder than ever, soldiers and knights were advancing towards the town, everywhere she looked she could see them, the steel of their weapons glinting in the sun. The water people were throwing water from the river to soak them and the ground, the earth people, manipulated the ground they walked on, churning it into a soggy bog. Men and horses alike sinking into the ground getting stuck, just in range of the fire people. Fireballs rained down exploding into huge plumes of fire and heat, men and horses screamed in agony as their flesh burned. The townspeople had unleashed hell, but the soldiers and knights kept pushing closer and closer. Anouk became aware of her name being shouted from behind, as she turned, she saw Anita running towards her, she was shouting, but most of it was lost in the noise of battle. Anouk started to tell her to go back, but as she watched, an arrow fell striking her in the chest, stopping, she fell to her knees. “NOOOO”, Anouk shouted as she looked on in absolute horror.

Anouk ran to her, the advancing soldiers forgotten. Dropping to her knees and taking her in her arms, “No, no, no”, she cried out loud, “Not you, my love, you can’t leave me”, she screamed as she held her tight. Anita smiled at her, “It’s ok, it doesn’t hurt much”, as she looked into Anouk’s eyes the pain started to come, her breathing becoming more difficult causing her to cough. Blood covered her lips, pooling at the corner of her mouth before trickling down. Now gasping for breath, scarlet bubbles frothed from her lips. She could feel her breath getting shallower, the hot wetness of her blood escaping the corner of her mouth, and the blackness creeping into her sight. Looking up she saw the floods of tears running down Anouk’s cheeks, the pain and sorrow etched into her eyes. “I love you Anouk, I will wait for......”. Anita’s body went limp in Anouk’s arms, her head tipping back, her eyes glazing over, no longer seeing the world.

Anouk pulled her closer, tears streaming from her eyes, great sobs forcing themselves up from her chest. “Don’t leave me, please don’t leave me”, she sobbed into her hair as she rocked back and forth. Ben knelt beside her, putting a hand on her shoulder, “Anouk, she has gone”. “Get away from us”, she snapped, continuing to hold her lifeless body, “I am so sorry my sweetheart, I couldn’t protect you, what good are these powers if you can’t protect your own loved ones”. Anouk started to sink into a very dark place within her soul, my parents are dead, my foster parents are dead, they want me dead, and now I have lost you, the love of my life, what will I do without you? Anouk sat and wailed out loud, tears gushing, unable to, or wanting to stop them. The noise of the battle slowly fading away as she dived headlong into her grief.

A short time later, she laid Anita down, looking deep in her eyes, the blackness, the futility, the suffering of all that had happened welled within her, only death seems to follow her. Well if they want death, that is what they will get, the power surged deep within her, every passing second it grew bigger and stronger. Her brain told her this was wrong, but her heart cried for retribution, more and more power coalesced within her, soon her whole body felt full to the point of overflowing. As Ben watched, he saw a dark look descend over her face; static began sparking as her hair broke free whipping about her head. Slowly she started to rise from the walkway, not by standing, as she was still in the kneeling position. The power exuded from her like a palpable thing, oh my god, she is going to explode, he thought suddenly. "EVERYBODY, GET DOWN, FOR GOD's SAKE GET DOWN". As he watched he saw her hover high above the walkway, her arms slowly extended, bigger sparks now flew from her, Anouk's eyes had gone dark with flashes of lighting tracing across them.

As Anouk started to spin, the power created a cyclone which she pushed out around the outer edges of the town, as she turned faster the winds picked up whipping around, collecting and churning anything outside of the walls. The cleared circle became a maelstrom strong enough to lift horses and men from the ground, as the winds grew wider out to the edge of the forest, collecting the siege engines, sucking anybody close enough to the tree line out of the forest. Anouk poured more power into the cyclone; dark clouds gathered spitting out lightning bolts, scorching anything they touched, splitting whole trees when they hit. Debris, branches, shattered siege engines and lost weapons added to the maelstrom causing men and horses to shred; lighting continued to flicker through the haze incinerating anything it touched. For the people in the town, the noise became terrifying, the air becoming thinner as the cyclone sucked at it. Within seconds not a living thing survived outside the walls of the town. Eventually, Anouk slowed and the wind became less, bodies and horses dropped to the ground all around the town, none moved. Anouk descended back to the walkway, her legs giving way, she fell to her side, unconscious.

Chapter 20

Anouk awoke slowly from her deep sleep, keeping her eyes closed, enjoying the warm comfort of the bed, she stretched with a groan. She could feel the presence of someone leaning over her, felt them move her hair from her face. A voice spoke soon after, "You are awake at last Your Highness, we have been so worried about you". Continuing to lay with her eyes closed she tried to get her thoughts in order, that wasn't Anita's voice, what about the battle? Did we win? Have I been badly injured? She did a mental check of her body, achy but no pain, she thought. Suddenly the memories started to flood back as she became more awake, seeing all over again, in her mind as Anita was hit in the chest with an arrow, memories of her dying in her arms, the look of pain as she passed away right in front of her. Anouk was weeping, tears pushing out of her closed eyes, spilling down to the pillow. She died and left me, she covered her face with her hands and sobbed, what am I going to do without you by my side, my love, she thought desperately. The person moved on to the bed and lifted her, cradling her as she wept, "I know, let it all out My Lady, you have to mourn her passing before you can celebrate the time you had". A soft knock came at the door, Dug's voice floated across the room, quiet and respectful, "Is she awake now"? Mary replied, "Can you give us some time please Dug, I will let you know when she is up", "Ok, but soon, we are all desperate to see her" he answered as he walked back to the kitchen.

Mary sat holding her for quite a time during which Anouk wept uncontrollably; eventually, she settled enough to speak, "Where is she now Mary"? Laying her head back on the pillow, Mary got a cloth from the wash-stand, as she bathed her face, she decided it was best, to be honest with her. "Anita was buried yesterday, you have been unconscious for the past four days", "Oh", was all she could say, thinking I couldn't even be at her funeral, what use am I? I couldn't save her, and I wasn't there to say goodbye. Anouk rolled over and curled up with her back to Mary, "Everyone is really worried about you, Your Highness, can they come in and see you. Put their minds at rest at least". She curled into a tighter ball, "No, I don't want to see anyone, tell them to leave me alone". Mary left the room, closing the door quietly behind her.

Mary popped in from time to time that morning to check on her, on one occasion, leaving food on the bedside table. Anouk remained curled up facing the wall, more than once she could hear her softly sobbing, not being able to do anything more for her; she left her to her grief. Just after mid-day she again entered the room and found Anouk stood fully dressed in her leather outfit, she was looking out the window with her back to her. "Oh, I was just checking on you, My Lady, didn't expect you to be up and dressed", she stood silently without answering. Eventually, not turning, she asked, "Where did they bury her"? Mary moved closer to her, glancing down at the food which hadn't been touched, "By the stream next to the practising grounds, she had told her dad that she had her happiest times there watching you practice".

Anouk didn't reply so she continued, "Benji made a beautiful headstone for her with an angel perched on top, to watch over her, he said". Anouk thanked her, and saying she wanted to go and visit the grave as she headed for the door, "I will get my cloak and come with you, My Lady". Anouk stopped and looked at her, Mary's heart melted at the look of sadness and loss in her eyes, "No, please, this is something I have to do on my own". Anouk opened the door and headed through to the kitchen, Ben, Shan and Dug were sat at the table, as she entered, they started to stand. But she carried on into the front room and out the front door without saying a word. The three stood staring after her, then looked to Mary, she shrugged saying, "Give her time, she is going to visit Anita's grave. I am sure she will come around".

Anouk knelt in front of the grave looking at the headstone, Benji had made a magnificent job of it, the angel was playing the harp whilst looking down at her, she read the headstone.

Anita Steen
18 summers
Died during the siege of Forest Town
Much loved Daughter and Sister
Partner of Her Royal Highness Anouk

The last line caused her to cry once more, tears running down her cheeks, quietly she spoke, "I am so sorry I failed you, sweetheart, you were and always will be my true love. I promise you that I will have our vengeance for what he has done to us. I swear to you now, I will go to Regis, and the King will die, he will pay for all the evil he has done to us, and everybody else in this realm". She remained at the graveside for most of the afternoon, talking to Anita, reliving their good times. As dusk started to draw in, she stood, looking down at the mound of earth, "It's time for me to go, my love, wait for me wherever you are now, we will be together again. Just not yet, I have things to do. Goodbye, rest now", she turned and walked away, promising she would be back to visit, someday.

She slowly walked back, taking in the damage that had been caused to many of the houses, there were still some arrows sticking up here and there making her shudder at the sight of them. The town's people she met, curtsied and bowed respectfully but didn't speak, nodding her appreciation she continued on her way. As she stepped into the house, she could hear loud voices coming from the kitchen; the men were being rowdy, probably had too many ale's, she thought. Mary's voice floated through, "Stop it, you men are awful, stop teasing me". As she entered, they all went quiet, Dug spoke first, "Can I have a hug now, My Lady", she smiled and nodded, Dug wrapped her in his arms, just holding her, not speaking. When they parted Shan and Ben had also stood, she hugged them both as well, "Mary, I think I can eat now, do we have anything"? She looked relieved, "Yes, yes, of course, I will get you something now". As she ate the men sat quietly drinking, so she decided to break the silence, "I have been thinking, the King, my grandfather, has been behind all the bad things that have befallen me, you, and this town. Tomorrow I will be riding for Regis where I will kill him and overthrow his regime. Anyone care to join me"? Everybody stared at her, Shan eventually spoke, "After the battle was over, what was left of his army turned tail and ran. There could only have been a handful of men that escaped. We went out to try and clear some of the mess out there, whilst doing it I came upon the body of the King, so I think you have already achieved that, My Lady".

Anouk's arm stopped with a piece of bread halfway to her mouth, "He was out there? So, he is dead, good. But I will still go to overthrow the regime and find out what has become of my aunt". Shan nodded vigorously to this when Dug chipped in, "But wasn't it odd that his body, although broken from the, ah thing, had an arrow piercing his chest through his armour. That must have been fired up close to get through his chest plate". Shan shrugged, "Dead is dead, and good riddance to him, he was always a nasty piece of work". Anouk finished her meal; she hadn't realized how hungry she was until she started eating, washing down the last mouthful with a goblet of wine. "Ben, could you see who among the gifted are willing to come with me, I will do this alone if I have to, but it would be easier with some help".

Ben nodded getting up from the table, "I will put the word out now, I think you will be surprised at the response, you are a hero in the town now". Anouk grimaced at his words, "I am not looking to be anybody's hero or Princess. I just want justice for Anita, Geraldine and all the other people who died here, things have to change. Oh, by the way, how is Gretta"? Ben stopped in the doorway, "She is just fine, although a little sad, many of her friends were killed in the attack. She has been asking about you, would be nice if you put her mind at rest and go see her".

Anouk, Shan and Dug sat for the evening discussing plans for the proposed march on Regis, Ben returned a short while later, declaring the word had been put out and was being well-received by all. Shan was especially keen to march on the capital town, as he was deeply concerned for the welfare of Geraldine. Dug raised a hand, "So when we depose the royal family and kick their perfumed asses out the door, who will rule the realm? Have you thought of that? Will you become queen"? Anouk looked aghast at the thought, shaking her head, "No, I will never rule, I don't want to be a princess let alone a queen. It is my sincere hope that Geraldine is ok, and she can take up the throne, if not, then a ruling Ossary maybe the way forward".

Whilst they talked into the evening, Anouk was watching Ben and Mary, noticing the little looks, smiles, and facial expressions passing between the two. Interrupting Shan who was describing the layout of the palace, Anouk directed a question straight at Ben, "Have you two got something to tell me"? Mary immediately coloured up turning away, and Ben became all coy looking down at the table. Dug sat back in his chair making a loud whoop, "I win, less than a whole evening, come on pay up". Anouk looked quizzically around the room as Ben and Shan slid a coin over to Dug, "We made bets as to how long it would be before you noticed Ben and Mary were seeing each other, as you heard Dug won", Shan informed her. "You men are so insensitive, was that what you were ribbing her about when I came in? I would have thought there were far more important things to concern yourselves about". The group continued planning into the night trying to think of every possible outcome; eventually, plans made they all retired for a night's sleep before the next adventure.

The next morning Anouk paid a visit to Gretta, sitting with her she explained what she intended to do, asking if she understood why it had to be done. Gretta was in full agreement, wishing she was young enough to travel with her. She gave just one piece of advice to her before she left, "Anouk, you are a kind and thoughtful young lady, the spark in you has somewhat dimmed due to recent events. Please, don't let your grief consume you, look to your conscience and deal with anything that happens with an element of compassion. Do unto others as you would expect to be done unto you". She promised she would before be returning to her house, and changing into her mother's leathers ready for the journey. Stepping out of her front door, she was totally taken back by the sheer number of people waiting for her. It looked as if all the gifted people and even some of the ordinary townspeople stood quietly looking at her. Horses were saddled, laden with supplies, and everyone carried a backpack. Some were sporting weapons, bows, swords and daggers, others empty-handed, the gifted ones she surmised. "I think you may have to give a speech before setting off", Ben said stepping up by her side. Anouk gulped and thought for a few moments, looking out at the sea of expectant faces. In a loud voice, she started:

"I am Anouk, a simple farmers daughter, over the course of this last summer I have come to learn many things. When I was a baby, my mother and father were murdered. As I approached adulthood, my foster parents were murdered, and I was condemned to death. I learned I was the daughter of a prince which through blood makes me a princess, I neither looked for this, expected it or wanted it. You all took me into

your town and cared for me, I found love here, only to have it savagely ripped away. Your town was attacked where many died, fathers, mothers, brothers, sisters and loved ones. We cannot turn back time, we cannot undo what has been done to us, but we can change how things are done in the future. If we stand together and fight for justice, we can look forward to a better tomorrow, for ourselves and our children. Today, we go to Regis to start making that change".

The assembled people cheered as Ben led Anouk down to her horse, the large brown mare whinnied at her approach moving against her. Instantly recognizing the horse, she turned to Ben, "But, this is Bonny, how did she get here"? Shan stepped out of the crowd, "I brought her, when I left Belcher I was in need of a horse, as Sam stole her from you, well I took her back and rode her here. As she is yours you should have her, I can use the horse you brought". Anouk reached up, rubbing her neck, "Didn't think I would see you again", Bonny dipped her head pushing back against her. She laughed out loud, "You haven't changed then, behave yourself, girl". Seating herself in the saddle she looked around, everyone who had a horse was mounted and ready. Riding alongside Shan; they headed towards the gate. The other riders fell in behind them with the walkers following after.

Over the next three days, they travelled by day and made camp by night, spirits were high, and each night they would all gather around the campfires, swapping stories or singing old songs. Anouk felt good for being back out in the wide world, having been cooped up in Forest Town for far too long. This was where she was happiest, in the great outdoors under the stars; everyone was careful not to mention Anita unless she brought her into the conversation. Sitting back on a log she watched Ben and Mary huddled together, love was blossoming, she could see from the expressions on their faces how they enjoyed each other's company. Reminiscing she thought, that should be us, Anita, we had so much more to give to each other. Shan plonked himself next to her, "Copper for your thoughts, My Lady". Smiling at him, "I was just thinking how much in love those two are becoming, I am glad they have found each other". Shan grimaced, "Yeah, Geraldine and I should be sat like that, I hope I get her back. Oh, sorry, I didn't think; I shouldn't have said that, not to you". Anouk placed a hand on his arm giving it a shake, "It's ok, you should be feeling like that, I only hope we can get to her before anything happens, you two are meant for each other". Shan nodded, staring into the fire lost in his own thoughts.

On the morning of the third day, Regis came into sight on the horizon. Shan was once again riding next to Anouk, voicing his thoughts he announced, "I shall ride ahead and meet with the remaining knights. If I still have any pull with them, I should be able to convince them to refrain from intervening, if not, you will probably find me in the dungeons", laughing at his own words, "Either way I will be inside the palace, good luck My Lady, see you on the other side of all this". Shan urged his horse forward and took off at a gallop towards the town. It was mid-day before they found themselves on the town road leading up to the palace, the road was quite wide allowing five horses to ride abreast, Anouk's horse was at the middle of the front row giving her perfect view up the road. No one was on the road apart from them, looking to the town she could see it was practically deserted. The odd person fliting across before disappearing into a house looks like they knew we were coming, she thought.

Arriving at the main gates to the palace, she could see they were firmly closed; several soldiers stood across the road blocking access. They were wearing armour, and each held a wicked-looking long spear in their hands, swords hung from their belts, and a couple had bows strapped to their backs. Anouk held up her hand, bringing her people to a stop a short distance from them, she sat and studied them for a few moments. Most were quite young, and some were physically shaking with fear, sliding down from Bonny, she patted her neck as she walked forward to close the gap. A gruff looking soldier walked forward to meet her, "Stop right there in the name of the King" he shouted. She stopped, holding his gaze, replied, "Funny, I thought the King was dead, so how can I stop in his name"? He ignored her remark sweeping his gaze over her and the group behind, "You are all to turnaround and leave this place, if you do not you will be forced to". Anouk slowly turned, looking out over her people, she winked at the front few before returning her gaze to the soldiers. "Well, as I see it, we outnumber you by about fifty to one, so that would be no mean feat to be sure". The younger soldiers behind had started muttering between themselves, "There are plenty more inside the palace, so I will tell you again, turn around and walk away".

Anouk decided she'd had quite enough of them and was anxious to get this sorted, "No, I am telling you now, move aside and allow us passage inside, or suffer the consequences". The young soldiers looked even more scared, shuffling their feet and mumbling to each other. "So be it", she announced loudly, bringing her arms out in front of her she began summoning her power. The air shimmered around her as it reacted to her will, as she brought her hands together, she formed a ball of stormy air. Pouring more power into it, the ball got larger; air could be seen like a raging storm churning within the globe. Lightning flashes sparked across it illuminating her face like a ghostly mask with each flash. The soldiers were all now in awe of the power before them and terrified, except for the old soldier, who now drew his sword. "Last chance to leave", she shouted, all but one dropped their weapons and ran from the gates out across the field towards the town. The older soldier started to lunge forward with his sword aimed at her stomach; she launched the ball straight at him. It collected the soldier causing him to fly backwards until he and the ball connected with the gates, a massive rending roar of exploding wood, metal and soldier erupted. The gates were blown wide open and left hanging on broken hinges; the soldier's broken body lay halfway across the inner courtyard.

As she made her way carefully inside, she was amazed to see there were no soldiers waiting for them, over to her right she could see the stables where the horses could be seen through the doors. But no knights or soldiers barred her way; Ben joined her looking as perplexed as she was, "Do you think it's a trap"? Anouk walked to the gate barracks and looked through the door, "Empty, I don't know. But it seems like there are no guards or soldiers left, and the knights' horses are still in the stables. I think the ones outside might have been all they had left, and they were very young". Her people were flowing in through the open gate filling the courtyard, "Ben, get the earth and water people to guard the gate, all the others wait in the courtyard. We will take the fire gifted with us into the palace". Ben started giving the order, and everyone sorted themselves to their positions, when all were ready Anouk set off towards the large imposing doors of the palace.

She was amazed at the size of the place, never had she seen such an impressive or imposing building in her life, mounting the steps up to the doors a figure appeared from around a corner. As the person strode towards her, she quickly realized it was Shan, "Didn't throw you in a dungeon then", she said mockingly. "No, they hadn't realized I was on the other side, but on a more serious note, they have thrown Geraldine into one. I am going to get her out, and I pity any fool who gets in my way". She agreed with him turning towards the doors again, "Well, shall we get this started". The doors swung open easily, as there were no locks, stepping into the grand entrance hall her breath was taken away, the floor was stone but polished to a high sheen. The walls adorned with paintings, rich tapestries and weapons of every sort, suits of armour stood proudly around the room. The furniture was all extremely ornate in a heavy dark wood, in the centre of the room was a huge rug woven with images of animals, she spotted images that looked just as Pata had described them to her.

Shan indicated a corridor to their left, "This way to the queen's quarters, we need to deal with her before anything else. Watch out for the royal guards, they won't back down so easily". Anouk followed closely behind Shan, with Ben and his sister Fina flanking her and several fire people followed after. The corridor was as extravagant as the hall, she couldn't believe people lived like this when others struggled even to feed themselves, where is the fairness in all of this she pondered quietly.

As they approached a corner in the corridor, several royal guards rushed towards them shouting, swords drawn and raised ready to fight. Shan met the first one head-on with a clash of metal as their swords collided, sidestepping away from them, Anouk raised her hands and sent a blast of wind down the sidewall knocking three from their feet. Pictures and tapestries fell from the wall crashing to the polished floor, a fireball sailed past her, the heat of it making her face smart. The fireball struck a guard full in the chest instantly igniting his clothes, the man screamed in agony as he dropped his sword, staggering around like a human torch. Anouk sent out another blast dropping the remaining two to the floor, Shan had won his fight and was advancing towards the guards as they picked themselves up, more fireballs sailed past hitting and igniting another two guards. Only one guard remained, dropping his sword he looked at them with wide eyes, his face frozen in fear, "Give up, and you will be spared" Shan told him. He raised his hands and dropped to his knees; head bowed in surrender.

The group continued to follow the corridor where it opened out into a large chamber, as they entered they saw at least twenty royal guards lined up outside a large door. An older man not in the uniform of the guards stood at the back next to the door, "I am Lord Commander Alfonse, you are committing treason with your presence here, lay down your arms or you will be killed". Anouk stepped forward, staring at the old man, "I think not, the time has come to an end for this regime, it will no longer rule over this land. The King is dead, and we will not stop until the queen is removed from her place of privilege and replaced with a more suitable one". Alfonse laughed, "You think you can take her place bastard, you haven't a clue. Kill them, men".

The room erupted into turmoil as the guards charged forward; fireballs flew across the fight igniting anything they touched. A sword swung at Anouks head would have connected had she not ducked, leaving her off balance, and falling to the floor. The guard seized his chance lunging forward with his sword, stabbing directly at her chest. Instinctively she rolled to her left away from certain death, just as fireball hit the guard full in the face, she watched his face appeared to melt and disintegrate before her eyes. Looking around, she saw Fina nod at her; she mouthed her thanks before scrambling away. Finding herself separated at the side of the chamber; three guards advanced towards her menacingly, swords and spears poised for a fatal blow. Gathering her power, she focused on them throwing her arms forward, blasting them with a wall of air, the guards flew backwards into the side of the other guards, bowling several to the floor.

A volley of fireballs sailed across the room striking several guards, dropping their weapons turned and ran through the ones who hadn't been hit, resulting in their clothes being ignited as well. In a very short time, the guards were routed, most burning on the floor, several impaled on their own weapons, as a result of Anouk's wind blast. Moving through the room, she noticed the Lord Commander's body wasn't to be seen, must have run back through the doors, she thought. They had lost two in the fight and Ben was sitting against a wall holding his side, Fina was kneeling beside him. Anouk rushed to them, "Ben, how bad are you hurt"? He looked up wincing as Fina packed the wound with cloth, "Ah, not too bad, although I will have to sit the last bit out I think",

Anouk nodded, "Fina stay with him, I have to go and have an audience with a queen".

When everyone was ready Anouk hit the doors with a blast blowing them wide open; papers flew from the desk just inside which slowly fluttered down like confetti. Standing in the doorway, she surveyed the room. An older but elegant woman stood just behind the desk, behind her was a large ornate window of many colours. Stood to her right was a weasely looking man who was cowering, to her left stood Alfonse. The Lord Commander stood ramrod straight with no expression on his face, in his hand was a sword, hanging down the side of his leg. Anouk and Amelia stared at each other for a time, not speaking, each sizing the other up. Amilia broke the silence, "So you are the bastard princess, I have heard so much about you, I don't suppose you would like to sit down and talk about this over a cup of tea, would you"? Anouk just stared at her, what arrogance this woman has, I dislike her already, she thought. "Oh, you appear to be overawed by my presence, ok, I will talk for now", she continued. "I have heard about your exploits on the battlefield with your witchcraft, defeating my husband's army and killing him, the King of this realm. That is punishable by death alone, but there is something else going on with you, isn't there"?

Anouk kept a deadpan expression, letting her dig the hole bigger for herself. "Yes, you have had quite the exploit in the bed-chamber I hear, with a woman I believe, what was her name"? Amelia raised her hand to the side of her face, a finger prodding her temple with a fake look of searching for her name, "Ah, Anita". The name dripped from her tongue with total disdain; Shan moved beside

Anouk, “Don’t you utter her name, she was twice the woman you are……”. Anouk shot a look telling him in no uncertain terms to be quiet, her patience was wearing thin and her anger welled inside, but she kept it in check, for now. Amelia had looked at Shan as he spoke, but she returned her gaze to Anouk, “So, for the offence of laying with a woman, the death penalty is twice as applicable. Where is the slut? She can be put down with you for your crimes”.

Anouk had been simmering with anger throughout her tirade, her power growing stronger with each insult levelled at her. But when she started to disrespect Anita, the blackness of the power moved in, clouding her judgement, manifesting into a ball of absolute rage within her. Anyone who could see her face saw her features become stone-cold like granite, her eyes darkened with flashes of energy flickering across them, Amelia was one who could see, total panic gripped her as she looked into the face of the young girl in front of her.

Amelia held up her hands in front of her, palms facing Anouk, “Maybe we have got off on the wrong foot, we should all sit down and discuss what is to happen next, like adults”. It was too little too late, Anouk’s power had reached it’s full potential, pushing her hands forward she released an intense, powerful burst of energy straight at Amelia, hitting her full in the chest. Amelia’s body was lifted and thrown backwards at great speed towards the window; she was dead before she reached it with her rib cage shattered and squashed. Amelia’s body hit the window, exploding it into a thousand pieces, flying through her body eventually landed on the grass next to the inner courtyard, in a bloody and broken heap. The blast had caught the two men either side of her, throwing them sideways, Glitch flew into a wall knocking him senseless, Alfonse flew the opposite way hitting his head on a bookcase, now lying unconscious on the floor.

Anouk dropped to her knee's breathing deeply, the power dissipating from her as she caught her breath. Fina rushed to her side, putting her arm about her shoulders, "Are you alright, My Lady"? Shan had knelt at her other side, his hand on her arm, both waited for an answer. Anouk smiled weakly at them, "Yes, I am fine, just a little tired. Give me a minute to catch my breath". Shan nodded, "Fina stay with her until she is on her feet please, I am going to find Geraldine downstairs", Fina agreed and Shan moved towards the door, "You and you, make sure those two are tied up tight, they may awaken at any moment", he ordered as he crossed the outer chamber.

Anouk made herself comfortable in a large padded chair, sat across from her was Alfonse and Glitch, both with hands tied behind their backs. She glared at Glitch for a long time making him squirm with discomfort; he kept his head down, avoiding all eye contact with her, hoping he would not incur her wrath. She turned her glare on Alfonse who defiantly glared back at her, sitting ramrod straight in the chair. "So, you are the King's Lord Commander, well he is dead, so I guess that makes you unemployed" The Lord Commander showed no emotion as he spoke, "I was his Lord Commander, I will not be yours if that is what you are thinking". Anouk laughed, "I will not be Queen, Lord Commander, that was never the plan, so in one way you are right. But you are a dangerous man to have walking about, we will have to see what we are going to do with you". Turning back to Glitch, "And you were the Kings advisor, we don't need you anymore, so what to do with both of you, it's a problem".

Movement at the door to the room drew her attention as Geraldine swept in closely followed by Shan, she was still dressed in the farmers dress she had on when she was taken. Mud and stains covered her dress, hands and face and her hair was down unbrushed. Anouk stood as she approached her, noticing the dried blood under her nose and around the corner of her mouth, she started to ask if she was alright. But Geraldine swept her into her arms holding her tight, as her face buried in her shoulder, the words disappeared in a muffled noise. Geraldine hugged her tight for a short time before moving her away to look at her. "Are you alright sweetheart? So much has happened these past few days", Anouk nodded, "I'm alright, but what happened to your face? The blood and bruise on your cheek".

Geraldine looked across at Glitch who was still cowering in his chair, "Ask him, ask him how he likes to hit women, especially those that don't agree with his warped idea's". Shan shot across the room grabbing Glitch's hair, pulling his head back, exposing his throat as his other hand rose with a knife clenched in his fist. "Hit women do you; you don't deserve to live you worthless piece of scum", the knife moved towards his throat. "Stop, don't kill him Shan", the words came from Geraldine, everyone looked to her. "I am the daughter of King Uther who is dead, as Princess I declare I am in charge of this realm until the Ossary can meet and discuss any succession", she paused looking around, all were listening. "My first orders are that Glitch is sent to the dungeons, for the crime of striking a Princess. He will be stripped of all titles and privileges. Lord Commander Alfonse, you are accused of treason against the King in that you assisted in his assassination, you will also be stripped of rank and privileges and held in the dungeons. Both of you will answer to the Ossary in due course. Take them to their new accommodation". Shan, Dug and several others escorted the two men from the room as Anouk and Geraldine watched, "Well now that unpleasant business is dealt with, it would be nice to get a bath, don't you agree, Anouk"? Anouk stood, shaking her head in disbelief, she is such a royal princess, does nothing bother her?

Chapter 21

A few weeks later, Anouk was sitting in the palace gardens lost in her thoughts; she had found a private spot where she didn't get disturbed too much. She hadn't wanted to stay in the palace, all the decadence, pomp and ceremony bored her, but Geraldine had insisted, she wanted her niece close and begged her to stay. How could she refuse her new-found aunt; after all, they only had each other, everyone else in the family had gone. Plucking at the fine material of her gown, her thoughts turned to what she was wearing, today she had on a frilly white gown, fitted at the top and blossoming out into huge skirts below, totally impracticable she thought, and don't get me started about the corset. She hated the thing, squeezing her torso so tight with her bosom shunted up for all to see, well most of it. Being acutely aware of it, she always chose gowns with a scarf so that she could cover herself. Mary had been assigned to her as a handmaid, although she was a lovely person, she really missed Anita. Mary and Ben had become really close, and he had stayed on at the palace helping where needed, Anouk fully expected them to get married before long. Dug and Cheryl were a couple now as were Geraldine and Shan. They all tried to include her as often as possible, but she felt like a third wheel around them. She was happy for them all, but in her sad times, she dwelt on what might have been for her, remembering the plans she and Anita had made.

Being at the palace was ok, but she yearned to travel, she wanted to see the things Pata had told her of, go to other lands and meet different people. I wasn't made to be cooped up in a splendid palace. I want adventure, excitement; I want to see the sea and travel on ships. A movement caught her attention; it was Garth, the gardener. At first, when she came to sit, he would respectfully avoid her, but she won him around with her friendliness and questions about the plants. Garth was a man of at least fifty summers, he wore simple clothes and walked with a hunched back. On his head was his ever-present straw hat, the brim of which was fraying and showing holes, as if the moths had been at it. "Good morning Your Highness", he said with a stiff bow, "Thought I saw you sneaking back here", he said with a cheeky grin. "You know me so well Garth; please come sit with me. You can tell me some more about the flowers", she replied, patting the bench beside her.

They sat for a time, Garth explaining about the plants and how to care for them, Anouk happy to listen, taking her mind off her brooding thoughts. In a rush, Geraldine swept around the corner catching them both by surprise; Garth leapt off the bench bowing as she approached, "I am sorry Your Highness, I, we, well, was talking". Geraldine waved her hand to stop his blustering, "That's perfectly alright, you must be Garth, Princess Anouk has spoken very highly of you", shocked he looked to Anouk who was smiling at him. "But I will have to ask you to leave now, as we have some very important matters to discuss", he bowed again and quickly moved away.

Geraldine perched herself next to Anouk taking her hands in hers, "I have received some very important news, I just had to find you to let you know first". Anouk could see she was very excited, "Well, don't keep me waiting, aunty", Geraldine grinned, squeezing her hands. "I will never get over someone calling me that; the Ossary has met and come to two very big decisions, the first is they have confirmed my ascension to the throne. I am to become Queen". Her face lit up as she told her, hardly able to contain her excitement, "I am really pleased for you aunty, I know it is what you wanted, I think you will make a good, fair and just queen. Just what the realm needs right now". "Thank you, sweetheart, and the second decision is one I put before them. I asked that should I be approved for Queen; I can name you as First Princess, which is a great honour. It was also approved my niece".

Anouk was taken aback by this, thinking, oh god is it not bad enough for me to be a Princess, now she has only gone and added to it. Out loud she said, "Thank you, does that mean I have to do anything extra around here"?. Geraldine laughed, "No silly, it is a title which gives you great honour and makes you first in line to the throne". She felt relieved at this answer because she still hadn't revealed her plans to Geraldine, which she felt sure were not going to be well received.

The palace was a hive of activity over the next few days, all the damage and mess from the brief fight had been cleared away, but there were a great many things to do before the coronation of Geraldine. All the hallways, tapestries and windows had to be cleaned, the throne room prepared for the ceremony and an army of gardeners worked on the grounds outside. It seemed to Anouk that wherever she went, there were people cleaning, washing and polishing or scurrying to and fro with their own important tasks to complete. By the third day she decided she'd had enough of the frenzy and asked Mary if she would walk down to the town with her, she agreed and said she would love to introduce her to family. They set off soon after and walked the short distance to Regis town, the locals all bowed and curtsied as she passed by, the children just stared in awe at a real Princess walking into town. Mary walked beside her, describing where things were and introducing anyone she knew by name, Anouk made time to speak with each she introduced, especially the children.

Eventually, they made it to Mary's house; it was a small, modest townhouse obviously in need of some repair. As they approached the front door, she saw two older children looking out the window, their eyes wide with disbelief. Mary opened the door, and they both stepped into a small kitchen area, in the centre was a table with four chairs, the floor was bare wood and what furniture there was had seen better days. The family stood in a group to one side, and Mary introduced each one to her, her father Ted, mother Jean and her siblings Tom and Tilly. Each curtsied or bowed and welcomed her to their home except Tilly, she was about twelve or thirteen summers old, slim build with a pretty face and long hair. Having got over her shock at a Princess coming to her house, she now had adopted a hard-cold look, staring straight at Anouk. "We were all nearly killed because of your family, why should I welcome you here"? Mary instantly replied, coming to her defence, "Tilly! You can't talk to her highness like that, now apologize at once". Tilly folded her arms, shaking her head, "Tilly!" Mary continued. Anouk held up her hand to Mary whilst looking to the child, "Tilly, I have never met you before, and I bear you no ill will. Can I ask you to sit with me and explain what it is that has befallen you and your family so that I might understand"? Tilly agreed to this, and the two sat down at the table.

After she had finished recounting the events of that day, Tilly sat back and crossed her arms again, looking between Mary and Anouk. The silence was deafening as Anouk sat and considered all she'd said, "Ok Tilly, I have to agree that was a terrifying ordeal for you and your family. I am pleased you are all home safe and sound despite it. But please lay the blame at the feet of the people responsible, your sister and I had no knowledge of this, as I am sure Princess Geraldine doesn't either. The person most responsible is a man called Glitch, he has already been stripped of all titles and thrown in the dungeons, the ones you were in for a short while". This news brought a smile to her face, "The King and Queen are dead, and Princess Geraldine will be taking the throne shortly, I promise you this town and realm will be a very different one, where no girls, boys or innocent people are thrown into any dungeon. Do you believe me"? Tilly sat nodding, her arms relaxing into her lap, "I will make you one more promise young lady, as soon as I return to the palace, I will make Princess Geraldine aware of the ordeal you have suffered, and arrange invitations for all your family to attend the coronation". The family gasped and gathered around the table, all excitedly talking about the honour of being there for the coronation.

On her return, Anouk found Geraldine in her chambers, "All ready for the great day tomorrow"? Geraldine looked up from what she was reading, "Where have you been? We were looking for you, your dress has arrived, and you need to be fitted to make sure it is the right size". Anouk grimaced at the statement and informed her of her visit to Mary's family and what had befallen them after her exit from Regis. She promised to take care of the family and add extra charges to Glitch's warrant, "Now go and try on your dress, please. I want you to look perfect on the day sweetheart".

Anouk returned to her rooms where she found Mary fussing over the new dress, "Look what has come for you", she said beaming with delight for her. The dress was sky blue with a fitted top and high neckline, thank god for that, she thought. The front of the bodice was embroidered with gold thread forming flowers; each flower centre had different stones which glinted in the light. From the waistline, the dress billowed out, falling to more embroidery around the bottom part of the skirts. It was indeed exquisite, but all she could think of was how much did that cost, this is madness.

The following day found Anouk standing in her room wearing the new dress; Mary fussed around her making sure everything was perfect, "Now for the finishing touch", she told her as she opened an expensive-looking wooden box. From it she took a tiara which twinkled in the light from the window, it was made of white metal and had numerous white stones set into it. Mary fitted it into her hair, fussing with it until it looked just right. "There, you look absolutely beautiful, Your Highness", Mary was pleased with her efforts. Anouk looked at herself thinking I look ridiculous, rather be in my mother's leathers, but out loud she said, "Thank you, Mary, it is time we were going to the throne room".

A quick walk found them entering the throne room; the hall was already packed with nobles, knights and some town's people. They all stared as she walked down the centre of the room, bowing and curtsying as she passed, whispers floated to her ears. "Look she is so beautiful" and "Oh what a fabulous dress", all Anouk could think at that moment was please don't let me trip up in this silly dress. As she walked through the people, she saw a familiar face, "Tilly", the young girl curtsied, "I am so glad you and your family have made it here. I hope you all enjoy the day". Taking her place in front of the raised platform Anouk waited for Geraldine to arrive, for a while the gathered people spoke in hushed tones, Mary whispered in her ear, "She's outside, it will begin in a minute", Anouk nodded turning to look.

Princess Geraldine entered wearing a magnificent white and navy-blue dress; she looked every part a Queen as she glided down towards the dais. In front of her walked the oldest Ossary member and behind followed Shan and Fina, as Geraldine made her way up onto the dais, Shan and Fina moved to beside Anouk. The Elder Ossary member stood and banged his staff on the floor three times; a silence fell over the whole room. "I am Seth, the elder of the Ossary, holder of the sacred staff, and here to swear in Princess Geraldine as Queen of this realm. If any person here has just cause to oppose this coronation, speak now". There followed a minute of silence, just the occasional cough to be heard. "So be it, no one opposes, we shall begin". He turned and stiffly made his way up on to the dais, handing his staff to a young surf, he took Geraldine's hands in his. "Princess, are you willing to take the oath"? She replied, "I am willing". "Do you swear to govern over this realm according to the law and custom of the land"? "I swear to do so" she replied. "Will you use your power to ensure law and justice be upheld without malice or ill will"? "This I promise before all who are here as witnesses to my oath". Seth released her hands and Geraldine took her place on the throne.

Seth moved to behind the throne, raising his arms; he held a golden crown sparkling with gems. Holding it over her head, "The oaths have been taken and accepted before all of you here present", lowering the crown to her head, "I crown you Queen Geraldine, may your reign be long and prosperous". The room erupted with cheers, many shouts of "Long live Queen Geraldine" echoed around the hall. Geraldine slowly stood up from the throne, balancing the crown lest it fall, raising her arms and waiting for the noise to abate.

When all was quiet, she spoke," I would like to thank you all for the honour of becoming your Queen, I promise to be fair and just, I will listen to any and all complaints or grievances. To that end, I would like to announce two changes to the law which has already been agreed by the Ossary. No longer will people with gifts of power be outlawed or called witches and sorcerers, from now on they are to be referred to as gifted people". She paused to see how this was received, most of the room nodding in agreement, no one shouted dissent. "The second law to change is that any person may lay with any other, no matter their sex. No longer will they be persecuted for their own decisions. I have named this 'Anita's Law', in honour of a brave, much loved young lady, who is sorely missed". Geraldine's eyes moved to Anouk; whose face was contorted with emotion in an effort not to cry.

The banquet wasn't being held for a while, so people gathered in Geraldine's offices. Anouk looked around, seeing Geraldine, Shan, Dug, Cheryl, Ben, Mary and Fina. Good, they are all here she thought as she got Geraldine and Shan to step away from the rest. "Geraldine, I have come to a decision, but first I don't want you to be unhappy about it". "Oh, sounds serious", she replied, putting on a serious face. "I have decided not to stay at the palace; I want to travel and live life outside of these walls". Now Geraldine was concerned, "But where will you go? What will you do? We have only just found each other, and you're going to go away"! "Aunty, I am not a Princess, I am a farmer's daughter, I was brought up on the land, feeding animals and being outside in the fresh air. I want to go and see the things Pata told me about, I want to have adventure in my life". Geraldine thought on this, the sadness showing in her eyes, "I will not stop you, but I will miss you so much my beautiful niece". Shan had not spoken, but look deeply concerned. Reaching out he took her by the shoulders and looked lovingly into her eyes, "I can see you have made up your mind, I don't agree with it, but it is your life to live. Promise you will look after yourself, and don't forget us my lady". Anouk pulled Shan into her arms giving him a hug, "I will, and I will never forget all of you. But you have to promise me that you will look after my Aunt". Shan smiled, "Oh, that's an easy promise and I will". Anouk reached up cupping his cheek in her hand, "Thank you for all you have done for me, I will be eternally grateful for having such a friend as you".

Anouk turned to Geraldine taking her in her arm's, giving

her a massive hug, "Will you tell the others a little later, let me get away first as they will undoubtedly try and stop me". Geraldine hugged her tighter, "Yes I will, just promise when you have had your adventure you will return to us, we all love you very much you know". Anouk released her looking into her eyes, "I promise, and thank you for what you did in Anita's name, I will never forget that".

Anouk waited a little while before disappearing away to her rooms, slipping out of the dress which she laid out on the bed. Taking the tiara from her hair she looked wistfully at it, am I doing the right thing? I have so many friends here. Sitting on the edge of the bed, she looked around the room; I could never have dreamed of living in a place like this and wearing such fine clothes. But this isn't me really; I need to go and see all the things Pata told me about, for his sake if nothing else, she told herself. Her mind made up she placed the tiara on top of the dress and turned to her other clothes.

Quickly she changed into her mother's leathers, gathered up her meagre belongings into a backpack, there was already food and water in the pack which she had obtained earlier. Pocketing the coins, she had been given by Geraldine, which consisted of quite a few gold ones, she tapped her pocket, thinking that should get me a long way. Slipping out of the room, she flicked up her hood and made her way through the palace. She could hear the banquet had started as she passed through the hallways and out of the palace, heading for the front gate.

As she approached the gate, a big figure stepped out of the gloom blocking her way, "And where do you think you are going without me, Your Highness"? It was Dug, standing with his hands on his hips, looking sternly at her. "Dug, my dear friend, you have helped me so much since Belcher. But I need to do this, and I have no right to ask anyone to come with me". Dug's face softened, "I swore to make sure no harm came to you, how can I do that if I am not with you"? Anouk stepped forward hugging him, "I will be ok, you above all others should know I can take care of myself, now". Dug hugged her back, and as she looked up into his friendly face, she noticed the wetness in his eyes, "But you are like a daughter to me, I don't want to watch you leave. I know the sadness is still with you, but it will get better, over time". She grimaced at his words, "Anita will be forever in my heart, and yes, I am sad, but that is not why I need to do this. I have to do this for myself and in honour of Pata's memory. Please don't try and stop me". Dug choked as he kissed the top of her head, "I won't, but please say you will find your way home to us", "I will", she replied as she released him.

Dusk was setting in as she walked the road away from the palace, Dug stood in the gateway, watching her go. *Well, this is the start of my adventure, let's see where it takes me,* she thought, disappearing into the gloom.

Epilogue

Anouk stood on the quay, looking out at the vast expanse of water. It was continually moving with little waves crested by white water. Just as Pata had described, she thought. She felt an immense feeling of excitement as she watched the shifting of the waters. A large ship was sitting at the quay. It was bigger than she had ever imagined it, made of wood and intricately carved at the back which was brightly painted in golds, reds, blues and greens. On top, it had three large wooden poles, as big as tree's pointed towards the sky, with horizontal branches wider than the ship. She stood and gawped at the incredible sight, trying to comprehend how man could build such a thing. Looking up, she had to crane her neck to do so; she could see a platform at the top of the biggest pole, I wonder what that is for?

Her eyes fell upon the name which was emblazoned across the top at the back in gold letters, 'ANITA'S DREAM'. She took a step back, stunned by what she was seeing. "Out the way missy, coming through", a gruff voice sounded behind her making her jump. Stepping to one side, she looked at the owner of the voice; he was an older man dressed in stripy shirt and baggy trousers, he and another man were carrying a massive trunk towards the ship. "Excuse me, I need to go on one of these ships. Can you tell me who to speak with please"? The men carried on towards the ship, but the older one called back, "Go to the Flying Dolphin Tavern, just a way up there", he indicated the direction with a movement of his head. "Ask for Cap'n Logan; he is the owner of this one".

Anouk walked the short distance along the front until she was standing outside the tavern, the sign was severely weathered, but a picture of a large fish could be seen jumping from the water. This must be it she told herself, as she entered. Her eyes had to adjust to the gloomy interior. There were plenty of people in the tavern, and the noise was quite overpowering, as was the stink of the ale. She approached the bar where a portly woman came over to her, "What's a lovely thing like you doing in a place like this, sweetheart"? "I am looking for Captain Logan, is he in here"? The bartender craned her neck looking around the room, "Aye, that's him over there in the far corner, the one with a white cap". Anouk looked over and spotted the man, "Thank you for your help". As she moved from the bar, the bartender called after her, "Sorry, if you are staying you got to be buying, house rules". Anouk looked back as she banged a flagon of ale on the countertop, she paid for the ale and carried it over to Logan's table.

As she approached his table, she passed another with several drunken seamen, one of the seamen reached out and slapped her backside, "Come and sit on my lap, wench" he shouted. Anouk instantly felt the power blossom, turning on the man her face full of anger and her eyes darkening with little bolts of lightning flickering across them. She fixed him with her stare, "Don't you ever lay a hand on me again, or it will be the last thing you do". The man recoiled in terror, "Sorry, I thought you were a tavern wench is all". Anouk turned away and continued to the Captain's table.

Captain Logan was an older man of at least fifty summers; he was of large build but looked fit from his active lifestyle. He had short white hair, and his face was brown and weathered from time spent on the sea, looking up at her approach she could see he had kindly looking brown eyes, which studied her intensely. She placed the flagon down in front of him and asked if she may have a word, he agreed, so Anouk took a seat at his table.

"I am looking for a ship which I can travel on to other lands. I am given to understand you have the one at the quay". Logan nodded, not speaking but continuing to study her, "Can I please book passage on your ship Captain"? He lifted his tankard and took a sip whilst considering her request, his eyes never leaving her. "And where is it you wish to go, miss"? Anouk hadn't expected that question, "Just across the sea, where ever your ship is going". "So, what are you running from, can't be a man. I saw how you handle yourself just now. I am thinking it must be something big, are you wanted"? Anouk recoiled at his question, "No, I just want to get away and have adventure in my life. If you are unwilling, then I will look for another ship, your choice".

Logan sat pondering for a short time, "Ok, I will allow you on my ship, but it will cost". Anouk smiled giving him her kindest look, "How much will it cost"? "One gold coin, and for that, I will sort you a cabin to yourself, that's the price, take it or leave it". Anouk stood up, "I will take it, when do we leave"? "On the morning tide, early, don't be late". Anouk turned to leave, pausing she looked back at him, "I saw your boat was called Anita's

Dream, who was Anita"? Logan smiled, "She was my wife and the love of my life, god rest her soul. It was her dream for me to have a Ship of my own one day, so when I got it, I named her after my wife's dream". Anouk smiled while a little wetness crept into her eyes, "You are a good man Captain Logan, I will see you in the morning".

Printed in Great Britain
by Amazon

60995606R00149